MW01027250

PLAGUE KING CHRONICLES

BOOK ONE

Also by Bree Moore

Shadows of Camelot

The Lady's Last Song

The Queen's Quiet End

Shadowed Minds Series

Prequel: Thief of Lies

Thief of Magic

Thief of Aether

Thief of Bones

The Lost Souls Series

Raven Born

Serpent Cursed

Coven Bound

Serpent Turned

Rebel Sworn

The Plague King Chronicles

The Quill and the Vial

Short Stories and Anthologies

Second Star

Beyond Instinct

BREE MOORE

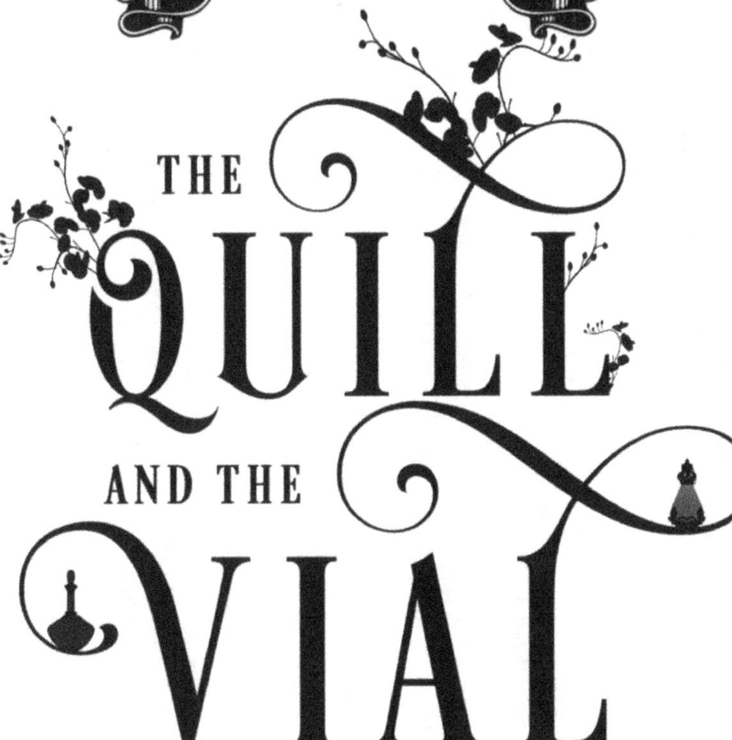

PLAGUE KING CHRONICLES
BOOK ONE

OCEAN OF ENDOS
NORWAST
THE DARKHOFF
PYRMOND
HUR SEA
OAK MIST WOODS
DOGON ISLAND
BRINDLEBERG
DELTRIE
LOSHAR
STARLIGHT FALLS
HAZOCK
SIRION
LUSCA ISLE
TYREE MOUNTAINS
THE HOBHORN
UTUN'S PASS
DULMIR
3 SISTERS MARSH
DAMARES
SILVERMOON WOODS
THORGOR
PETREA
DACIA
LANARK, ISLE OF THE BLESSED

THE STEPS OF EYD
LEGEND
KINGDOM CAPITALS
CITIES
NOTABLE LANDMARKS
THE WATCHER'S GRAVE
LUTON
AVONIA WOODS
MUSPORT
CROTOS
AFTEAN SEA
EASRICH
CROTOS CHANNEL
ENTEREA
BLOITS
IWATE
THE RIFF
MAGASP
THE IVORY GUILDS
DELAIN
SIRION BAY
CERRO

https://www.authorbreemoore.com/

This is a work of fiction. All of the characters and events portrayed are products of the author's imagination.

THE QUILL AND THE VIAL

An Innate Ink Publishing Book

Cover art by Just Venture Arts https://www.justventurearts.com/

Map art by Cartography bird https://www.cartographybird.com/

Developmental Editing by Cae Hawksmoore

https://reedsy.com/cae-hawksmoor

Copy Editing by Claire Ashgrove https://reedsy.com/Claire-Ashgrove

ISBN: 978-1-956668-26-1 (Hardcover)

ISBN: 978-1-956668-18-6 (Paperback)

ISBN: 978-1-956668-21-6 (Ebook)

Pronunciation Guide:

Alighieri: AL - I - GEE - RI

Donovanu: DO - NO - VAN - OO

Draigh: DR - AY

Enterea: EN - TE - REE - A

Eyd: EED

Fimbulvintr: FIM - BUL - VIN - TUR

Ionsa: EE - OWN - SA

Jayce: JAY - CEE

Lothian: LO - THEE - AN

Lyadne: LEE - AD - NEE

Mystri: MIS - TREE

Neldor: NEL - DOOR

Prieta: PREE - TA

Savage: SAV - AGE

Tanulia: TA - NU - LEE - A

CHAPTER ONE

Plants lied.

They whispered twisted truths and hid falsehoods among their blossoms and roots.

Jayce tried to ignore the mutterings that wafted through the air and found their way onto her skin through the gap at the wrist of her leather gloves as she crushed leaves and measured out tinctures.

Even the gloves weren't enough to stop her ability from telling her what the plants wanted her to hear.

Jayce ground the last of the ingredients with her mortar and pestle, making a thick paste that smelled of cinnamon and a strong bitterness that seeped into her nostrils.

Wormwood never smelled nice. Didn't taste nice, either, hence the cinnamon. She used a flat wooden stick to take the mixture from the stone bowl and scraped it into a shallow wooden container, then moved to screw a lid on top.

In her haste, she bumped the open jar, and the remedy sloshed onto her gloved hand, seeping through the fabric.

Jayce jumped and yelped, stripping off the glove, but it was too late. The liquid had saturated her glove and contacted her skin, and Jayce's head filled with words.

Wormwood. Resentment and regret poison your heart. Find solace in my leaves—

Jayce shook her head and gritted her teeth, bracing against the frigid cold that spread across her skin where the spilled remedy had soaked into it. The herbs wouldn't harm her topically, but her ability to hear them could drive her mad, not to mention the chill that flooded her body and made her shake.

She ran to the sink, trying to ignore the clamor of the other ingredients she could distinctly hear. The rosehips chanted like a group of gossipy ladies.

She thinks she knows. She doesn't know. She knows nothing.

Jayce grabbed the pump handle and gave it a few vigorous thrusts, then plunged her hand beneath the too-strong stream and sprayed water down her front. She slowed her pumping, then reached for the strongest soap she owned. Lye burned her skin with a painful tingle, but it cleaned away the tiny bits of plant matter and the final traces of infused oil.

The clamor in her mind quieted to whispers, and on the third washing, the whispers finally fell silent.

Still trembling, Jayce wiped her hands on a thin linen towel, then removed her wet apron to examine her blouse.

It hadn't gotten too wet, and it would eventually dry as she made her rounds in the city.

She hung up the apron, her gaze drifting to the black case that haunted the top of the highest cabinet in the apothecary. Dust had gathered thickly on the top and sides, and she ducked her head, shoving away the shame building inside her gut. She had clients to attend.

The Dawn Chant had long been sung in the capital city of Lothian when Jayce finally finished re-preparing the tonic that had spilled. She would be late on her rounds, but she couldn't make them without the tonic that relieved the symptoms of the suffering.

She took one last look around the apothecary. All her remedies for the clients she would visit that cycle sat lined up on the counter in glossy wooden containers or shiny brown bottles.

Jayce donned a clean pair of gloves and gathered her remedies to load into a flat-bottomed basket. Containers clinked together. She took her wrapped lunch from the counter and tucked it in a worn satchel, checking that she'd remembered extra gloves and a paper ledger, a charcoal drawing stick, and two carefully wrapped glass spheres she could only pray to the Three she wouldn't need.

Satisfied she had everything, she left the shop and turned a sign on the door.

THE APOTHECARY IS OUT.

Jayce walked down the street, grasping the edges of her shawl and pulling it tight. Chills still trembled across her skin, even though the bright sun shone down on the clean streets of Lothian, capital of the realm of Neldor. People bustled about busily.

Queen Lyra had already sung the Dawn Chant, but its magic lingered in the air, seeming to coat Jayce's skin and gifting her with a surge of much-needed energy. Her blood moved with more vigor through her fast-beating heart, revitalizing her. Jayce breathed deeply, and a smile worked its way onto her lips as she walked along.

People parted around her as if they were waves and Jayce the prow of a boat, some even going so far as to cross the street or move their skirts out of the way. Many eyed her with wariness, while others, the ones she had treated for various ailments, had expressions of gratitude.

It came with being an apothecary during plague times. Even as cases had diminished over the ages and the terrifying infestation of living dead had been managed, people still held their suspicion close and refused to be familiar with someone who maintained contact with those who fell sick.

Jayce held her head high. She could handle a few nasty stares and the gossip that floated in her wake. Her skin held no gray pallor, her lungs were healthy and strong. She had no excessive thirst or rapid pulse. She was vibrantly healthy. However the sickness passed between people, it hadn't gotten hold of her.

A man in a worn brown coat stumbled against the front of the bakery ahead. As Jayce passed, he grabbed her arm, whirling her around.

"Please," he croaked. His eyes darted around at the crowd, then locked on hers, twitchy and frantic.

Was it just her, or did his eyes seem a tad bloodshot? Most likely he'd spent the night drinking at a tavern.

"Excuse me," Jayce said, shaking off his hold, anxious about being delayed in such a manner.

"They say you can help," the man said.

Jayce paused and faced him again, curiosity getting the better of her. "Do you need help?" She was inviting trouble, but she never could resist a problem that needed solving.

The man pulled up his coat and shirtsleeve with several shaky jerks of his hand. He revealed an uneven patch of skin, pale gray compared to the healthy tan on the rest of his arm.

Jayce's gaze darted around the sidewalk. "Put that away," she hissed. She didn't want to start a riot on the streets. She moved a little closer to the man. "You know what that is?"

Tears welled in the man's eyes, and he nodded. "I'm going to die, ain't I?"

She wouldn't give him false hope, but she could make him comfortable.

"What's your name?" she asked, instead of answering.

"Jones. Raegar Jones." The man wiped his hand across his nose, sniffing.

"Tell me where you live, Raegar," Jayce said, taking out her charcoal and parchment.

"You ain't going to see me right away?" the man asked, pulling his brown linen cap off his head.

"I can't. The Uppertown clients get seen first, then I can work my way down to you." Jayce put a careful hand on his arm and softened her voice. "This is only the first symptom. You have time."

The man's hopeful expression twisted, and he ran his hands through his hair, pulling on it hard. He gave a guttural shout.

"Sir—" Jayce began, hoping to calm him.

"Why is it always about the nobles? You're not even one of them. You're one of us, or used to be. Now I'm starting to wonder if you're even an apothecary, or if you're running some kind of scam to get the nobles to pay you. You're a hack."

Jayce reeled a few steps back, stumbling on the uneven cobblestones. "I assure you, I'll come by later to check on you. I have clients expecting me."

"Forget it," the man spat venomously. "You know I can't pay much. By the time you finish with your previous rich clients, I'll probably be dead."

Raegar Jones jammed his hat back on his head, squashing it further, and stormed down the street, pushing through the crowd that had gathered.

Jayce eyed those who remained, straightening herself and turning away to continue her journey to Uppertown, the section of Lothian where the nobles and wealthy lived. She felt the eyes on her back accusing her as she walked away.

Jayce slowed hard. *He's wrong*, she told herself as she walked through the market. *I'm not just in this for the money, even if I am in debt.*

Awnings unfurled before her eyes, the colorful cloth catching the first rays of sunlight as they peeked around the top of the Hobhorn. She tried to resist, feeling the tug of urgency to get to her appointments, especially after her encounter with Raegan, but one particularly pretty turquoise rock caught her eye, and she gave in and stepped toward the stall.

She took off one glove and picked up one of the pieces. The coldness of the stones was far preferable to the coldness of her plants. The rocks and gems said nothing to her, and Jayce reveled in their stoic silence and beauty.

"I have a special discount for beautiful women," a voice said from under the awning. A man stepped out, sweeping straight brown hair from his eyes and polishing a large purple gemstone brooch with a cloth.

Jayce dropped the bracelet. "It's all cheap replicas, I'd wager," she said with a teasing tone, holding her basket in her elbow and sliding her glove on with a practiced motion.

Nels Martin laughed and tossed his hair again, looking down at the jewel he held. "It's good to see you. Have a lot of clients this cycle?"

"Enough to keep me busy," Jayce said, her finger gliding across three necklaces on display. "You know these are the best in the valley, right?"

"You mean best in the realm," Nels shot back, putting the brooch down and leaning across his table of wares. He glanced both ways, as if he held some great secret he didn't want anyone else to hear. "You heard about the latest cure?"

Jayce rolled her eyes. "Who hasn't by now?"

Nels licked his lips. "Do you—do you think it works?"

Jayce glanced away, playing with a loose thread on the leather that covered the basket's handle so she could touch it without hearing the words of the reeds that had died to make it. "You know it's bosh, Nels. Like every remedy that they've touted before."

"But have you known anyone who has taken it? Seen its effects?" he pressed.

"I'm sure I will soon. People are fools, lined up to be experimented on by people they hardly know," Jayce said.

Nels straightened and picked up the brooch. He placed it on a velvet pillow at the center of his display. "It's gotta be better than the last one at least, you think?"

Jayce adjusted her grip on her basket. "I'll let you know what I find out."

"I'm just waiting for the cycle when you tell me you've found it. The cure, I mean."

Jayce's mouth dried up.

She jumped when Nels spoke again.

"Take care of yourself. I don't want to hear that the plague's finally caught up with you." His voice choked a little at the end, and then he leaned in, and his lips brushed her cheek.

Jayce stood there in shock, her hand halfway to her face. Nels busied himself on the other side of his stall, rearranging the already neat rows of rings.

"Sell lots," Jayce said, the words from her own lips sounding far away in her daze. She walked away as fast as she could, nearly running into the first few people she crossed paths with. Nels was better off pursuing someone else, and she'd have to make sure he realized that.

Her legs ached as she finished her climb up the hill and knocked on the door to the house of Lady Tanulia, a middle-aged woman with dark hair and a biting sense of humor, who only needed a salve for a condition that caused patches of itchy dry skin.

Jayce handed the pot of salve to the maidservant who answered the door and waited until the maid returned with payment, which Jayce tucked into a leather pouch specifically for collecting her dues.

Eighty percent of it would go to the debt collector, on account of the life-debt Jayce owed to the queen.

Jayce's belly pinched at the thought. According to her ledgers, at the rate she made money, she'd pay off the life-debt when she was a hundred and three, and not an age sooner, unless she came into a sudden fortune. Inherited a realm, more like.

She didn't like to think about why she was in debt, and she cleared the thoughts away as she approached the next house a few doors from Lady's Tanulia's place.

Lord Syfas had summoned her last week to inquire about a worrisome gray patch of skin behind his left ear. As expected, the patch had indicated the first sign of the plague.

He'd been immediately quarantined, and the staff in his home reduced to the bare minimum. Luckily, he was without family, and there were no children or wife to send away. Unluckily, as soon as word had gotten out that he'd contracted the plague, his shipyard had been given to a fortunate, though inexperienced, cousin. Lord Syfas, far too young for such a fate, was left to waste away from a plague that had no cure and watch as his legacy was squandered.

"I'm here to see Lord Syfas," Jayce said to the man who opened the door.

The manservant hesitated. "Lord Syfas has no further need for your services. He has been cured."

Jayce startled, grabbing her basket to keep it from sliding off her arm. "That's impossible," she said. She pushed past the manservant to enter the manor.

"He has no need for an apothecary, miss. He's in perfect condition," the manservant said, sounding apologetic.

"I'll examine him for myself, thank you," Jayce snapped. She rushed down the hall to the first drawing room, but the furnishings had been rearranged. No bed.

She stumbled away from the room, looking to the manservant, who gave her a look of politeness that barely contained the exasperation he must feel over her barging into his employer's home.

"He takes his morning tea in the dining hall," the manservant supplied.

Jayce walked, her steps less harried and more measured. A cure. Nels, as well as most of Lowertown and Midtown, had been overrun with rumors about a cure. One that finally seemed to work. One that took the frightening gray pallor from the skin of the plague victims.

But no one knew anyone personally who had taken it. It was lord this, lady that, such-and-such soldier. They were all second-hand stories that no one could confirm, and Jayce wondered if things had gotten so desperate that people were making up stories just to give them hope.

"I can feel your thoughts from here. They're like a violent storm. Come, see for yourself," Lord Syfas called.

Jayce froze in the doorway of the dining hall, staring at the man who only the cycle prior had been bed-ridden and wheezing. The man she had been able to provide only small comforts and empty reassurances.

Now he sat hale and hearty as she'd ever seen him, eating a full meal with gusto. He grinned when he saw her, then patted his mouth with a napkin and swung his arms wide as he stood from the table.

“Miss Jayce, good news! I am healed!”

CHAPTER TWO

"I can see that you certainly seem better than last cycle, my lord," Jayce replied, stunned. She cleared her throat. "Can you tell me what remedy was applied?"

Lord Syfas clapped his hands and rubbed them together. "Gremin, fetch the bottle, would you? It's a miracle, Miss Jayce. An absolute miracle. Before I tell you, I need you to prepare yourself, lest I am forced to use my calming ability on you." His bushy eyebrows rose, and after a moment's hesitation, Jayce took an obligatory calming breath and smiled at the much-revived lord.

"Excellent. Good work, miss. You'll be pleased to hear that the rumors are true. I've had only two doses of this miracle cure. After the first, my breathing eased. After the second, well, you see the results!" He spread his arms, pulling up the sleeves on his rich blue coat, turning his head so she could see the patches of gray skin had, indeed, receded.

Gremlin returned and handed Jayce a blue glass bottle with a bow. No labels or etchings indicated what might be inside.

Jayce shook and uncorked the bottle, startling Lord Syfas, who flinched but said nothing. She sniffed. Sweet, floral notes wafted into her nostrils. Along with something… metallic? She closed her eyes, parsing through the unintelligible whispers that floated into her senses with the scent of the mixture.

"Hold this," she said to the manservant, handing him the open bottle and cork.

She put her basket down, the contents disheveled from her run through the manor. She pinched the finger of her glove and pulled it off.

Fully aware that Lord Syfas and his manservant both tensed as she lowered her pinky, Jayce closed her eyes and touched the brown liquid that glistened on the surface of the solution.

Coldness arrived first. A stinging, frigid sensation like touching a metal pole in the middle of winter. The kind of cold that made her skin stick to the metal and for a moment, made her fear it might tear the first delicate layer off. Unforgiving cold, spreading from her finger, up her arm, to her heart and stomach, making her nauseated.

Somehow, the cold allowed the plant words to unravel from nonsense to words.

Jayce smelled copper and tasted it on her tongue as she touched the drop on her pinky finger to the tip. Bitterness flooded her mouth, drying it as she ran her tongue around her cheeks to get the fullness of the taste.

Wormwood wept. Toad's foot chattered. A dozen other plants she had tried in remedies for the plague called out to her, clamoring for attention.

Whoever made this remedy had used a rose extract to cover up the smell—it wasn't good for much else beyond beauty products. What was that lingering, cloying sweetness? She tried to pick out the words, willing the plant to surface and tell her its secrets.

She ran her finger around the rim, gritting her teeth against waves of chill that washed through her as she searched for any other elements that might clue her in as to what was in the bottle.

The plant that had eluded her hissed its name, a crackling, quiet sound like a dying fire.

Noxbrosia.

Jayce froze. She had heard of poisons being used in remedies, but only the most scant of doses, used to purge the system. Could noxbrosia be used in a similar manner? She'd only studied the plant long enough to be aware of its poisonous properties, and the books she'd read hadn't mentioned any healing reactions.

"What is wrong? Something is wrong. Tell me," Lord Syfas said, and his magic pried at Jayce with a tug that tried to *make* her reveal what she was thinking.

"Hush!" Jayce snapped, touching the mixture to her tongue again, fighting back a shiver.

I cling to the mind and muddle the senses. I disturb the nerves and lock the bones. I clear the skin and drain the blood.

The plant hissed its truths to Jayce, and she sifted through them, looking for the lie. There was always a lie.

Maybe it wasn't a lie at all, but a manipulation. Clearing the skin of the grayness that accompanied the plague was just getting rid of a symptom, not targeting the root problem. What did the noxbrosia mean by *drain the blood*? Did it mean a sort of cleanse of the pathogens present, or did it mean the blood would behave improperly and pool somewhere in the body or get pumped too fast by the heart, potentially leading to internal bleeding?

More research would be needed. She stepped away from the manservant and the bottle he held, clasping her hands in front of herself.

"I apologize for my abrupt behavior, my lord," Jayce said, rubbing at the slightly bald spot on her right eyebrow. She had a bad habit of rubbing it when she felt stressed or anxious, and the fine hairs had never grown back.

Lord Syfas breathed deeply. "I do, as well. It was uncouth of me to attempt to extract information from you in such a manner. You have always been forthcoming."

"To put it delicately, Lord Syfas, do you know anyone who might want you dead? Because this remedy is poison."

"Poison? How am I not dead already, then? I've had two doses," Lord Syfas said, doubt clear in his voice.

"It seems to be a low dose, meant to lead to a sort of gradual demise. Though I admit it is possible the outcome was intended differently. May I examine you, my lord? I will be brief," Jayce said.

Lord Syfas' brows furrowed together, but he nodded, sitting.

Jayce crossed the room and looked into his eyes. Bloodshot. She measured his pulse and his breath, noting that both were elevated. His skin was clear, that much was true. The tell-tale gray color that was the first symptom of the plague had gone completely, and there was a healthy ruddiness to his cheeks.

Although, the ruddiness leaned more toward a fever flush, and the rest of his skin appeared paler than she'd initially thought. Could she just be paranoid? Someone *might* have discovered a remedy, or something near enough. Why had she jumped to gruesome conclusions?

If someone had found a remedy, it would improve things enormously. She didn't have to be the one to discover it.

"How do you feel, generally?" Jayce said, taking out her notebook and writing down her observations, trying to keep her own complex emotions out of the equation.

Lord Syfas shrugged. "Better. Isn't that enough?"

"Are you experiencing any headaches? Racing heart? Shortness of breath?"

Lord Syfas frowned. "A bit. Worse after taking my dose, but I assumed that just meant it was working to drive the plague from my blood."

Jayce looked hard at her paper, forcing her eyes to keep from rolling. Medicine didn't chase away illness like a dog herding sheep. The best kinds supported the body's own healing mechanisms, and anyone claiming their remedies cured all ailments, or very powerful ones, by purging it from the system... Well, they were after money, plain and simple.

"The last thing I need from you is this: who gave you this remedy?"

Lord Syfas glanced at Gremin, as if to confirm before replying. "A messenger arrived late last cycle. No one I knew, but they said the remedy came posthaste from the palace, and that I'd been chosen to be part of the trial. I asked if it was the same as the one we'd been hearing about in the rumors, and the messenger smiled and told me yes, it was."

Jayce put her quill down and raised her eyebrows. "So, I'm to believe that you allowed a stranger to enter your home after dark, believed his claim that he was sent by the queen herself, and knowingly drank this mystery liquid without consulting either physician or apothecary?"

"To be fair, I sensed no guile. My ability would have detected subterfuge. It often has in the past, and only a skilled liar can thwart me," Lord Syfas insisted.

"Then perhaps the messenger believed what they'd been told. It's a simple workaround," Jayce said, more to herself than to the nobleman sitting in front of her.

Lord Syfas sputtered with indignance, rubbing a hand across the salt-and-pepper stubble on his face, then his entire frame drooped.

"Yes, you have a point." He looked shamefaced. "But you would have done the same in my place. You've taken great care to reduce my symptoms, Apothecary Jayce. But even you do not have a cure. So, you must understand my desperation to avoid dying, or worse, becoming one of the moribund. You must understand how my hope kindled when I was offered another chance."

Jayce could understand—because Lord Syfas was using his ability to project the exact emotion he felt in her direction. It made Jayce queasy, and she shook out her skirts as if to distract herself from the uncomfortable sensation of feeling another's emotions.

"I do. I understand," Jayce said, though in her head she cursed hope and the ignorant and desperate things it made people do. She'd learned her lesson five ages ago and would no longer give hope permission to overpower her common sense.

Jayce took a deep breath before continuing. She hated this part of her job. She hated giving anyone bad news and hated even more the feeling of inadequacy that came when she had to tell someone there was nothing more she could do.

"Lord Syfas, you must understand that I want you well. I wish to see you well more than anything. The plant used to make this remedy will kill you. If I am correct about this so-called remedy, you will eventually bleed to death as your vessels open of their own accord and drain blood from your pores. It will not be pretty."

"Neither is dying at the hand of this plague, if I am to understand correctly. And what if I turn into one of the moribund?" Lord Syfas asked.

His eyes had widened, still bloodshot. Was it possible for them to be more so? The color had drained further from his face, accentuating the fever flush even more. She would need to check on him later that night. Did she have anything that would help flush the poison from his system? Perhaps burdock root...

"Drink lots of water," Jayce said. "Avoid alcohol, that will only make it harder for your body to rid itself of this poison. Some people do get well, Lord Syfas. Would you give up your chance to defeat this for an experiment?"

"If it helps others, I think I would," Lord Syfas said.

The emotional wave his powers emitted gave Jayce a surge of determination not her own.

The declaration startled Jayce, and the quill left a splotch of ink where she'd been about to record his agreement to her recommendation not to take the noxbrosia remedy.

"What was that, my lord?"

"I would like to continue the remedy. If I am more likely to die or become one of those awful things than to live, I will take this risk. Note it down if you must. I am prepared." His jaw tightened.

Jayce clenched her own jaw, biting her tongue to keep from insisting that he not take the poison. She couldn't tell him what to do. He had a right to his own body. If he wished to experiment with it, then so be it.

Jayce blew on the ink to dry it, then looked up at Lord Syfas and his manservant. "May I at least trouble you for a portion of the remedy to take back to my apothecary? I would like to experiment on it and further decipher the ingredients."

After all, if it contained minerals or anything animal-derived, her powers alone wouldn't detect it.

Lord Syfas gave a curt nod. "Of course. Gremin, fetch another bottle and send the original with Miss Jayce for her research. If I run out and need more, I will try to contact the servant who gave me the original bottle."

Tension whooshed out with Jayce's next breath, and her shoulders dropped. "Do you happen to have their name, or...?" she asked, re-dipping her quill.

"Nothing of the sort. They said they would contact me later to see how I was feeling. If I find out, I'll certainly let you know," Lord Syfas said, settling back in his chair and clasping his hands over his stomach.

Did he seem unusually drowsy, or had the intensity of their conversation worn him out? Jayce put her quill, ink, and ledger in her satchel, tsking herself for her paranoia. He wouldn't get better in a cycle, no matter how good the remedy.

The manservant returned and handed her the little blue bottle.

Jayce's stomach turned as she grasped its warm, glass surface. "Gremin, please send word to me if his condition changes in any way. Otherwise, allow him to go about his duties as he feels fit. I wouldn't tell anyone about this supposed cure until we understand it further. I will be sure to share my findings."

Gremin nodded.

Jayce placed her satchel over her shoulder and picked up the basket. She inclined her head at the nobleman still reclined in his chair, eyes closed as if dozing. It still troubled her, but she'd wasted enough time chasing shadows.

"If you'll excuse me, Lord Syfas, I have other clients to see."

He waved her off, murmuring a muffled sort of farewell, and Gremin escorted her to the front door.

Jayce's mind wandered ahead to the other customers she had to see that cycle, wondering how many of the sick had also taken the mysterious, poison-based remedy.

She set out up the street toward another house, concocting potential remedies in her head to counteract the poison, her mind going to the dusty alchemy set at the top of her cabinet. This certainly warranted cleaning it off and firing up the burners again. Despite the clenching dread in her chest, she had to try to discover the origins of the remedy. She couldn't let it go unchecked.

The rest of the cycle went downhill from her encounter with Lord Syfas. Three more of her regular clients, all in Uppertown, had consumed the remedy. One had taken it that morning and practically threw Jayce out when she suggested the remedy could fail.

Disheartened, Jayce finished her rounds, moving through the next two areas of the city, keeping an eye out for blue bottles while talk of the latest miracle remedy seemed to follow her.

There had been false remedies promoted before, mostly by charlatans posing as medical experts preying on the hope of the masses. Most of these remedies originated in Lowertown with the poor population, and few made it to the nobles before they were exposed.

But none of them had caused harm. Jayce didn't have evidence that this new remedy was harmful, either, but she feared it was only a matter of time.

Her tumultuous thoughts and regret weighed down her heart and made her feet drag. She hadn't been able to track down Reagan Jones, the man with the plague who had approached her that morning. Either none of the people she had talked to knew him, or he didn't want to be found.

In either case, there was nothing to be done for him unless she saw him again.

Jayce walked slowly through the dusk-darkened streets, reaching her apothecary in Midtown as the final notes of the Evening Song hung in the air. She entered, removed her boots and stockings, and went straight to the counter to count out the marks she'd earned. Two out of every ten went in a small pile she would later add to her own funds. The remaining eight went to the realm, for the debt and taxes she owed. After counting and putting away the money, Jayce sat down to rub her feet.

No sooner had she relieved her feet, than a knock came at the door. She opened to a messenger with a somber face bringing news of the untimely and shocking demise of Lord Syfas.

CHAPTER THREE

There was nothing that could have been done for Lord Syfas. He had died in his armchair, while reading by the fire. Apparently, the death had been sudden, which surprised Jayce more than the death itself. And he had not become a moribund. Was that a side effect of the poisonous remedy? Could its true purpose be in preventing the turning of a plague-dead person into one of the animated, violent undead things that had overrun the capital when the plague was first introduced?

From Jayce's limited knowledge, noxbrosia was known for slow deaths. Something in the remedy's makeup must have accelerated Lord Syfas' death, and she wouldn't know what until she had a moment to use her alchemistry training and test the remedy.

And if she discovered the remedy was intended to prevent the formation of moribund by killing its victims prematurely? What then? Murder was wrong, but those creatures of death were horrific, and nothing stopped them except burning or beheading. Could she advise her own clients to take a remedy that promised a swift, clean death while there was any chance they could recover?

Recovery from the plague was rare and seemingly at random. Men, women, and children were equally affected and just as equally died or lived. A smaller percentage turned into moribund, but any percent was enough.

But killing people before one knew if they would live or turn or die? She couldn't condone it. Wouldn't.

She was getting into her head again.

Jayce sipped from a mug of lukewarm, heavily watered-down tea. She drank chamomile, a safe plant that whispered, rather than shouted, and left mostly nice words on Jayce's tongue and lips, even if they were entirely nonsensical. They calmed her, and her thoughts eventually calmed as well, allowing her to make a plan.

As soon as she heard of Lord Syfas' death, she'd returned to his manor to examine him. The symptoms of the plague had come back in full force; his skin was entirely gray, his lungs had collapsed, and blood ran from the corners of his eyes.

But had he died from the poison or from the plague?

Since she didn't know who had made the remedy to ask them what their purpose was, she would have to sort out the ingredients and try to determine it herself.

Jayce donned her apron and climbed a makeshift stool to the top of a shelf in the back of the apothecary. She moved

dusty, empty jars and boxes until she could finally grasp at the black metal box.

She made her way down and set the box on her worktable in the center of the lanterns that lit the area.

The metal box gleamed darkly, seeming to watch Jayce as she moved around the room gathering items. The last thing she set on the table was the blue bottle containing the remedy that had killed Lord Syfas.

Jayce stared at the gathering of things on the table. It contained two of the most precious things she owned—a copper and glass alchemist distillery set with all the necessary containers and piping, along with a billows attachment.

She supplied her empty stomach with some of the morning's cold porridge, swallowing words and their chill with each miserable bite. She had to eat to live, and she couldn't always avoid eating plants. She finished off with a slice of cheese before she assembled the alchemistry set. Crickets outside her window had fallen silent by the time she finished cleaning each piece and getting every screw and piece of tubing in place. She ran plain water through the alchemistry set, checking that the elements still heated and there were no holes to patch.

There were, in fact, holes to patch, and she spent what felt like ages searching for the glue and patches she kept on hand for such a purpose.

Finally, she uncorked the blue bottle and dripped some of the solution into a bronze dish. It pooled innocently, waiting for her to test it, to change it. With a building sense of the thrill of discovery, Jayce added the first element to test the solution: heat. She lit the burner and turned it up slowly until the drop of solution fizzled. She watched the reaction and noted the evaporation time. When the solution was gone, she turned the heat off and checked the bronze pan for residue. She found a strange powdery substance she could move around the pan with a metal scraper.

Some kind of mineral, shell, or bone, she assumed. She tipped the bits of powder into a clean vial and proceeded with other tests, portioning out small measures of the remedy Lord Syfas had given her, fully aware of how little she had to work with.

Pages of notes later, Jayce leaned against the table and hung her head, her mind filled with pieces but no connections. The powdery substance appeared to be bone, commonly used in folk remedies in smaller towns and villages. Not something she'd expected to find at the center of the realm. Additionally, the remedy had changed color when she'd added an acidic solution, indicating it was a base. She'd made several observations, but none of them seemed to point to any one conclusion.

It was as if five different people of differing backgrounds had each brought an ingredient to put in this remedy, and many of the ingredients she'd discerned seemed to have no purpose at all except to possibly mislead her into drawing the wrong conclusion about whoever had made the remedy, and for what purpose.

Lord Syfas had said the remedy came from the palace, but what if the servant that had delivered it lied to him? From what Jayce knew, Queen Lyra would not sanction a remedy that took away all chance for her subjects to recover, even if it did prevent the formation of the moribund.

Jayce needed to do more research on the properties of noxbrosia and how someone might have gotten hold of the rare, poisonous plant, but she didn't have access in her cramped apothecary. The nearest library she knew of was in the Oakmist Woods, which was a several-cycle walk, and she couldn't leave the capital city without express permission from the bailiff that handled her debts.

Jayce warmed a kettle of bone broth and poured herself a mug. She huddled in a chair, exhausted and upset that all of her efforts had led to nothing, just like the last five ages. Nothing but debt and doubts.

The front door of the shop rattled, and something banged on it, jerking Jayce from the tide of emotions. She sloshed a bit of broth on her blouse as she sat up, staring wide-eyed at the door and wondering who would call at such a late hour.

CHAPTER FOUR

The door at the front of the shop opened. Whoever had arrived ignored propriety and let themselves in.

"You couldn't wait two moments, Nels?" Jayce snapped, coming around the counter and shelves that partially obscured the front door from view.

She halted when she saw the man who had entered was not a friend, as she'd assumed, but a bailiff of the realm. Almost as if she'd summoned him with her thoughts of leaving the capital.

"Sir Dray, I-I didn't know this was a collection cycle," she stammered, changing direction toward the counter where she stored her client ledgers and the money set aside for collection.

"Oh, it isn't," Sir Dray drawled. He ran a hand over his greased-back black hair and tugged on the short ponytail tied at the end. "This is a social call."

"Oh," Jayce said, her hand dropping. She gestured toward the back room, where the alchemy set was still set up. "As you can see, I'm a bit busy for company."

Dray glanced toward the back room with interest. "Haven't seen that out for a while. You chasing remedies again, darling?"

Jayce sighed. "Something like that."

"You know, you could sell this place. It would pay off a chunk of your debt," Dray said, glancing at the ceiling and around the room.

Jayce shook her head, a knot tightening in her throat. "Where would I live and make my remedies? I couldn't work out of an apartment."

"What if you didn't have to work?" Dray said, moving closer, rubbing his thin mustache and putting on a charming smile—all teeth and no warmth.

Jayce looked at him, confused. "I have to work. You of all people know how much debt—"

"Your payments barely make a dent in your life-debt, not to mention the interest. I have a proposition for you."

Jayce waited for him to continue, her fingers curling and uncurling at her sides, tension hanging in the air.

Dray walked past her and leaned against the counter between the front room and the back. "I heard the rumor mill discussing your argument with Lord Syfas right before his untimely death. He was the picture of health, they say, and then one argument with you and he's dead." Dray tsked. "Such a shame."

"We didn't argue. We disagreed on his course of treatment, is all." Jayce licked her lips.

"Come now, Miss Jayce. He refused to pay you, perhaps? Or offered favors instead of money?" His grin was oilier than his hair, and Jayce wanted to strike the expression from his face.

She worked her jaw, clamping down hard on the desire. Dray wasn't the kind of person she could speculate to about the noxbrosia remedy Lord Syfas had taken. She didn't trust him as far as she could throw him. Even telling him about the so-called remedy before she had done more research could cause more trouble than it resolved.

Dray chuckled and straightened, stepping closer to her, too close for comfort. "Look, I know you didn't poison him. You don't have the spine for cold-blooded murder. But if the talk overwhelms common sense among these folks, or if his family wants to press charges, you're going to need protection. That's what I came to talk to you about."

Jayce cocked her head and raised her eyebrows. "That's thoughtful of you. Were you thinking of posting a guard or speaking at the next council meeting?"

Dray showed all his teeth and rubbed his mustache again. "Now how would either of those things benefit me? You've got to think harder, Jayce. This would be a partnership, with both of us getting things we want out of it."

Jayce crossed her arms. "I don't have any more money to give you, Dray." She had the distinct feeling she was being backed into a corner by a predator.

"The most valuable thing you got is your pretty face." Dray knocked a finger under her chin, then leaned in, his face sliding next to hers until his mouth was next to her ear.

"Marry me, and I'll make sure no one else lays a hand on my wife. You see? We both get what we want."

Jayce ducked past him and braced herself on the counter behind her. "With all due respect, Sir Dray, I don't intend to marry at the moment. A few rumors won't convince me to make hasty decisions about my future."

Dray nodded, his demeanor deceptively calm. He rested his hand on the pommel of the sword sticking from his belt, looking around the shop.

"You could keep doing your work," he said, gesturing around. "Make your potions, sell your remedies. I wouldn't keep you from it."

"You would inherit my debt," Jayce reminded him, desperate to put him off.

Dray frowned, as if he hadn't thought of it. After a moment, he nodded. "You're right, I would. But together we could pay it off in less than half the time it would take you alone. I make more than an apothecary. You could sell the place, move in with me."

Jayce tilted her head, then rubbed a hand across her forehead. "Why do you want to marry me, Dray? There's no shortage of pretty women for you to foist your attentions on. I'm sure you have half a dozen just waiting for you to make your intentions known. Why would you want an orphan with no family? A woman with no prospects and a life-debt that will sink you even further?"

Dray's face changed, shifting from congenial to dangerous in an instant.

From Jayce's perspective, a monster seemed to have come to life behind his eyes, and she suddenly knew why no women had come forward to tempt the queen's bailiff.

Dray gritted his teeth as he spoke, biting off each word and giving them a sharp edge. "I have certain... requirements of my life partner. I prefer a beautiful, intelligent, quiet woman. One who will bear me sons and daughters with magic abilities that will bring honor to my name and the crown. I could go on, but suffice to say, you fit all of my preferences and then some."

Jayce breathed in, drawing strength from the familiar smell of the apothecary and all its dead plants. The gentle shushing of the floras' secret language seemed almost audible in the air, and it bolstered her, as if she weren't actually facing this monster of a man alone.

"I-I will consider your proposal. But I need a favor," Jayce said quickly, breathlessly.

Dray perked up. "Go on."

"I need to visit the library at the Draigh monastery. I'd just be gone a few cycles. Approve my travel request, and when I get back, we can talk some more."

Dray laughed, pacing. "You know how easy it would be for you to give me the slip if I let you leave here? I'm not so much a fool." He spun on a heel to face her, approaching her so quickly she couldn't move out of the way, and he grabbed her arms. "Agree to marry me, and I'll take you anywhere you want. A library, the coast, a realm across the sea."

"I'm not interested in marriage, Sir Dray," Jayce said, wrenching herself from his arms and breathing hard.

Dray pursed his lips. "Very well. I would have much preferred it if you had chosen the more amenable route, but you force my hand." His eyes held a dangerous glint. "I will give you three cycles to consider my proposal. In the meantime, I will reject any travel request you submit, and I will do nothing to stop the rumor mill concerning your implicated involvement with Lord Syfas' death. Additionally, you should know that I have the power to call your life-debt due whenever I want. We both know I'm your best, if not only, prospect. Don't make this harder than it needs to be, Jayce."

He turned on his heel, not waiting for her response. The wooden door slammed in his wake.

Jayce sank to the floor and leaned against the wall beneath the counter. She dug the tips of her fingers into her eyes. If she didn't get convicted for Lord Syfas' death and Dray made good on his threats, any future she could imagine for herself would be lost, spent in prison or sent off to the Hobhorn mines.

She hated that she considered agreeing to his proposal, even for a moment.

The first thing Jayce did was make herself a cup of chamomile tea to calm her nerves. She needed to think clearly, to come up with a plan. She wished she had someone to talk to, but this late, most folk were headed to bed, and she wasn't certain who she could call on even if it weren't after nightfall.

A moment after she sat, a second knock sounded at the door. She jerked, spilling the warm tea on herself. It soaked into the front of her shirt on top of the broth stain from before, and the plant whispered to her.

I induce sleep. I make one beautiful. I am a beautiful flower. Why shouldn't I impart beauty?

"You're just a flower," Jayce muttered. "A weed, almost." She breathed through the brief coldness spreading across her skin that accompanied plant speech.

Dead plants regurgitated the final words they had spoken in life. The dried chamomile flower heads had a sort of vanity about them that Jayce, in her damp and frustrated state, found incredibly annoying.

“Just a moment,” she called to whomever had knocked. She dabbed at the wet spot spreading on her front.

She stared toward the front of the apothecary, terrified to answer the door. Every time she opened it lately, more bad news arrived. At this point, she expected the reaper himself to be waiting for her.

“Jayce, it's Nels! Let me in.”

Jayce flew to the door.

She fumbled with the latches but eventually got them all and threw open the door, out of breath and tears already pricking her eyes.

She leaned into Nels without a word, and he made a surprised sound, then wrapped his arms around her without saying anything.

After a moment, she pulled away and let him into the apothecary.

Nels looked around the pillar to where Jayce’s project lay strewn across her worktable, but he didn't ask about it. Instead, he leaned against the counter and waited.

"Did you hear about Lord Syfas?” she asked.

Nels looked shocked. “One of your clients? No. What happened?”

Jayce relayed the events of the cycle before. She didn’t have to leave anything out about Lord Syfas’ death.

“And someone has decided to use his death to get something they want.” She bit her lip at that last part. She hadn’t intended to tell him about Sir Dray.

"Someone is blackmailing you?" Nels asked.

She shook her head. "You know what? Don't worry about it. I'm sure I can handle—"

"No, you can't. Not something this big. Let me guess, it was that oaf Dray? I've always thought there was something piggish about the way he looked at you." Nels' hands tightened into fists.

"Leave it, Nels. I know what you're thinking."

"You can read minds, now?" His eyebrows raised.

Jayce laughed, breaking through some of the tension.

"Tell me honestly, Jayce. Do you want me to leave it alone? Because I will. But if you're lying because you have this delusion that you can handle it yourself, I—" He swallowed. "I care about you." His voice and eyes softened even more.

"I'm not trying to leave you out of it on purpose. I just don't know what you can do about the situation. He's threatening to either let the rumors get me convicted of Lord Syfas' death or call my life-debt due. Either would put me in prison or the mines."

"What could he possibly want in return? You don't have money." Nels scoffed. "Sorry," he added quickly.

"He wants to marry me." Jayce closed her eyes to Nels' shocked expression, rubbing her brow and wishing her budding headache would vanish on its own. She had some mountain mint ointment that would help... She headed for her workroom, grabbed the ointment jar off her counter, and unscrewed the lid.

Nels followed, ranting. "Marry you? He is blackmailing you, so you'll marry him? I mean, I get where he's coming from, I'd marry you in an instant, but I wouldn't..." He trailed off, flushing as he realized what he'd just said. He ran a hand through his hair, glancing anywhere but at her.

Jayce finished with the ointment, replaced it on the counter, and breathed in the invigorating menthol scent while trying to ignore the whispers of the mint. Perhaps she should have dealt with the headache another way.

"None of this is very helpful," Nels said.

"No, it isn't."

He snapped his fingers. "You have to go to the queen. She'll set it right."

"It's my word against Dray's. She's not going to listen to some random apothecary, especially not one suspected in the recent death of a noble."

"But you're not some random apothecary, you're Jayce Keenstone. After what you and your brother did to try to save the realm..."

Jayce's vision tunneled, and Nel's voice grew distant. She grabbed the counter, feeling as if she might drift away without something solid to hold on to. Blinking rapidly and deepening her breath, she clung to the rough wood and the smell of mint until her mind cleared. She shook her head.

"You all right?" Nels asked, his hand landing on her shoulder.

Jayce shook him off. "I am fine. It's just been a long cycle. I don't think going to the queen will work, but I need permission to leave the capital, and Dray won't give it to me. Going straight to the source is my only hope. I'll join the petition line after I get through my rounds tomorrow."

"I bet if you drop your name with one of the guards at the gate, you'll jump to the front of the line," Nels said, looking at her with concern.

"I don't have any of the power you seem to think I have," Jayce insisted. "That was a long time ago."

Nels shifted his stance, putting his hands on his hips and glancing at the floor before looking up again and tossing his shaggy hair out of his face.

"You could marry me instead. Put Dray off that way."

He looked so hopeful Jayce had to bite back the laugh that bubbled up in her chest.

"No way. I'm not asking you to save me, Nels."

"It wouldn't be a burden," he added.

He raised his eyebrows in such a comical way that Jayce gave in and laughed, and Nels joined her.

As the laughter died down, Jayce shook her head and sighed. She stared at the one person she'd managed to befriend through all these ages spent alone in the apothecary.

"You're a far better option than he is, I'll grant you that. But Dray would just call in my life-debt, and then we'd both get sent to the mines."

"I would do it for you in an instant," Nels proclaimed with a bravado that Jayce knew he didn't feel.

"I'm asking you not to," she said, adding a bit of sternness to her expression and her voice, and then, seeing him wilt, she added, "Promise me you won't take this as a rejection."

Nels' throat bobbed. "I promise. If you promise to find a way out of marrying Dray. I'll kidnap you if I have to. Stage your death, whatever it takes."

Jayce laughed through the tears that threatened and let a smile break through the sadness weighing down her heart.

"I think I can promise you that."

CHAPTER FIVE

Jayce stood in a short line of people at the bottom of the castle steps, waiting for an audience with the queen. She hopped from foot to foot, chilled and anxious that the sun was going down and the line had hardly moved.

They closed the doors at sundown so the queen could sing the Evening Song. If she didn't get in before then to tell the queen about Sir Dray's threats and the troubling poison-filled remedy circling through the capital and presumably coming from the palace, she would have to find a moment tomorrow. Another day would increase the likelihood that Dray would catch her trying to report him and...

The evening bell tolled, announcing the cycle's end, and the queen walked out onto the balcony above, her blue and silver dress resplendent in the cycle's dying light.

"My people," she said in a loud tone that carried across the square where Jayce stood. "I regret that I cannot visit with you this cycle. Perhaps tomorrow. For now, hear my song and find rest in it."

She opened her mouth and sang a song that sounded both familiar and ancient.

Through her frustration, Jayce nearly wept at the relief brought on by the queen's magic voice. She wished she could bathe in the perfect tones, in the promise of rest that the notes provided.

When the song ended and the queen returned to her palace, ornate doors closing behind her, some of the peace drained back out of Jayce, and renewed determination replaced it. She marched up to the castle doors but halted as the two guards standing at attention lowered their spears.

"Petitions are finished for the cycle. Return tomorrow," one of them said, voice more feminine than Jayce expected. She knew there were females among the queen's soldiers, but she'd rarely met one.

"The queen must hear what I have to say. It's essential," Jayce said, planting herself firmly and resisting the urge to shrink from the guards' cold stares. She didn't want to say specifically what she had come for. If the remedy was known in the palace, it wouldn't cause any harm. But if it wasn't, and there was a conspiracy, possibly even against the crown, she didn't want the rumors to come from her.

The female guard lowered her spear but waived Jayce off. "We hear that every cycle, miss. No offense, but it's rarely as urgent as they make it out to be. Get in line in the morning. Sleep on the cobblestones, if you must. Unless you're a personal friend of the queen, she won't be hearing you this cycle."

Jayce opened her mouth, then closed it. She couldn't claim any friendship, but could Nels be right? If she told the guards who she was, gave them her name and reminded them of what she'd lost in service to the realm, would they let her in?

The very thought of proving her identity and the memories attached to it made her head feel light, and she swayed far enough to one side the female guard reached out a hand as if to catch her.

"Miss, are you well? Should we fetch an apothecary?"

"I am an... an apothecary," Jayce murmured. Why had her vision blurred at the edges? Why had the crowd stopped chattering?

"What's going on here?" a deep, male voice asked.

It all rushed back at the sound of that voice, her heart racing, her brain telling her to run. Why should she run? Her vision cleared, and sound crashed down on her as Sir Dray's face came into view.

Emotion rushed through Jayce's chest and into her head like a torrent. She blinked away tears and drew herself to her full height.

"Nothing. It's fine. I'm fine," she insisted, her voice too loud. She spun on her heel and fled down the street, not caring that she made a spectacle of herself. Her eyes and lungs burned as she ran through Uppertown toward her shop in Midtown, and her mind raced faster than her feet.

Had he seen her standing in line to meet with the queen? If he had, he'd assume that she meant to report him, and he'd no doubt head her off in the morning. He would either plant lies in the queen's ear before Jayce got to see her, or make sure Jayce never made it to the queen's presence.

And what if Dray knew about the poisonous remedy? He knew Lord Syfas had died but hadn't said he knew the man had taken the so-called miracle cure. What if marrying her was his way of protecting her from whoever was behind the cure? Could he be so benevolent?

And who would the queen believe? A simple apothecary with nothing but a life-debt and no family to her name? Or one of the royal bailiffs that handled the realm's debtors?

Shadows replaced sunlight as the golden orb slipped lower in the sky, almost at the horizon.

Jayce slowed her footsteps to a walk as she reached the market between Uppertown and Midtown, hunching in on herself, feeling a chill despite the warm summer evening. She dodged groups of gossipers and shoppers finishing their wares, ignoring the last-offer cries of merchants trying to get rid of the more perishable items at the end of the cycle.

As she turned to go around another cluster of shoppers, she caught a darting figure from the corner of her eye.

She wouldn't normally have given it a second thought, but her skin prickled with fear. The fine hairs on her neck rose, and her gut twisted. She breathed in and out to calm herself, then turned slowly, scanning the thinning crowd in the streets, but none of the faces caught her eye. She turned forward once more and quickened her pace, picking up her skirts to free her stride.

The shadow flashed again a few blocks later, and Jayce measured her steps and her breath, trying not to panic. She caught a glimpse of a cloaked face in her peripheral. Why would someone wear a cloak except to hide their face?

She was being followed. With only three blocks to go and the streets growing more barren by the moment, Jayce broke into a run. Footsteps behind her sped up as well, though they still sounded muffled, as if the person didn't want to draw attention to themselves.

Fumbling with the key to the apothecary, Jayce jammed the metal into the doorknob and turned. Her breath hitched with desperate noises that could have been words if she'd had more air. But cursing the doorknob didn't make it turn any faster, and she nearly caught her own skirts in the door as she slammed it shut behind her and locked it.

She backed away slowly, watching the door. Her gaze darted to the window on one side, expecting any moment a face would appear. Several shadows walked past, making her jump, but none approached.

She had nearly relaxed when the door handle jiggled. Her breath froze, her entire body seizing.

It could be Dray, coming to check on her. Or Nels, who she'd welcome. But Nels would call out, letting her know it was him.

Jayce backed up against the counter that separated the front room from her workroom.

The handle jiggled again, more violently this time, and then a form did appear before the window.

Jayce yelped and ducked under the counter, hiding in the shadows, not certain the person on the other side of the glass could see her. But she hadn't washed that window in some months, and the glass had some grime on it from the street. She couldn't identify the onlooker, but they wouldn't be able to get a good look at her, either.

Jayce licked her lips and begged the Three to make the person leave. Whoever it was.

Long after Jayce saw the shadowy form move away from her shop, she sat hunched in her corner, legs and back cramping. When she finally felt comfortable enough to move, her muscles and joints complained, and she moved into the back of the shop. She lit the smallest candle she had, afraid if the person came back and saw a light on, they would confront her.

About what? The remedy? If whoever made it didn't want word getting out about what the remedy actually did, would they kill to keep her silent? Or just threaten her? Even if Dray wasn't involved, someone else might have heard about Jayce's connection to Lord Syfas' death, and if they had also seen Jayce waiting in line to see the queen, they might do anything to stop her from revealing their hand before they were ready.

But what would someone have to gain from giving out this poison and saying it came from the castle? Was it someone who wanted recognition, or someone who wanted to test their poison before they gave it to the queen?

Jayce's gut churned from both hunger and a sense of intuition she couldn't shake. She needed to find out more about this remedy, especially its key ingredient, the *noxbrosia.* Texts on the rare plant would certainly be held in the monastery library, she just had to make it there before Dray or someone else caught on to her suspicions and tried to stop her.

She could leave. Tonight after it grew dark. And hope that no one watched the shop.

Perhaps she was overreacting. But she would rather overreact, just to be safe, than risk having her reputation and all future prospects ruined. She would be in violation of her debt, but she could write a letter, address it to the queen, and pray to the Three that the queen would be merciful.

No more marriage proposals. No more hiding in her shop, hoping the plants would speak a cure into her fingertips.

Suddenly filled with purpose, Jayce moved about the shop, gathering supplies, clothing, and the herbal preparations and ingredients she didn't want to leave without. The latter she funneled carefully into thin glass vials, corked them and added them to a long row of leather pockets in a wrap made to hold the unique containers.

That done, Jayce rolled the leather holder up and tied it to the top of her bedroll. A metal cup, plate, knife, and spoon went into a cloak, completing her pack. When she picked it up, she nearly fell over, and realized the extra clothing she had packed—two skirts, two blouses, socks and undergarments—were the only things she could compromise. She reduced it down to just her undergarments and an extra blouse, reasoning that the skirt would wear all right and she could wash it at an inn if needed.

She tied a strap around the whole bundle, then stood back and admired her work. It looked a bit pitiful leaning against the table by itself.

Atop the table, her gleaming alchemistry set stood abandoned. She hadn't put it away in her distress the night before, and this morning had been a rush. Leaving it unattended and exposed made her heart clench, so she forced herself to wipe down and dry the pieces before placing them carefully in the metal case where they belonged.

Everything else, though nice, was just furniture and things. And the garden full of plants out back would have to look after itself.

Last, Jayce picked up a quill and scratched a brief note to Nels. It said far too little, and it was a poor excuse for a goodbye to the only friend she had, but she had to tell someone why she was leaving and where she planned to go. As a last-moment addition, Jayce added a line asking Nels to lie should Dray ask if he'd seen Jayce. Make something up, anything to convince the bailiff that she hadn't actually left town.

She signed her name, then placed the folded parchment under an impressive, glittering specimen of purple-hued crystal that Nels had given her once. Amethyst, he'd called it. Jayce kept it on the short bookcase in the front of the shop, and when Nels came looking for her, he would use the spare key he knew she kept under a matching rock in the garden. He would find the note.

Silently, Jayce said goodbye to the apothecary, sweeping her hand along the edge of the worn worktable, touching the shelves and the few books she owned that she couldn't possibly carry if she wanted to move fast.

And she would have to move fast to evade the reaches of a man like Dray, or whoever had followed her that night.

Jayce slipped through the back door, pack in hand, then made her way through the garden she'd tended so carefully the past few ages. She trailed her gloved hand through bushes and vines, stopping last at the chamomile plant that she'd planted not that long ago. Its little yellow and white flowers opened toward the afternoon sun above.

"Goodbye," she whispered. For now. She would be back, once she knew about the noxbrosia and who could have gotten enough to put in the remedy that had been given to several of her clients.

Jayce took the back way out of the city, going through the quiet parts of Lowertown and avoiding streets with taverns where there would still be people awake and watching. She couldn't afford to have anyone see her with a pack, clearly ready for travel outside the city, and to have word get back to Dray before she'd even set foot outside city limits.

Jayce adjusted the gloves on her hands and marched down the dusty road. She whistled, trying to remember images from maps she had seen in order to orient herself in a helpful direction to reach the monastery she had only heard of.

A wind whipped up, driving heavy clouds over the sun, and Jayce shivered. She passed nearly no one on the road. At least the rain would erase her tracks and prevent Dray or anyone else from coming after her, giving her time to put more distance between them.

The wind blew, and a gap opened in the clouds above, revealing pinpricks of pinkish light in a deep indigo sky. The Purple Bell Moon season was nearly at a close. Soon the moon and stars would take on the reddish hue of the Blood Moon, the hunting moon, and the turn of the seasons from warm to cold.

Jayce gazed at the stars, sending wishes up like prayers to the Three, wishing she could escape to the space between the stars and not have to deal with poison, politics, or men and the troubles they brought.

CHAPTER SIX

With the lavender-colored moon high in the sky, Jayce dragged herself into the town of Eastmill. Her tired feet and eyes had found new energy each time a fleeting shadow reminded Jayce of the figure who had followed her to the apothecary earlier, and it didn't help that a man on a horse followed at some distance. She kept expecting him to pass her, but he seemed to hang back, almost as if he intended to remain behind her, which only made Jayce's nerves cling closer to the edge of her sanity.

The Silver Gardener still had its lights on and people moving around inside, despite the late hour. Energized folk tunes floated through the open doorway, reassuring Jayce that she wouldn't have too many unsavory characters to worry about, aside from whoever could be following her.

Jayce dodged exuberant locals singing along with the bards that took up one corner of the main floor, rounded a pillar in the center of the room, and made her way to a counter at the front. She took up an empty stool and raised her hand to catch the barmaid's attention, holding up a dull bronze chip. The maid nodded, served a pint to a man several seats down, then approached Jayce.

"What'll you have, love?" The woman clipped her vowels in a way typical of people from Brindleberg, all the way on the shores of the Shur Sea.

"Stew and bread and water, please," Jayce said, sliding the chip across the counter.

"It'll be two of those, then, if you want meat in your stew," the woman said, eyeing the coin.

Jayce took another coin from the pouch at her side and slid it across, wincing internally at the cost. She shouldn't have spent it on inn food, but her belly ached with a hunger that dried venison couldn't touch. She'd have to visit this town's market in the morning and get more food for the journey through the woods. She had a slingshot, but she wasn't much of a marksman.

When the barmaid came back with a mug of fizzy purple bell wine, a steaming bowl of stew, and a hard roll, Jayce sheepishly asked for a room, having forgotten before.

"We're actually full-up tonight," the woman said, apologetically.

Jayce drummed her fingers on the counter. She'd have to find quarters at one of the other inns after she ate.

She sniffed at the stew, then dipped the spoon in and sipped at the thick gravy. Rich, but tasteless. She ate several spoonfuls, choking past the dull words of the root vegetables and squash that spoke to her despite their cooked state, before she finally gave in and reached for her pack, which she'd placed on the floor between her legs.

If she had to endure plant whispers regardless, she might as well make the stew taste better. She pulled out the leather wrap holding her plant vials, and laid it out on the empty stretch of counter beside her. She tugged out a paper sleeve from a small pocket on the outer edge.

She sprinkled salt first, a fine grey salt harvested from the hills of the Hobhorn, a rarer commodity now that the mines were considered to be in the domain of the Plague King.

Thinking of the Plague King, even for a moment, almost caused Jayce to lose her appetite. She forced herself to eat a few bites, but even though the salt improved the stew it still lacked flavor. Jayce couldn't resist the temptation of her favorite herbal mixture. She sprinkled the barest dash of rosemary, thyme, and brindleweed over the stew, stirred it in, and took a taste. She shivered as the plants' whispers washed over her, sending goosebumps over her skin with an accompanying chill.

The warm and comforting stew quickly banished her chilly thoughts. It amazed her how a few tiny leaves could change the flavor of a dish so dramatically, especially when she went cycles or weeks without adding them to avoid the whispers of the plants. She slurped the entire bowl fast enough that she hardly noticed the slight language of the dead plants on her tongue, though the chill of her magic canceled out the stew's warmth.

The stew did an excellent job of chasing away the chill, and the bread had a nice, nutty taste and a pleasant chewy texture. She wiped her bowl clean with the last bit of bread, chased it all down with the fizzy, fruity drink, and let herself enjoy the jaunty tune winding through the inn played by the bard group.

They were talented, and Jayce was a little too ready to leave her worries behind as she got caught up in the music. The drink, fermented as it was, went to her head and made her senses float away enough that she didn't notice when a large, bearded man flanked by two capital soldiers crossed the inn's threshold until the conversations died and the music trailed off.

The master of the inn left the table he'd been visiting and clasped his hands in front of his round, aproned belly. "It isn't every cycle the queen's own bailiff graces our door. We're honored to serve you and your men. Kiri, bring a pitcher for these fine, working gentlemen." The innkeeper smiled pleasantly, playing his role.

Sir Dray sniffed as he glanced around the inn. His eyes skipped over Jayce as she turned her head slowly away. She was just another traveler, a young woman with nondescript features and brown hair. There was no reason he'd pick her out of this crowd, except...

Her gloves.

Jayce shoved her hands beneath the counter and tugged at the fingertips, trying not to let the struggle get to her. It wouldn't come off. Panicked, slightly inebriated, and cursing herself for a fool, she slid off the stool and crawled across the floor toward the nearest table where a single man sat. She curled herself tightly against the single leg at the center of the round table, careful to avoid the man's stretched out feet.

Her arms clasped around her legs, hugging them tight to her as she waited for Dray to tire of searching for her.

Booted feet approached the counter, and Jayce froze. Her pack remained on the ground where she'd left it. It looked non-descript enough that Dray might ignore it. Her leather vial-holder, on the other hand, was unique to her trade. She cursed herself for forgetting to put it away. Would he recognize it? Or would he glance over it and leave?

She held her breath. The boots moved again, closer to the counter, and tilting her head slightly she caught a glimpse of Dray's hands roving over the vials in their leather pockets.

"She's here," Dray murmured to the man beside him.

Jayce ducked back, blood pounding in her ears, and she gripped her legs tighter, her mind reeling with thoughts of imprisonment, the taste of salt on her lips. She would be sent to mine that salt for the rest of her cycles if Dray caught her. That was the best-case scenario.

Dray's face floated into view, his expression morphing from curiosity to a smirk that made Jayce recoil even farther. His hand shot out and wrapped around her arm. He dragged her out from beneath the table.

"Found you, little mouse," Dray jeered. "Got her, let's go," he said to the men who had accompanied him. They weren't soldiers at all, but men with swords and leather armor, looking like the mercenary types that took dirty jobs for dirty money.

She wriggled, gasping as Dray's hands tightened further, and her eyes roved the crowd, locking gazes with the man whose table she had hid under.

Unlike the eyes of the other onlookers, who either stared in shock and curiosity or glanced away in shame, his eyes were wide and almost seemed to recognize her.

But that was impossible. She had no idea who this man was. How could he know her?

CHAPTER SEVEN

Jayce's gaze flicked to the door for only a moment before she lunged. She yanked her bags from the floor and prayed to the Three Sisters she could move fast enough to get away.

Dray moved at the same time, his bulk blocking her path. Jayce ducked under his grab and ran, dodging around tables and the stunned patrons of the inn.

Run. Run. RUN! Her mind screamed.

Jayce stumbled out the door and past the two stunned guards that had arrived with Dray. Facing the darkness, she blanked on which way she should go. To another inn? See if a family might take her into their home? She knew no one here. She had nothing to offer unless someone was sick.

Her pause cost her dearly.

Rough hands caught both arms from behind. She fought against Dray's grasp until he shoved her around the side of the building where the shadows would hide them from casual passersby. He shoved her against the outer wall of the inn, making her cry out. He muffled the sounds of her distress with one meaty hand pressed over her mouth until she stilled, and then he removed it.

"How did you find me?" Jayce managed, still tasting him in her mouth.

She resisted spitting and settled for glaring at the man in front of her. His hired hands kept watch for any trouble from inside the inn.

"You think I don't know about your silly note exchange system with that rock merchant? I've been watching you for a long time, Miss Keenstone. I know your every routine. I know where you keep your spare key. After our odd little meeting at the castle entrance, I wondered if maybe you'd gotten it in your head to report me. Or maybe you have some information on Lord Syfas' case that might prove your innocence. Either way, I decided to question you. Despite the late hour, I figured you could be awake. Imagine my surprise when I found the apothecary abandoned and the note to your friend telling him to cover up for your illegal travels to the monastery. And that got me thinking, why would she want to go to this library so bad?"

Jayce hung her head. She'd hardly made it more than half a league down the road. How had she fooled herself into thinking she could get to the monastery and back without him noticing?

Dirty black boots kicked dust onto Jayce's skirt. She looked up to see Dray gesture to his men, who grabbed her on either side, jerking her arms back and forcing her to look up into Dray's face.

He managed to look almost sympathetic. "You're going to wish you had kept your head down and stayed out of things. Because now my boss thinks you know too much, and he's not pleased."

Jayce opened her mouth to ask who Dray's boss was and why he'd care about anything she knew, when Dray's fist connected with her stomach, driving all the air out of her lungs. She doubled over, wheezing.

Her legs crumpled, but the men roughly yanked her up, straining the muscles in her shoulders. She cried out, still panting with the pain that had bloomed in her stomach.

"First, I will teach you not to run from me. Once you understand that concept, perhaps you'll be more open to marriage." Dray's lip curled, and he readied his fist for another strike.

"Why are you afraid of me? I'm nobody," Jayce shouted. "Or do I know something, after all? Who are you working with, Dray? Where did you get the noxbrosia?"

It was a shot in the dark, but Jayce watched Dray's eyebrows lift. His eyes widened slightly, and his mouth went slack for an instant before he regained control of himself, raising his fists again.

"You would do well to stop prying into matters that do not concern you," he growled.

"I do hate a man who hits a defenseless woman." A new male voice came from behind the men holding Jayce.

Their grips relaxed, and Jayce jerked away, darting past Dray's grasping arms into the dark and running headlong into a solid form.

The man whose table she'd hid under.

He pushed her gently away but held on to her arm, his eyes softening as they stared into hers. There was that flicker of recognition again.

"She is a criminal," Dray shouted, storming toward where Jayce and the man stood. "She's hardly an innocent woman. Stay out of this situation you know nothing about."

"Nothing she has done warrants this kind of treatment. Dragged from a public place and beaten in an alley? She did not attack you, that I saw. Can you stand on your own, milady?" the stranger asked. "I won't allow him to hurt you while I'm here."

Jayce remained frozen, hardly daring to breathe or move, the pain in her stomach still throbbing. She didn't think any damage had been done internally.

"You don't know me," she said, voice raspy from a scream she didn't remember releasing.

"Don't bet on that," the stranger said. "Jayce Keenstone, correct?"

Jayce's brows furrowed together. She finally straightened, edging out of the stranger's grip and farther from Dray and his men.

"How do you know my name?" she asked.

The stranger hesitated. "It's quite a long story, one better told over food and drink. I say we deal with the situation at hand and then get to know one another. Does this man have cause against you?"

"She has a debt that she refuses to pay," Dray snapped.

"I have paid on time every turn!" Jayce's voice went deep, filled with conviction and truth. Her own fiery conviction reflected back at her through the stranger's gaze. "I did not run from my debt, Dray. As you well know. I ran from your threats, and I have urgent business you kept me from attending."

Dray gave a harsh laugh. "Leaving the city without declaring intent leaves us to assume you meant to flee without paying and frees me to do as I will with a criminal such as yourself."

"According to the law, what is the punishment for leaving without declaration?" the blond-haired stranger asked, punctuating each word.

Dray gritted his teeth. "Five cycles in the stocks," he muttered reluctantly. "And a fee for each cycle the debtor is in violation."

Those kind eyes turned back to Jayce. "You won't be truly free until this debt is paid, will you?" the stranger asked.

Jayce shook her head. Dray would show restraint only until they were out of this man's sight. If the man followed them to the capitol, he would wait until she was imprisoned. There would be no escaping his wrath then.

"Very well. Her debt. How much?"

Jayce nearly fainted. There was no way this stranger intended to pay for her freedom. He hadn't an ounce of hesitation in his expression. In fact, he *winked* at her.

CHAPTER EIGHT

The stranger angled himself toward Dray, standing closer to Jayce than before, but now she could see Dray's expression.

Dray guffawed. "It's a life-debt, you imbecile. What did you think you would do? Pay it off and sweep her away from a life of drudgery tied to the coffers of the realm? She earned her place. Be on your way and let her keep it."

The stranger looked at Jayce, who resisted the urge to duck her head in shame. She wouldn't be ashamed of the effort she'd made to find a cure that had put her in this debt in the first place. She doubted this stranger cared enough about her to actually pay off the exorbitant sum. What could he hope to gain from making such a grievous financial error?

"How much?" The stranger said again, quieter this time but with no less conviction.

Jayce made a strangled sound. "Sir, I can't let you do this. It's a huge sum of money. You can't possibly—"

"I will determine that when someone has told me how much," the man said, firmly.

Jayce wanted to hate him for his confidence. Surely no one had that much laying around to hand over in the cause of a stranger, but he didn't seem to be posturing. He didn't brag. Simply stood there, looking expectantly at Dray.

"Y-you can't be serious!" Dray finally managed. "No one would pay a stranger's life-debt. Few could."

"The amount please, bailiff. You are a bailiff, are you not?" The stranger raised his eyebrows.

Dray grumbled, then took a ledger from a pocket inside his blue cloak. He opened the rolled-up paper and scanned the document, running his free hand along the page.

"Keenstone, Jayce. Amount owed, 187,646 djewls." Dray let the parchment roll back up on itself. "You have that in your pockets?"

"Near enough." The baron drew a much smaller piece of parchment from his own pocket. This one bore a seal. "I anticipated meeting you soon, though I imagined under much different circumstances. This is a certificate from my treasurer. You'll find everything in order, confirming that I do, in fact, have the means and the intentions to pay the debt."

He was serious. He really had the means and intention to free her from her debt. Jayce's breath caught. It was too good to be true. If she allowed this man to pay her debt, would she be more indebted than she had been before?

What would he ask of her, and would she be willing to pay it?

And the fact that he had come prepared with these documents, and said he'd planned to meet with Dray about her... What did this man want with her?

"Then get a quill and let's be done with it," Dray growled, not sparing Jayce another glance.

"I'm sorry, I can't let you do this," Jayce said, stepping away from the baron, putting her hands up defensively. "This is so incredibly generous of you, but it's none of your affair."

"Having second thoughts about our wedding?" Dray said, wiping his arm across his mouth.

"I insist," the stranger said, eyebrows coming together in confusion. He leaned in closer. "I assure you my intentions are honest, and I will not hold this against you in any manner."

"I have a hard time believing that," Jayce replied, lowering her voice to match. "In my experience, no one gives like this without expecting something in return. Even if they look nice."

"I see why you would think that. What if I promise not to require anything of you that you aren't comfortable with? I simply wish to speak with you, and I can't easily do that if you go to jail. Or the stocks."

Jayce bit her lip, considering. His expression and tone seemed sincere, but she knew better than to completely trust a noble throwing money around. Unfortunately, he made a good point. If she didn't trust him enough to pay off her debt, she would be hauled back to the capital, under the same threats from Dray and deeper in debt than before.

She wouldn't be able to research noxbrosia at the library, and while she might find more clues in the capital, her search would be delayed by her time in the stocks, making it possible for whoever had made the poison remedy to murder more innocent people.

Jayce finally nodded. "Very well. I accept."

The baron summoned the innkeeper to serve as witness, and the innkeeper came out, wringing his hands in his apron. When he caught sight of the baron, and then Jayce's disheveled state, he cringed.

"How can I be of assistance?" he asked.

"A large sum of money is about to change hands, Tumnus. We need a quill and a witness," the baron said.

Tumnus bobbed his head in agreement and invited them to take a seat inside the inn. Once they were all settled, he insisted on reading over the contract.

"Have to be sure you aren't tryin' to sell this poor girl or nothin'. No offense," Tumnus said firmly.

Jayce forgave the man immediately for not stepping up for her sooner. He'd likely been thinking of his other patrons and the longevity of his business. He seemed like a kind man, and Jayce couldn't fault him for sacrificing her to protect what he had. Especially when he'd likely assumed Dray was just doing his job.

"No offense taken," the baron replied cordially. He sat straight and calm, brushing something off his white suit.

Dray muttered something under his breath about the delay. He sat next to Jayce, the two men he'd brought with him standing behind her as if they were worried she'd get up and run at the first possible moment.

She had to admit she'd thought about it.

Satisfied with the contract, Tumnus handed it over to the baron, who wrote Dray's full name on the top line, his own name, and the amount of Jayce's debt.

Jayce watched the exchange, gut churning. But despite her wariness of the baron's intentions, she couldn't help but feel anticipation. She'd never imagined that in her lifetime she'd see the cycle when her life-debt was paid off.

The baron passed the contract to Dray, who signed with an illegible scribble, then blew on the ink to dry it.

"She's yours, then." Dray clapped his hands, rubbing them together.

"Certainly not," the baron said, smiling at Jayce. "She is her own."

Dray stood, pushing his chair back with a scrape on the floor that made Tumnus wince, and motioned for his men to follow. Just before leaving, he leaned down to Jayce.

"If you know what's good for you, you'll stay far away from the capital. Don't go digging around. You won't like what you find, and the baron won't always be there to save your hide."

Jayce looked up at Dray in alarm, catching the sneer on his face before he turned and left the inn.

Her hands trembled, and her head swam. Could Dray have known what she was going to the monastery to research? How would he have guessed? Was it because of her association with Lord Syfas?

Jayce stood. Her head felt hot, and her stomach still ached from Dray's strike.

"Did you mean what you said?" she blurted at the baron. The words weren't at all the grateful ones she'd meant to express.

The baron broke off his conversation with the innkeeper and blinked at her in surprise. "Whatever do you mean?"

Jayce rubbed at the bald spot on her right eyebrow, then clasped her hands together. "That I'm free to go? To do whatever I will?"

"Of course. Though I had hoped you would speak with me for a moment. I've been looking for you for some time."

Jayce closed her eyes. Why did she feel dizzy?

"Please, sit. I'll have Tumnus bring some cordial," the baron said.

Jayce hesitated, glancing to where her pack lay slumped over, abandoned at the bar.

"Tumnus, please have her things brought over here. And a nice wine. And a damp rag for that cut on her head," the baron smiled.

Tumnus bobbed his head and went to fetch the things the baron had requested.

Jayce raised a hand to her head as she sat down again, touching the sticky spot behind her temple. Dray had hit her with the hand that bore his seal ring, she remembered. That explained the way her head had felt like it exploded when he struck.

The baron breathed out. "Whew. What a night. I did not expect so much excitement when I followed you out of the capital."

"You followed me?" Jayce asked, nearly standing up again. She needed to get out of here. She could only think of one reason the baron might know her name, and it wasn't something she was interested in exploring with a stranger, no matter that he'd just saved her from an unwanted marriage, prison, and a life-debt.

"Tell me what you want," she blurted, then stuffed a hand against her mouth. *The Three forgive my big mouth.*

"You assume correctly. I don't normally make a habit of dropping exorbitant amounts of money for the benefits of strange women. Though maybe I ought to. It has turned out to be highly satisfying."

His language was rich and varied. He sounded as if he'd attended the university, and perhaps he had, as a baron's son.

Jayce's own education had consisted of reading borrowed books, a short apprenticeship to a local herbwoman, brief access to the alchemists employed by the queen, and talking to plants. It hardly qualified her in the eyes of other apothecaries, much less more distinguished company.

"You *are* Jayce Keenstone, are you not? I know I asked before, but I figured I ought to make certain," he said, tilting his head to catch her eyes.

Jayce fidgeted with a tear in the top layer of her skirt. Something else to fix. She didn't know what to say to this baron.

He's just a baron, Jayce. You speak to others just like him daily. Sit up straight, look him in the eyes. For some reason it was different when the baron wasn't her patient.

"How do you know my name?" The words came out more forcefully than she'd intended, thanks to her nerves.

The baron laughed and shifted in his chair. "I know more than that. I've been studying you. Or rather, I've been studying the Plague King and the records associated with the queen's attempts to cure the plague he cast over us. Your name came up an awful lot, and I had to speak with you. For my research."

"For your research," Jayce said slowly. It dawned on her what he meant, how he would have seen her name. He knew they had failed to defeat the Plague King. He knew about her brother. And from the look on his face, he wouldn't give up until he'd pried those memories from her in the name of his research.

CHAPTER NINE

A panicked film blurred Jayce's vision. Her breathing hitched. Her body stood, obeying some command that she hadn't given.

Run. Run. RUN. Her mind repeated. Just as it had with Dray.

This man, this baron, was as dangerous, just in a different way. He would make her go back to that mountain, to the place where her brother had died.

No, not died. Changed. Transformed into something else. Something she could hardly bear thinking about.

"Where are you going?" The baron's distorted voice filtered in through the panic.

A hand landed on her arm.

"You said yourself I was free to go, so let me!" Jayce screamed. She flung his hand away, picked up her pack, and bolted for the door.

The damp spray on her face was nearly enough to shock her into halting. It hadn't been raining before. But the baron calling from behind startled her into a sprint.

Her boots splashed through the water on the road, and her pack thudded against her back. She should have left it behind, should have changed her name when she returned from the mountain without her brother five ages ago.

Goddesses above, why hadn't she changed her name?

Thunder rumbled, louder than Jayce expected.

The baron grabbed her arm again, shouting something unintelligible.

Jayce yanked from his grip a second time, slid her pack off her back, and swung it toward him. He stumbled back into the middle of the road.

Thunder rumbled again. She hadn't seen any lightning, and the thunder didn't stop rolling, sounding more like a horse's hooves coming up on the road.

"Look out!" Jayce shouted.

The baron reeled around. He slipped in the mud and fell on one knee as a carriage bore down on him, the two horses pulling it galloping recklessly through the rain-filled night. The driver in front shouted for her to move, his face lit in an eerie, bouncing light from a lantern tied to the front of the coach.

Her hearing cleared, and she finally registered what he was saying.

"Move out of the way!"

Jayce grabbed the baron's arm and dragged him up. She couldn't carry his full weight, but her effort enabled him to get his feet under him once more. He stumbled back with her, out of the path of the carriage.

Momentum carried them off the road together, and Jayce's heel struck a rock. She fell into the mud, dragging the baron with her and getting crushed as they landed.

Her breath knocked from her lungs, but she twisted, shoving the baron off her as she spit gritty water from her mouth and glanced over him for any wounds.

The carriage slowed some paces ahead. The driver dismounted and ran toward them.

"Are ya hurt? Please, goddesses, don't be hurt!" the driver said, skidding through the mud.

Jayce stared at the baron's muddied face, his matted curly hair, and the ridiculous grin on his face.

"Are you hurt?" she asked, her mind slowly clearing and realizing that she was lying on top of him, somehow. She rolled off him, struggling to her feet.

"I'm all right. A little banged up, maybe."

"Praise the Three," the driver said, sending a litany of whispered prayers up to the heavens. He turned and headed back for the carriage, leaving Jayce and the baron staring at each other in the near-dark.

"You're all right, then? You're not hurt?" the baron asked.

"No!" Jayce cried. Emotion crashed over her like a wave. She'd made a fool of herself. She wanted to bury her face in her hands, but she busied herself instead, gathering her pack, which had been thrown to the side so violently by their fall that it had come undone and her cloak containing her dishes had unraveled partway. Hopefully, her vials of plants weren't all broken. She started back down the muddy road with the baron walking at her side.

"Can you tell me what happened back there? Did I say something wrong?" the baron asked.

"No, I..." Jayce twisted her hands together. She closed her eyes, trying to find the words. "People who know about my past aren't usually kind."

"That's why you ran?" the baron asked, sounding incredulous. "Did you think I would be angry with you? Hurt you? Because I can assure you, I—"

"No!" Jayce said, cutting him off. She grabbed her skirts in her fists and gave a frustrated groan, feeling as if she could tear her hair out. Why was this so difficult to talk about?

The baron followed, jogging to catch up to her. To his credit, he didn't speak.

"I left the capital because I needed to find some information. I need rest, and I don't have time or energy to explain my past to a complete stranger."

"You have been through a lot," the baron said, his expression thoughtful. "I should have been more tactful. Would you give me a chance to redeem myself?" He smiled wryly, dragging a thick strand of damp, unruly curls out of his face.

Jayce stopped walking, ignoring the rain trickling down her skin. "I don't even know your name."

The baron bowed at the waist. "I am Savage Alighieri. At your service."

Jayce inclined her head. It was an odd name, and unfamiliar to her. Surely a baron with as much money as this one had at his disposal would be better known in the capital, but politics were a weakness of hers.

She breathed in and let the air whoosh out of her, then held out her hand. "Jayce Keenstone, apothecary."

Looking amused, Baron Alighieri took her hand in his, turned it over, and planted a kiss on it.

Jayce squashed the giddy, girlish feeling that rose inside of her at his show of chivalry. No one did romantic things like that anymore. Certainly not noble to commoner. She reeled around and continued her march forward, hoping the flush in her cheeks would leave before the baron caught up to her.

The inn glowed warmly in the short distance. Jayce bit her lip, hoping Tumnus would allow them to stay.

He did, with some smooth-talking from Baron Alighieri, who seemed to know the innkeeper. They spoke with familiarity that only came from frequent contact.

"Tumnus just told me the inn is full tonight. I know we just met, but I have semi-permanent quarters here. The room is more than big enough for two..." He trailed off, watching her with cautious eyes.

Jayce's shoulders sagged as she crossed the threshold into the common room. Many people had gone up to their rooms, leaving the common area far emptier than before. Fatigue dragged on her. She could go to one of the other inns and hope to find a room this late. She could more easily leave in the morning without the baron realizing she had gone.

Her stomach clenched at that. Before, it had clenched at the thought of trusting him. Now, it clenched at the thought of leaving without telling him. *Make up your mind,* Jayce told herself.

As much as she hated the idea of feeling indebted to the baron, she couldn't ignore the potential resource he might be if she could trust him. A man of status and wealth perhaps had friends at the monastery where she intended to do her research. It might be worth getting to know him better, but she would have to tell him outright that information about what had happened five ages ago was off-limits. Would he be so amenable then?

Baron Alighieri smiled, dabbing at the mud on his face with a damp cloth. "Well?"

"I'll sleep on the floor, and we will have a screen brought up to divide the room," Jayce said in a rush.

"Yes, to the screen, brilliant idea. No, to the floor. You'll have the bed, obviously," the baron insisted.

"I'm not sleeping in your bed," she countered, readjusting her grip on her things.

"I'll ask about a cot and some food and brandy. I need a decent drink after the events of tonight." He chuckled.

He had an admirable, easy-going manner to still be able to laugh after all they'd been through. It made Jayce think of Nels, who always seemed to have a positive outlook no matter how dismal things got.

She could do worse. Like Dray.

"All right. I agree," Jayce said at last. "About the room and the brandy, please."

She managed a small, polite smile, wincing at the pain in the side of her head. It had worsened after the fall to the ground, and concern that she might have a concussion made her head pound even more as she made a mental list of herbs she could take for it, if her vials were still intact.

Jayce's eyes drifted to the baron's damp, curly hair, staring as it swayed against the damp, once-cream suit he wore. It had mud on it, and seeing the dark spatters made her inspect her own soaked and muddy skirts. She didn't have a proper change of clothes at all.

She ascended the last of the stairs and walked into the room at the end of the hall that the baron unlocked.

He closed the door behind them, and immediately went behind the dressing screen provided in the room.

The baron is undressing with me in the room! Jayce stood awkwardly dripping on the floor, unsure whether it would be most polite to look away or exit the way she had come.

Baron Alighieri seemed unconcerned. "Did you grow up in the capital?" he called as his damp suit and shirt were draped over the top of the screen.

Jayce gripped her arms, suddenly chilled. "Tell me about you first."

"Fair enough," the baron said good-naturedly. "No, I grew up north of here in a town of little fame. My parents didn't want me to grow up spoiled, I suppose. We lived simply, until they sent me to school."

Interesting. Jayce wouldn't have guessed he'd been raised away from politics. She wanted to ask more questions, but it seemed only fair to give him something in return.

"I grew up on the outskirts of the capital."

"Lowertown?" Baron Alighieri asked.

"Outside of that, even. Almost not in the capital at all," Jayce replied, focusing her attention on a small table near the wall. It held a stack of parchment, a quill, a candle, and a handheld mirror.

She walked over, picked up the mirror, and turned her face each way. Mud, blood, and tears coated her brown hair and streaked her thin face. She needed to eat more. Trying to pay down her life-debt had forced her to make certain sacrifices.

Sacrifices that she no longer needed to make, thanks to the baron. She hadn't been able to process it before, but a weight suddenly lifted off her, and relief overwhelmed her, bringing tears to her eyes. A sob threatened to break forth, and Jayce breathed deep, putting her hand over her mouth. She searched for some response she could make to the baron, anything other than sobbing in his presence.

Jayce cleared her throat. "Alighieri is an odd name. I haven't heard it spoken in the capital. Who are your parents?"

The baron laughed. "That question has a complicated answer. Suffice it to say, Alighieri is a name you'll be hearing far more often when I finish the project I'm working on." He emerged from behind the screen, dressed in a flowing white shirt and vest, green breeches, and thick, fluffy stockings.

His blond curls framed a tanned, oval face, strong jaw, and bright blue eyes that Jayce hadn't noticed during the intense situation in which they'd met.

Baron Alighieri spread his hands. "What do you think?" He grinned.

She'd been staring. Jayce blushed. "Very... fine," she admitted.

His expression fell. "Only fine? I went for comfortable, but fashionable, and all I get is fine?"

"Not that kind of fine! Like, finery. Luxury. You look nice," Jayce corrected, fingers fidgeting in front of her.

"Ha. Nice is hardly a better compliment. I like luxurious though. That's *nice*." He raised his eyebrows, and Jayce had the distinct impression that he was making fun of her. She rubbed at the smooth patch on her right eyebrow, then forced herself to stop and clasped her hands together again.

She'd noticed how he'd skirted her earlier question about his parents. Had he avoided answering properly, or was she being too paranoid?

"Are you going to get changed?" he asked, gesturing at her wet clothes.

Jayce lifted her arms helplessly. "I didn't bring a change of outer clothing. Only under… things. I'll just drip dry here near the door."

"You will not," Baron Alighieri exclaimed, moving immediately to a wardrobe in the corner between the dressing screen and the bed. "What kind of host would I be if I let my guest catch a terrible blither while under my care? I'm no lady, but I'm certain a few of my things might fit while we send yours to be washed and dried."

"Oh no, that's not necessary," Jayce said, shaking her head. She didn't need his *clothing* after everything that he'd done for her.

He ignored her protests and tossed a shirt in her direction, large enough it might swallow her whole. A pair of breeches followed, and a belt, and another pair of the same stockings he wore, so plush that Jayce wanted to rub her face on them to see if they felt as soft as they looked, but she resisted.

“That’s premium spapsas wool. You won’t wear anything finer in your life,” the baron said.

Jayce disappeared behind the dressing screen, hunching in on herself as she peeled off her wet clothes, one article at a time. She made sure each part of herself was only uncovered for the briefest of moments. Nothing could be done for the stay she wore—she hung it to dry.

After tucking in the billowy shirt, she threaded the belt through loops in the pants. Last, she tugged the socks on, shuddering with pleasure at the cloud-soft wool.

Whatever stroke of luck Jayce had found, she hoped it held long enough for her to enjoy it.

CHAPTER TEN

"You're right," Jayce said, emerging and picking up her feet, admiring the beautiful stockings. "I think I'm walking on a cloud. When I'm wealthy, remind me to commission a dress made of this stuff."

She froze. When had the maid entered?

The middle-aged woman with streaks of gray in her black hair already held Baron Alighieri's wet clothes and looked expectantly at Jayce.

"Belsa will launder your clothing, Jayce. She's sent for a cot to be set up as well." Baron Alighieri rubbed the back of his head with one hand, glancing over Jayce's appearance. "Guess my clothes are a bit big."

"Not much," Jayce said, fully aware of his gaze on her. Her cheeks heated. "I only wish I could have had a bath. I'm filthy."

The baron slapped his forehead. "How did I not think of that! I can call for one to be drawn up. Belsa?"

"Yes, Baron?" The maid's eyebrows had risen nearly past her hairline.

Jayce could only imagine the rumors that would start. Did the baron not think about his reputation, either? Alone in a room with her, a woman he had saved from a bailiff of the capital?

"No!" Jayce exclaimed, flustered at the idea of soaking naked in the baron's quarters. "No, that's all right. I can wait until morning. Thank you, Baron, for your generosity."

"All right, then. Belsa's brought the wine, and I still have questions for you. Questions you promised to answer. The fire's been stoked, and I had a cushion brought for you. And snacks!"

The baron's eyes lit up at the mention of food, and he walked hastily through a door in the side wall, popping his head back out when Jayce didn't follow. He motioned for her to join him.

Hesitantly, Jayce conceded, giving the maid an exasperated look.

The maid's mouth twitched upward in an almost sly smile. "You'll find the baron most amenable, milady."

"Does he do this a lot, then? Entertain young women?" Jayce hissed as she passed, tugging nervously at the end of her borrowed shirtsleeves.

"Oh, no. He almost never has guests. It's nice to see him with someone." Belsa shrugged and took Jayce's wet skirts, shirt, corset, and stockings, and draped them over her arm. "I'll have these back in the morning."

"Thank you," Jayce said, her cheeks burning with embarrassment at what the maid could possibly be thinking of her.

Through the door she went, entering a sitting room of sorts. Or was it a library? A study? Bookshelves lined the walls, filled except for a few half-empty shelves. A table with a writing set atop it took up space on one wall, and an armchair stood lonely near the fire.

Two deep blue, velvet cushions sat before the fire with a large tray of crackers, cheese, and assorted meats and fruits on it. A carafe of wine and two cups sat on the floor beside it all. A miniature feast.

Despite the stew Jayce had gulped earlier, she found herself craving the comfort of food.

She ripped her gaze away from the food and wiped at the corner of her mouth before her saliva could escape, watching as the baron lowered himself on one of the cushions and crossed his legs. Her eyes drifted back to the food, and emotion rose in her throat. Had anyone ever done something so nice for her? Why should she remain suspicious of someone who clearly had only kind intentions?

Because he's being too *nice.* her gut seemed to whisper, and her suspicion tainted the cozy tone of the setup before her. *Find out what he wants.*

"Everything all right?" Baron Alighieri asked in a deep, reassuring tone.

Jayce shook her head, a hook-sensation pulling at her gut. She placed a hand over her stomach. "You've been far too kind, Baron. I don't deserve any of this. And I know you think I have information for you, but I'm not important. Not a bit. The fuss all those ages ago was over my brother, and I'm sure you know how that ended."

She clipped her words at the end, wishing she hadn't mentioned Javin. Wishing she hadn't said anything at all as the baron's eyes saddened.

He patted his cushion at his side. "Please take a seat, if you would. And call me Sav."

Jayce sat across from him, staring into the fire. She didn't know if she could stand to look at him. Not after her outburst, and certainly not after he'd asked her to call him what sounded like a nickname, of all things.

The baron took a deep breath. "I don't mean to bring up memories that must be painful. Or rather, I do wish to hear what happened from you, so I might record it, but I don't wish to cause you pain. If you would..."

Jayce glanced at him, then did a double take. A fresh trail of blood had leaked down his temple and the side of his face, nearly reaching his chin. She scrambled to her feet.

"I have something for that. I'm sorry—I should have noticed sooner," Jayce stammered.

The baron touched his temple, eyeing the blood with curiosity. "I didn't even notice. Must have hit a rock when I fell on the road."

Jayce ran from the room amid the baron's protests and grabbed the leather pouch containing her herb vials and salves, praying as she unrolled it that they weren't all broken.

She re-entered the study, counting the broken vials and pots. One wooden pot of salve had cracked, but she could salvage most of it if she got another container. Only four of the twenty-four plant vials had broken, and they were all common mountain or river plants that she could easily obtain within a short walk. She breathed a sigh of relief.

Broken glass clinked as she shook it carefully into a pile on the floor.

Sav—or Baron Alighieri, she forced herself to call him—watched with quiet curiosity.

"Sorry about that. I'll clean it up in a moment," Jayce insisted.

"I'll ask Belsa to do it. I'm paying her, after all," the baron said, gently.

Jayce tugged on her gloves and unscrewed one of the pots containing her burdock and yarrow salve, then gestured at the baron. "If you would just... tilt, yes, toward me." She felt ridiculous leaning in so close. But why would she? The baron was just another patient.

He did as she indicated and remained as still as a statue while she applied the salve.

"That feels rather nice," he said, sitting with closed eyes for a moment after she'd withdrawn.

Jayce shrugged. "It's a basic salve. Nothing special."

She wiped the whispers of the plants from her fingers, then reached toward the pot again to dress her own wounds, but the baron took the pot from her.

"Now, then, it's your turn. Tilt your head just so." He smiled as if enjoying himself. Like it was a game, rather than two adults addressing real wounds.

"Thank you," Jayce murmured, allowing him to stroke the thick salve on shallow cuts across her cheeks, the top of her hand, and the bruised area on her head.

"I've gotten it in your hair," the baron admitted, setting the pot down and picking up the cloth she'd used to wipe her fingers.

"Unavoidable. I would have done the same, perhaps worse," Jayce said, laughing lightly and tucking a strand of hair behind her ear.

If only she had some toadsfoot. It would ease the nerves fluttering through her system, even if it did give her headaches. She reached for the wine carafe, her hand brushing the baron's as he lifted it and filled a cup for her.

She blushed, removed her soiled gloves, and took it from him, her hand shaking.

"You're dodging, Lady Jayce."

"Just miss," she blurted. "I don't have a title."

The queen had tried to give her one, and Jayce had refused. She hadn't wanted it. A title made a poor substitute for a family.

She wiped her mouth, which was wet with wine. Didn't people say it made one feel floaty and pleasant? She wasn't floating yet. How much did she need to drink to make a proper idiot of herself so this baron would believe her when she said he was wasting his time?

The baron steepled his fingers. "You have little cause to trust me, as I'm a stranger and a man at that. To assure you of my intentions, I'd like to share how I discovered you, and why it's important."

He cleared his throat, then sipped at his wine. "I was sent to study medicine, but my interests were in history, legends, and lore. I buried myself in the library, received poor marks in my medical classes, but drew the attention of the monks who taught history and record keeping. My penmanship certainly helped."

Baron Alighieri laughed dryly, then glanced at Jayce and coughed. "So, I changed my studies to history and graduated with top marks. But what I became obsessed with while I was there, once it began, was the plague. Perhaps a crossover between my history studies and my medical studies. Once I returned to Neldor, I poured over every record available, then received access to the locked records. The ones containing information about a certain prophecy."

He turned his gaze from the fire to Jayce, passion burning in their blue depths, a passion so strong her breath caught. She knew that sort of fire for knowledge. Had experienced it herself when she had confidence that she would be the one to find a cure.

But she had failed. And she didn't want to be the reason Baron Alighieri lost his passion. He'd be better off asking someone else to help him.

"I already told you; I can't help you. I have essential research to do at the Draigh monastery," Jayce said firmly.

"You mean Draigh. It's pronounced like stay," Sav said with a bemused expression.

Jayce flushed. "I've only read the name in books," she admitted. "Draigh?"

The baron nodded and turned to the snack tray with a contemplative expression as he stacked meat and cheese and crackers on top of each other. He hesitated before bringing the stack to his mouth, however.

"I plan to write a book, you see. I've already started it. A history of the plague, but writing it as it's happening instead of after the fact. Imagine," he said, putting the stacked crackers and cheese down and shifting forward, excitement filling his expression. "If I were to follow you about for a time, ask you questions about your research and the treatments you prescribe. An apothecary's perspective would be highly valuable."

"You could ask the queen's apothecaries. They are far more advanced, and I'm sure you'd get more interesting information for your book from them," Jayce said, sipping the wine again.

"Ah, but none of them were there when you... well, I've gathered you don't want to talk about that for now, and I promised to respect it. From my limited research and investigation, I've learned that you were there when certain key events happened. Events that possibly hold the key to more answers."

Jayce shook her head, her mouth suddenly parched despite the wine she'd been sipping. "Dwelling in the past isn't helpful. And as I told you, I'm singularly focused on my current research."

"Which concerns what?" the baron prompted, dropping his chin into his hand as if listening to her talk was the most engaging pastime in the world.

Jayce considered him, pursing her lips, then set down her cup and clasped her hands in her lap. "noxbrosia."

The baron's brow furrowed. "I can guess it's a plant, but I haven't heard of it."

"I know very little about it, except that it's poisonous, and someone has put it in a recent remedy for the plague. I need to find out how someone obtained it, where it grows, and more about its properties to make sure I understand it before I accuse someone of intentionally harming those who are sick."

The baron's eyes widened. "Have people died?"

Jayce nodded. "The remedy is new, but I have evidence it might have caused the death of one of my clients. I couldn't waste any more time to see if others died as well. The plant is known for its poisonous properties. It's forbidden to be sold in any market in the realm, and though I know it grows natively in Neldor, I'm unsure what area. If I could find out more about the plant, it might point to who would have come up with such a thing. At the very least, I could ask them why they chose to put poison in a tincture meant to cure."

The baron sat up and spread his hands. "You amaze me. Your knowledge and drive to discover the truth behind this. I hoped when I read about you that you would be such a person, but you have surpassed all expectations, Jayce Keenstone. I'd be honored to go with you and aid in your research."

Jayce's heart skipped a beat, and she took a breath to steady the surge of excitement she felt. She cleared her throat. "Have you been to the library at the Draigh monastery?"

"I have, yes. I've done a fair amount of research there in the past age." He smiled at her again.

"Do you have... connections there?" Jayce asked, hesitantly.

"A few of the monks are friendly with me. I believe one of them will have just returned from his pilgrimage to the Sanctuary of the Three in Thorgor. If you have need of any special attention or restricted volumes, I'm certain he'll be great help, especially if I put in a word or two."

"Then I accept your offer of aid, Baron Alighieri. And you may ask me questions along the way for your own research, so long as you agree to abandon any subject I find uncomfortable," Jayce said.

"Immediately and without question," the baron agreed. "If you will agree to call me Sav."

Jayce snorted and picked up her wine cup again. "You drive a hard bargain, Baron."

"Sav, if you please," the baron insisted, picking up his own cup. He raised it toward her. "To research partners and discovering truth."

Jayce obliged to the toast, bringing her cup up to meet his, their fingers brushing briefly, and then she drank, watching Sav from the corner of her eye and wondering if she had, in fact, made the best decision, or if she'd come to regret letting the noble-born historian accompany her to the monastery library.

CHAPTER ELEVEN

They didn't talk much after that. Jayce claimed fatigue, and not just as an excuse. She felt exhausted.

The cot set up on the other side of the room looked comfortable enough, piled with as many blankets and pillows as could reasonably fit, and at her request, the baron dragged the dressing screen between it and the bed.

They went to sleep without saying another word to each other.

In the morning, the scratching of a quill brought Jayce out of her strange, dark dreams and into the quiet room that smelled of wood and smoke.

A gentle beam of light filled with glittering dust motes slowly flooded oak floorboards. Jayce stretched and winced at the bright light, her head starting to pound from its rough treatment the night before. Likewise, she prodded the tender area on her stomach and stretched out her sore muscles.

She climbed out of bed, tucking in the enormous shirt and retying the belt to hold everything on her body. She donned a pair of soft leather gloves as well, not knowing what the cycle would bring.

"Good morning," the baron called out, the quill sounds stopping as he addressed her.

Jayce quickly combed her fingers through her hair and braided it.

"Good morning, Baron," she replied, tying off the braid. She padded around the dressing screen into the main part of the room.

"I've told you, call me Sav. That baron nonsense won't do now that we're colleagues. I don't much hold to the title anyway; it's more of a formality, since I haven't actually inherited any land yet."

She would have to get used to it eventually. Jayce breathed in. "All right, then, Sav. Are you ready to leave?"

"Before breakfast?" Sav seemed aghast at the idea.

Jayce twisted her gloved hands together. "No, I suppose not." Her stomach felt too funny for eating, all nerves about traveling with Sav and how she'd avoid his questions about her past. Perhaps some of that could be calmed with a decent breakfast.

"I'll call for Belsa," Sav said, getting up from his seat and going to the door. He rang a bell just outside, and a few moments later, a quiet knock came.

Belsa entered with a tray, her quick eyes darting between Jayce and the baron. "Did you sleep well, miss?" She seemed to have noticed the dressing screen, and some of the mischief faded from her eyes.

Jayce grabbed a scone from the tray and bit into it, crystals of sugar from the topping coating her lips. "Very well, thank you," she replied, spitting a few crumbs. She laughed, covering her mouth as more crumbs fell out.

Belsa and Sav both stared at her, a smile teasing Sav's lips, dismay taking over Belsa's expression, as if she'd fancied Jayce a mysterious and intriguing companion for the baron, only to discover she was ordinary.

Belsa brushed at her apron, folded her hands, and straightened. "Will that be all, Baron?"

Had she emphasized the baron's title? Perhaps to remind Jayce who she was with?

Jayce took another bite of the fluffy pastry. Blueberry and lemon burst on her tongue, and she forgot about the maid's scowl.

"Have them saddle the horses in about an hour, Belsa," Sav said.

"Of course," Belsa said. "Should we expect you for the lunch hour?"

"Please pack a lunch and some non-perishables. I believe we are going on something of a journey. Don't expect me back for some cycles," Sav said, pushing the pot of ink, quill, and scattered parchments aside as he tugged on the edge of a much older parchment covered in drawings.

Drawings of the Hoborn mountains, with scrawled text on either side as if the artist had made notes to themselves.

Where does the Plague King live? The nearest one read.

"Did you draw this?" Jayce asked, her throat tightening.

Sav glanced at the drawing she referred to, then swept it into a pile with several other pages of notes, stacking them together so the mountain was covered.

"Just a doodle," he said, giving her a quick smile.

Jayce frowned. Clearly not—the linework had detail she could never manage. Sav, it seemed, was something of an artist as well as a researcher. Why did he have such a detailed drawing of the Hobhorn? What did he know about the origins of the plague?

Whatever his purposes, they had little to do with her more immediate concerns. They needed to get to the Draigh monastery and find everything they could about noxbrosia, so they could discover how someone might have gotten hold of the rare plant to put it into the remedy.

Belsa cleared her throat. "Is there anything else you require, Baron Alighieri?"

Sav tipped the serving woman and excused her, then clapped his hands together, making Jayce jump. "Excellent! She brought the drinks I asked for."

Jayce eyed the steaming mugs on the tray, which Belsa had set on the bed, and picked one up, sniffing. The brown liquid looked creamy, and it smelled sweet with bitter notes.

"What is this?" Jayce asked, blowing on the surface of the drink.

"You've never had hot chocolate?" Sav asked. He picked up his mug, took a big breath in, and his head tilted back. "Oh, man, you're in for a treat. They ship it in from Enterea. It's the perfect thing on a rainy morning. Especially after what you went through last night. I don't like the silvertop

extractions—they taste like bitter weed water even with sugar. But this is excellent."

Jayce sipped tentatively.

Cacao.

Heart. Blood. Love. Lovers drink me to swell their...

Jayce snorted, nearly choking on the swallow of hot chocolate she'd just taken. She covered her mouth, some of the drink dripping into her hand. It had a flavor like nothing else she'd tasted.

Sav gave her an odd look and handed her a napkin.

"You okay?" he asked.

Jayce set down the mug and mopped her hand and chin, still laughing. "Sorry. It's... I had a funny thought. Is the chocolate—is it a plant? Cacao?" she asked.

Sav finished chewing. "I think that's what they call it. Cacao. I thought you hadn't tried it. How'd you guess?"

"Plants... speak to me," Jayce said haltingly. "I hear their name, they often speak of their properties, sometimes they say nonsensical or untrue things. That's why I've had to learn about them in the traditional ways, as well, to compare my notes with what the plants say and determine what is truth and what is a lie."

Sav looked impressed. "I knew you were gifted with plants, but no one mentioned it was a goddess-gifted ability. You could do this from birth?"

"Yes."

Receiving magical gifts from the Three at birth was the most common way magical abilities appeared in an individual, but they could also be gifted later, usually to those who dedicated their lives to the service of the Three and visited their shrines in Thorgor.

Once she got past the whispers the chocolate was delightful, and before too long, she'd lost herself in the cup, sipping greedily until she got to the slightly bitter dregs at the bottom, which she left alone, knowing the voice of the Cacao would be stronger if she drank them.

"Oh." She leaned back on one hand and closed her eyes. "It's a good thing I don't eat like that every morning. I'd be round as a boulder."

"I thought you'd like something special after last night," Sav said.

Jayce cracked her eyes open lazily. "You're too nice," she murmured.

"I don't think there is such a thing. I just like making people happy," Sav said.

"Well, what makes you happy?" Jayce asked, reluctantly opening her eyes wider and straightening. She felt like she'd roll across the floor if she tried to stand. She hadn't been this full in a long time.

"Everything," Sav said, smiling as if he knew that answer would annoy her.

Jayce rolled her eyes. "Okay, keep your secrets."

"Ready to ride?" Sav asked.

"I've only ridden a horse a handful of times," Jayce said. She frowned, remembering the last time she'd ridden one.

One horse had returned without its rider.

"Well, it'll come back easily, I'm sure. I'm surprised you've ever ridden one. That's not common among... well, common folk. No offense."

Jayce bristled slightly at the reminder of the difference in their stations. "None taken. It's a fact. I learned to ride under... special circumstances."

To his credit, Sav didn't ask her what those circumstances were. Ever since her explosion last night, he'd seemed to have gained an understanding of what topics to push and which to avoid—an uncanny sort of empathy. If their differences weren't so obvious, and if he didn't want to pry into her past like a starving squirrel with a nut, she might have been inclined to trust him more.

Sav stood, crossed the room, and picked up a pair of freshly polished boots by the door. He grabbed a second pair that Jayce recognized as her own.

"Belsa brought these back early this morning. She said your clothes are still drying. We can pick them up on our way out."

Jayce gathered herself together and forced herself to reconstruct her pack. She wrapped her travel dishes, reapplied the salve, and placed it in the leather vial pack, which then got rolled up and tied to the cloak bundle along with the blanket she'd brought.

Sav had a strange pack—a stiff leather bag with multiple straps—into which he piled books and parchment and maps, along with a quill case and a pot of ink. He clipped it closed at the top and pulled it over both shoulders.

"Like a satchel, but easier to carry," he explained to Jayce when he caught her staring. "They call it a backpack in the Guilds."

"You attended at the Ivory Guilds?" Jayce replied, more shocked by that than the odd bag.

"Yes. Have you ever been?" Sav asked.

Jayce shook her head. She'd never been anywhere, not south of the Hobhorn, not north or east of the Oakmist, not even west. She'd never seen the sea, never stood on a cliff.

She had little interest in travel, preferring the sanctuary of her apothecary and other familiar places.

"Well, I hope you do some cycle. They're incredible. I miss them terribly."

Sav went outside, and Jayce followed him to the stables behind the inn, where three animals stood waiting, tied to a post. A stable hand finished fixing a bag to one of the horse's backs and bowed to Sav.

"Baron, the horses are ready."

Sav tossed the young man a mark. "Thank you, Tyrrin. Did Belsa bring Miss Jayce's clothes, by chance?"

"She did. Said you were leaving for a few cycles and would want 'em. She said to come back soon, and she'd have a cuppa waiting for you."

"She didn't happen to pack any for us?" Sav asked, glancing sheepishly at Jayce.

"She did, Baron." Tyrrin grinned.

Sav sighed with relief. "Good. I wouldn't want to go weeks without my favorite drink. I'd miss it too much."

Jayce didn't mind admitting that after tasting it only once, she'd miss it, too, and she hoped Sav would share.

"Tyrrin here can help you mount," Sav said to Jayce, then turned back to the stable hand. "I think she'll like riding Elsa."

"Are these horses yours?" Jayce asked.

"Yes, in fact. They were gifted to me. Elsa is the smaller black and white, Abigail is the gray, and the shorter, stockier one in the back there is Maggie. She's a stubborn ass. And I mean that in both senses. But Abigail helps keep her in line, hence why they're tied together."

Jayce noticed the lead line connecting the two animals as Sav gestured between them.

The stable hand approached Jayce and asked for her pack.

Jayce turned it over, allowing him to strap it to the donkey. Then she approached the black and white horse, murmuring in a gentle voice. "Hello, Elsa. Please let me ride you. I don't weigh much, and I'm nice." From the corner of her eye, she spotted Sav pulling his bottom lip in, as if he were trying not to laugh out loud. Let him laugh.

Jayce managed a foot in the stirrup, but only made it halfway up before she had to drop back into the dirt. She tried again, straining until she was red in the face, but no such luck. She glanced helplessly at the stable hand, who smiled good-naturedly and came over to boost her up.

"Lead on," Sav said, gesturing ahead from atop his horse, Abigail.

Jayce finished settling herself and squeezed Elsa's sides with her calves, vaguely remembering the brief instruction she'd received ages ago.

Sav brought Abigail up on the left side of Elsa, and they took off down the trail. An expectant silence filled the air between them.

He didn't ask. Jayce respected him for that. But the fact that she *knew* he wanted to hear her story filled her with dread, and she could hardly focus on the road in front of her, much less what her horse was doing. She almost led it off the road twice before they'd even lost sight of The Silver Gardner.

She glanced at Sav, wondering what he was thinking, following her to the Draigh, probably hoping to convince her to tell him despite the fact she had refused. Guilt pinched in her gut and squeezed her chest. His entire purpose in paying off her debt had been so that he could freely talk with her, that he thought she held some secret key to whatever research he was conducting for his book.

He clearly didn't understand that some stories had greater costs than could be paid with money.

CHAPTER TWELVE

Hoofbeats thudded rhythmically as the horses plodded toward the patch of forest lining both sides of the road ahead.

Jayce looked at the puffy, almost translucent clouds in the sky, the trees in the distance, and at her horse's mane. Anywhere but at Sav, who kept glancing her way. She could tell he wanted to ask her something, and she wondered if she'd given him too much credit for his respectful silence earlier.

"So, what's with this remedy?" Sav asked, locking his gaze on the side of Jayce's head.

She felt the stare almost tangibly and fidgeted with the attention. "What do you need to know?"

"From what I've gathered, the remedy was given as a cure for the plague, correct? And you don't know who created it? But what's in it, and why do you need a library to track down a murderer?"

A farmer pulling a massive hay wagon rattled up the road. Sav and Jayce steered their horses almost into a ditch trying to give the man enough room to pass.

Oak.

Sustenance and strength can be found in my fruit. I–

Jayce leaned her head away from the leaves dangling in her hair and touching her cheek. A flash of coldness filled her head, and she shuddered.

"My magic tells me the main ingredient is noxbrosia, an extremely rare plant in Neldor. I have only heard of it in passing, and there's almost no information about it available in my books. It is forbidden to grow, sell, or trade this plant. That's how toxic it is."

"So how did someone get hold of it, and why did they include it in the remedy?"

"Exactly!" Jayce exclaimed, finally meeting Sav's gaze. "I don't even know if they intended for the remedy to kill. Perhaps noxbrosia has some property I don't understand, but my magic didn't reveal anything other than its poisonous properties and something about it cleansing the blood. I'm hoping the monastery's collection will contain a record from a time when the plant wasn't banned and someone wrote down deeper observations on it. Or if we can figure out where it grows, we might be able to determine where it came from, and from there, postulate who recently traveled to obtain some."

It was a stretch, and Jayce didn't have the investigative abilities she would need to find a trail if it went cold. But this was her only lead. She had a feeling Sir Dray knew something. The way he'd warned her off returning to the capital had been rather ominous, almost as if he knew she'd be in trouble if she went back and didn't want her to get hurt. But he hadn't exactly been kind about it either.

He could have let her go when he realized she'd left, but he'd tracked her to beat her, maybe even kill her. What if he'd been following orders from someone who didn't want Jayce to discover the truth about the poison and had second thoughts because Sav had shown up?

Not only did she owe him for paying off her life-debt, she possibly owed him her actual life, which made her feel even more guilty about not telling him the story of her past.

"Jayce?"

"Hm?" Jayce glanced up from the horse's main, startled. Had he asked her something?

"Why didn't you consult with the other apothecaries in the capital? I know the queen employs a fair number, and I would assume they'd be glad to discuss their findings with you."

Jayce snorted. "Then you don't know those men very well. They have wisdom, to be sure, but they are quite stingy with it. To consult with them, I'd have to pay them or apprentice with them, and having apprenticed with them briefly before, I have no desire to do it again."

"You apprenticed with the royal apothecaries?" Sav whistled. "You must have great skill to be recognized that way."

A whiff of rain came on the breeze. Jayce glanced up at the darkening clouds blowing in from the northeast above the trees. Another storm, like last night. She avoided looking at Sav again, realizing that by revealing that fact of her past, she'd come close to provoking questions she didn't want to answer.

"Where are we sleeping if it rains tonight?" Jayce asked.

Sav reached down and patted the neck of the donkey walking steadily beside his horse. "We packed a tent."

Jayce made a face. It couldn't be a large tent. They'd be sleeping... side by side?

Sav must have noticed her expression. "If it's good weather, I'll sleep outside. Baron's honor. I'll only come in if it's pouring. I can handle getting a little damp."

"That's not fair. It's your tent. I couldn't—" Jayce suddenly had a lump in her throat that she could hardly swallow past. "I don't think I ever thanked you properly for what you did last night. My debt must have nearly emptied your coffers. I don't know how you afforded it or why you thought me worthy of such a gesture, but I-I am in your debt."

Sav crossed his arms in front of himself, slashing through the air with them. "No, I insist that you do not think of it that way. I won't have you trying to pay it back or some nonsense, so don't even get that idea in your head. I got a research grant from my school, and I'm putting it to good use."

"There is no way your research grant covered my life-debt," Jayce replied, aghast. He'd spent his research grant, plus his own money, to free her from debt just to talk to her, and she couldn't even tell him what he wanted to know.

He cleared his throat, glancing away from Jayce. "I've been looking for you for some time. I found your name in a document I shouldn't have seen, but people sometimes leave things lying around that shouldn't be. I took advantage of such an incident and made my way to the capital as soon as I could to find you."

"But how did you know I had left the capital when I did? You seemed to be in exactly the right place at precisely the time I needed you," Jayce said.

Sav flushed and rubbed the back of his head. "I may have followed you, trying to figure out if it was you."

Jayce gaped at him. "That was *you* following me to my apothecary that evening? I was terrified! You couldn't have approached me then, asked what my name was?"

"You seemed rushed, and then when you got to the apothecary, you turned all the lights off, and I figured you'd had a long cycle, and I would talk to you in the morning. I stayed at an inn across the street. It was something of an accident that I glanced out my windows that evening and saw you leave. I wondered why a young lady would flee the city in the middle of the night on her own, and I certainly didn't want to lose you. By that time, I'd put the pieces together and figured out who you were, but again, I didn't want to frighten you."

Amusing, then, that he had unnerved her despite his intentions, but the amusement vanished quickly as Jayce's mind worked out the rest of the details around this man seeking her out.

"How do you know so much about me? About my life-debt?"

"If one has the right resources and contacts, one can find out a great many things others would think unreachable. Your noxbrosia plant, for instance. Being illegal to grow or possess, any information on it is likely held in the restricted section of the Draigh library. You're going to need to get someone on the inside sympathetic to your cause to let you see the records without written permission from the queen herself."

Jayce wilted, and her relaxed posture caused her horse to slow, making her fall behind Sav. "I don't know anyone at the monastery. I've never been there," she admitted.

He twisted in his saddle. "That's why you brought me, isn't it?" He flashed her a smile. "I'm good for more than my looks and my money, you know. I have friends there. Some enemies, too, but mostly the annoying kind. As I said, one of the monks of the Order of the Three is a good friend of mine. You'll like him."

Jayce urged her horse forward again, catching up to Sav.

The road narrowed for a stretch, and Sav ducked under a tree branch that sagged low, like it had broken in the storm.

Jayce kept an eye out, not wanting to run into any more errant branches. She couldn't shake her unease about the man riding beside her, the fact that he seemed to know so much about her and she knew nothing about him.

"Why were you looking so hard for me? Leaving your school, searching the city, paying off my debt just to talk to me. I'm not anyone special, Sav. Anything you want to know about me, you could probably pay the right person, and they'd tell you everything you wanted to know."

"But they weren't there. When you faced the Plague King, and your brother—"

A roar in Jayce's ears drowned out what Sav said next. Jayce kicked the horse's sides, and it bolted into a gallop, racing down the center of the road. Panic darkening the edges of Jayce's vision, she yanked on the reins to slow the horse down, but it veered toward the edge of the road instead. Branches whipped Jayce's face, scratching her and filling her head with whispering voices.

Oak. Maple. Birch.

Shouting from behind her. Sav. Clarity returned to Jayce's thoughts, and she pulled hard on the reins again, but not before a huge, low-hanging branch swept in front of them and the horse ducked. Jayce grabbed the branch and let it carry her off the horse's back. She landed on the ground.

She started to untangle her braid from the tree, a threatening hum filling her ears. She frowned, straining her hearing, wishing she had her brother's enhanced senses. The hum grew louder, and little black things whirred into her vision, surrounding her in a cloud.

Dozens of hot-needle pokes all over her arms and face, through the thin fabric of her shirt and even her legs. The runaway horse became the least of her worries as she swatted at the fat, angry insects swarming around her.

Blister bees.

CHAPTER THIRTEEN

Jayce woke to blurred vision and a pounding headache. Her blood chilled in her veins, leaving her trembling as if ice flowed through them, and voices whispered in her head, garbling the lies and truths that plants told.

She gasped, sitting up fast, and immediately regretted it for the stabbing pain in her head. She rubbed her cheek, which had numbed with the cold from her magic. She'd been laying in a bed of moss.

Her vision crossed and blurred again. She groaned.

Sav came up a nearby embankment carrying a small pot that sloshed water from its brim. He stopped suddenly, seeing her.

"You're awake! Thank the Three." He knelt, gazing at her, giving her a relieved smile. "I'm no doctor, but it didn't seem safe that you were out that long."

"How long?" Jayce demanded, still rubbing her cheek. It stung, feeling gradually coming back into it.

"Well, Elsa threw you, then she ran to the river and rolled in the water for a bit. I left her to check on you. Luckily, I don't think anything is broken. But again, not a doctor." He shrugged helplessly.

Jayce wiggled her legs and rotated her ankles, raised her arms and twisted her wrists. Her shoulder complained loudly from getting wrenched when she'd grabbed the branch, but not enough to indicate anything more than a mild strain.

Rosemary for inflammation. Jayce twisted her torso, breathing deep and feeling her ribs. A wave of nausea washed over her, and she froze, measuring her breaths and adding *mountain mint* to her list of herbs she needed to take.

And then there were the blisters. They all sang to life at once as Jayce accidentally brushed her sleeve across the back of her hands.

"Oh, no," Jayce moaned. Her hands shook with the fire racing across her skin. The massive, angry pustules had filled with a clear fluid. The worst ones were already filling with puss.

Sav leapt into action. "There's a river nearby. The cold water will take the worst away. Elsa walked right into a fallen blister bee nest. I didn't see it because I was so enthralled with what you were saying..." He shook his head. "We can talk about that later. For now, river."

"There's soap in my pack. It will help the blisters. Would you get it for me?" Jayce talked Sav through finding the soap, which she'd made with milktree sap, honey, and lavender, all soothing for the skin.

Sav returned with it, holding his hands out to help her up.

Jayce took his hand, wincing as his fingers brushed the blisters, making them fester. Her instinct to duck and protect her face had saved her eyes, lips, and other tender places. She only had a few on her head, neck, and one on her cheek.

"Can you manage all right? No feeling dizzy or anything?" Sav checked as he guided her down the riverbank.

"I'll be all right. Stay within calling distance," she said.

"I'll start a fire," he said, putting the soap down on a rock, then leaving her alone to bathe.

Jayce watched his retreating back, grateful she hadn't been alone when the bees attacked and grateful she hadn't gotten more injured when the horse threw her. She hadn't even asked if Elsa was okay.

Jayce left her clothes on a rocky part of the shore and lowered herself into an area of the river where the water swirled slowly before rushing down. The instant the cool water touched her skin, she sighed in relief.

She soaked until her skin wrinkled and her teeth chattered, reveling in the nature sounds around her. Tiny whippoorwills and the distant call of a mountain eagle, the shushing of leaves as the breeze blew through them. Sunlight dappled the leaves when she entered the water, but by the time she left, the dark clouds hid the sun, casting everything in shade and making her shiver.

She shook the extra water from her limbs and twisted her hair until it stopped dripping. She dressed as quickly as she could manage, wrinkly, numb fingers fumbling with the fine fabrics of the clothes she had borrowed from Sav. Putting gloves on was painful with the few blisters on the tops of her hands, but she wanted to touch as few plants as possible.

Jayce picked up what remained of the lavender-scented soap and half-walked, half-crawled up the loose-soil bank, slipping on foliage and grateful her gloves kept the plants' words at bay. She still wondered at the multitude of whispers she'd heard with her face on the moss, but she didn't want to think about it at the moment. Not until she did something about her headache.

When Jayce emerged from the top of the hill, Sav stood from his crouch beside a merry, crackling fire. He had a little pot set up on a flat rock in the fire.

"It's boiling. I figured you might want tea? Or maybe you'd need it to dress your wounds. They say to boil water when there's been an accident." He shrugged, wearing a pitying expression as he watched Jayce move stiffly over to the base of a tree near the fire and sit, leaning back against it.

"I do need tea, yes. And my salve. Can you bring that leather pack to me?" Jayce said, feeling worn to the bone. Her body was fighting off infection from the blister bees.

Sav laid her pack at her side and took a seat on the mossy area, watching as Jayce unwrapped the leather pack and ran her fingers along the glass vials. She tugged out the rosemary and mountain mint, along with a potent ginger she'd bought from a foreign merchant over the summer.

Ginger didn't grow in Neldorland. Or at least, she hadn't found it anywhere. She'd meant to try growing it herself, but clients and other concerns had overtaken her intentions.

She shook the dried plant bits into her gloved hand, then eyed the fire, which was close enough she felt its warmth but far enough she couldn't easily reach the pot that bubbled high with heated water.

"Let me," Sav said, jumping into action. He cupped his hands under hers until she dropped the handful of herbs into it, and he relayed them to the pot, brushing his hands off after.

"How long does that need?" he asked, putting his hands on his hips and surveying the fire. He grabbed a long stick with a blackened end and poked at the wood, feeding the flames.

"Only a few minutes. The pot should be taken off the heat. Do you have another rock nearby?" Jayce asked. She licked her lips, realizing her mouth was parched. She needed a drink, but she didn't want to order Sav around like he was the servant and she the noble.

Sav used a thick mitt from his packs to grab the hot pot handle and remove it from the flames. He placed it on a second, bumpier rock near the fire. The steam twisted into the air, filling it with a spicy, familiar scent.

Jayce leaned her head against the smooth tree bark at her back, letting the tree's bold voice wash through her for a moment. The coldness was almost pleasant with the fire in her skin.

Birch.

I cleanse and purge the black from limb and innards. My bark is my strength. There's a man on the road.

Jayce pulled away from the tree, startled. The tree had *talked* to her. Not just spouting what it wanted her to hear. It had spoken to her about something other than itself.

Just how hard had she struck her head?

CHAPTER FOURTEEN

Jayce intentionally pressed her head back against the birch's trunk, wondering if she'd misheard or if the tree might say more, but it only repeated what it had said before, ending with that strange phrase that sounded more like a warning than a lie.

There is a man on the road.

It could be a lie. Couldn't it? After all, she'd never had a plant *warn* her.

Jayce squirmed and pulled away from the tree, then sighed and stood. Her curiosity wouldn't be sated by sitting there thinking about it.

"I thought I heard someone on the road," she said to Sav, feeling bad about the lie but not wanting to alarm him with the strange experience she was having with her magic.

Sav looked up from the steeping tea, surprise on his face. “What? I can look. You should sit down.”

True, her head was swimming, but Jayce had to see for herself. She waved Sav off. “I can do it.” She forced herself upright and tried to walk in a straight line. Good. She wasn’t seeing double or tripping over things that weren’t there.

Sav’s shirtsleeve brushed Jayce’s blistered arm, and she hissed in pain.

“I’m coming with you,” Sav insisted.

“Someone should watch the fire,” Jayce argued, putting her gloved hand on a nearby tree for balance.

“It’ll keep,” Sav said, following close but not touching her arm again.

They cleared the trees and looked both ways on the road. It seemed deserted, the dust from the most recent travelers long settled, the sun quickly disappearing beyond the horizon, bruising the clouds with dark purples and blues.

But there were no crickets or toads chirping as they did in the evenings at the end of the Purple Bell Moon season, and the lack of sound set Jayce’s nerves on edge.

She eyed every shadow with suspicion, but nothing moved.

To his credit, Sav didn’t question her sanity as she scanned the darkening road for signs of life. Eventually, Jayce’s shoulders slumped.

“Guess I didn’t hear anything,” she said. *I guess the tree did lie to me.* All plants lied. She had to remember that.

“Even if you had heard correctly, why did you feel the need to check the road?” Sav asked.

Jayce shrugged. "Just a hunch, I guess." She turned away from the road to head back toward camp, and her stomach fluttered, activating all the alert signals in her body.

Slowly, she turned her head. Weak as the dying sunlight was, she could barely make out the form that ambled between the trees on the far side of the road, just off the beaten path. The outline seemed blurred, almost glowing a muted gray color.

Not the color of any regular, living man.

Panic clutched at Jayce's chest and clawed its way up her throat, garbling the word of warning that tried to come out.

Sav gave her an odd look, then glanced back the way she stared. His entire face went sheet white.

Moribund. The awful creatures that people transformed into after being infected with the Plague King's sickness, if they didn't die. Seven ages prior, after the plague had struck, the capital had almost been overrun with them, until Queen Lyra had found her voice again and driven them back with the help of her army and a gas compound one of her alchemists had invented.

Jayce edged around a tree, putting herself out of the moribund's line of sight.

She had two of the glass holders of the gas in her bag, cradled in the special pouch she'd sewn for them. She hadn't used one in ages, and the thought of getting one out now made her fingertips burn as if she'd grabbed a handful of grass from the ground and held onto it until it withered.

Breath gasped through her, accompanied by her pounding heart. As the moribund ambled out of the shadows, Jayce caught a clearer view of his face, and her entire body clenched.

Jones. Raegar Jones, the man who had approached her a few cycles ago on the street. The one she'd refused to treat in order to maintain her rounds and the satisfaction of her customers. She'd only seen him once, but she recognized him. How could she have given up trying to find him so easily? She might not have had a remedy, but her tinctures had been able to extend symptoms, prolong life. He might have had a chance if she hadn't been in such a rush to see paying clients.

Was it a coincidence that she was seeing him now, after the plague had changed him? Or had he somehow followed her, a sense of revenge leftover from his living self leading him to her?

She glanced around for Sav and found him across from her, behind a slightly thinner tree that barely hid him.

She bit her lip and considered her options. They could wait here, growing stiff and cold, and hope that the moribund wandered off. Or she could make a dash for her bags and pray to the Three that she was fast enough to toss one of the handheld gas chambers at the moribund before its unnatural burst of speed allowed it to catch her or Sav.

Across from her, Sav tilted his head just enough to peer around the edge of his tree, and then he straightened with a small gasp.

Jayce widened her eyes, asking him silently what he'd seen.

It's getting closer, Sav seemed to mouth.

Jayce didn't know if Sav had ever encountered a moribund. Judging by his current reaction, she guessed that he had no idea what to do. The denizens of the Plague King sometimes attacked and other times didn't. It seemed utterly unpredictable. When they did attack, everyone present ended up sick. But only some of them turned into a gray-skinned moribund before they died.

Jayce couldn't take the risk of getting infected. Counting down from five, she lunged from her safe place behind the tree, low-hanging branches slapping at her face as she ran.

Sav cried out, not understanding what she was doing, and Jayce nearly cursed out loud. He'd draw the thing right toward him.

She entered the fire-lit clearing and pounced on her bags, ripping them open with little care. She unwrapped clothes and tossed them aside until she found the knotted bundle she was looking for.

After fumbling with the knots, she grasped one of the glass spheres filled with glittering flakes. Those flakes held a compound that, when exposed to air, would cause a great gust of gas to rush out and envelop anyone standing nearby.

Living humans and animals were relatively unaffected, but the moribund would wither to a dried husk.

Jayce steeled herself to use the sphere again, ignoring the cry of her heart that screamed at her for not having a cure yet. She shouldn't be killing. She should be healing, but her gift had failed her in that regard, and all she'd gained from past attempts were a life-debt and a dead brother.

This was all she had left.

As she stood, the hairs on the back of her neck prickled with a sort of premonition. She bit back a cry and spun around, coming nearly face-to-face with the moribund.

Its face was wretched, black veins pulsing beneath its grayed flesh, a dark hole in place of its mouth.

It reached toward her, and Jayce faintly heard Sav calling out to her before she slammed the gleaming glass globe down and stomped on it for good measure.

The glass shattered, crunching beneath her boot, and the chemical reaction billowed into the air in a glittering yellow cloud.

Jayce instinctively covered her face with her arms. Even though the compound was said to be harmless, she still hadn't figured out everything that was inside it and didn't want to take in more than she had to.

"Jayce! What in the holy names of the Three was that?" Sav said, staring at the spot where the moribund had stood. A shriveled corpse rested on the ground, looking mummified and horrible. A slight mustiness clung to the forest air.

Jayce straightened her gloves and tucked the borrowed shirt back in at her waistline. "That was a moribund," she stated, still in shock herself.

"No, the thing you threw at it. And why." His voice cracked, and his expression grew desperate. "Why did you kill it like that?"

"I couldn't very well let it touch either of us," Jayce said, kneeling at her disheveled pack and re-wrapping the remaining sphere. She pointedly ignored the mummified body behind her.

"I've never seen anything like—I mean, I knew it was bad here. I've read about it, but I've never—"

From the sound of it, Sav was pacing, his footsteps crunching over the dead leaves on the forest floor.

"Why did you have to kill him? I could have *studied* him."

Jayce threw her clothes down and stood to face him. "While you were safe in your gilded ivory halls in Enterea, we were here, fighting *these*. At one point, we couldn't even go into the streets after the sun went down because the capital was so filled with the moribund."

She curled her fingers in on her palms, trying to squeeze out the pain in her chest. She kept her eyes locked on Sav, who seemed sorry he'd said anything, but she wasn't going to let him off the hook after an ignorant comment like that.

"When the queen's voice healed at last and she sang for the first time, we saw less of them. It was as if they couldn't stand the life in her voice, and her magic drove many away, but it wasn't enough. And then one of the alchemists created this compound, and they put it in spheres and gave them to everyone they could reach, and the city took on the moribund. And we won. So, forgive me for not wanting to go through even a portion of that again for curiosity's sake."

Jayce finally tore her eyes away from Sav's, unable to take the pity in them. She swallowed.

"And the compound—" Sav began.

"Doesn't cure the plague. Doesn't even alleviate it. And the man who invented these died, if you'd believe it, leaving useless notes written in his own shorthand language. They still have a team working to decipher them. I'm given a ration of the spheres because of the risks of my role as an apothecary, but we're going to run out, and when that happens, we won't be able to fight them anymore."

Sav nodded, still frowning, but he seemed more curious than judgmental now. He glanced down, brushing a twig off his shirt as the silence stretched between them.

Exhaustion swam through Jayce, and sensation seemed to return to her body in a rush as the adrenaline left her system. Her various pains flared up, first in the blisters along her arms, then the aches in her ribs, shoulder, and head.

Jayce winced and lowered herself to the ground, scooting far away from the moribund's wrinkly, dried body.

"I'll take care of that," Sav said quietly.

Jayce stared into the fire as Sav found some branches to roll the shriveled, feather-weight body onto a makeshift litter and drag it away into the woods. A while later, he returned, and dug a small shovel from his pack. He nodded at her as he returned to the forest and buried the husk of the moribund.

CHAPTER FIFTEEN

After the moribund attack, Jayce and Sav sat sipping their cold, slightly bitter tea. It had steeped for far too long, and the evening air had cooled it, but the flavored liquid grounded Jayce. Even the coolness and the whispering of the plants didn't bother her as much as it normally did.

The trembling in her hands had finally stopped, and the energy had leeched from her limbs, dulling her senses, bringing them down from their heightened state.

The tea swirled across her tongue with a distinct bitter taste that would have been made much better with honey, but she didn't have the energy to even ask if there was any in their food pack.

She fumbled with the tin cup, her bandaged hands bulky but manageable.

At least the tea soothed her stomach and lessened the pounding in her head. She drank while Sav tended to Elsa. She had many stings across her back, head, and flanks, and even down her legs, and she kept twitching and giving little whinnies of pain.

Jayce didn't know anything about animal medicine, but a horse was a mammal, and she figured the horse's skin was close enough to human skin to benefit from the topical remedies she knew. She instructed Sav in crushing plants from various vials with the river mud, making a thick, dark paste that he rubbed where every nasty pustule-like blister rose.

Once Elsa had settled, Jayce asked Sav to bring her the cloak she'd packed, and she rolled it up to use as a pillow between her head and the tree. There. No contact. She could ignore the weird voices for a while.

She drifted in and out while Sav discovered what Belsa had packed them for lunch. He went back and forth for a while, sharing his discoveries and effectively keeping Jayce awake. She knew she needed to stay alert after hitting her head again, but the cool afternoon lulled her worries and sent her dozing.

Sav's chipper voice brought her back every time.

Once everything was unpacked—a veritable feast—Sav settled himself against the same tree trunk about a half foot away. He dished Jayce a plate of cold, roasted chicken breast, bread covered in an olive-cheese spread, and an apple tart.

He lifted the bread from the plate. "This tastes amazing. Give it a go, then." He gestured for Jayce to open her mouth.

She gave him a pointed stare, raising her eyebrow. "I can feed myself, you know."

"I wasn't sure, with the hands..." He indicated her bandaged hands, which he'd wrapped just before getting lunch out.

She reached for the plate, and Sav obliged, putting it in her lap. He handed her a cloth napkin as well, and when she struggled to tuck it in her shirt by herself, he helped her.

Eyeing the contents of her plate, Jayce ate the chicken first. Her stomach growled as she considered what remained: the bread and cheese spread, and the apple tart.

The silvertop wheat in the bread would talk to her. The apples would sing. Even the olives would have something to say. And coldness would wash through her as their whispers filled her head, and...

Jayce shuddered and tried to ignore the saliva pooling in her mouth and the grumbling of her belly.

"Is something wrong?" Sav asked.

Jayce swallowed, avoiding his curious, and concerned, gaze. What would she say to herself as an apothecary?

You need to eat to keep your strength up, to help your body fight the blister bee venom.

She'd received a lot of stings. That many could make her sick if she wasn't careful.

With a gloved hand, she raised the piece of bread to her mouth and sank her teeth into it. Salty olives burst on her tongue, babbling on about the virtues of being an olive. Silvertop, as usual, considered itself much more important than it was.

Entire civilizations would have failed without me.

Really? Jayce rolled her eyes, but kept chewing, bracing herself against the rush of cold that slithered across her tongue, filled her mouth, and poured down her throat.

With a large gulp of water, she washed all the words down, shivering against the cold of the plants' language.

"So." Sav clasped his hands over his stomach and leaned back against a tree. "What is the plan when we arrive at the Draigh tomorrow?"

"I-I was just going to ask to see their records on noxbrosia," Jayce said, taken aback by the question. She set her plate to the side, her stomach feeling full and satisfied for the first time in a long time. And the cold hadn't been so bad, had it? Nor the whispering.

"And what if they say no?" Sav asked, sitting up, his eyes intent on her. "What then?"

"Then we return to the capital, and I'll try to see the queen again," Jayce said, tugging on the hem of the stay over her shirt, trying not to appear as flustered as she felt.

Sav shrugged. "I was just wondering how far you would go for the information."

Jayce stared at him. "What other option is there? We can't force them to let us see forbidden records."

"No, but we could find another way in. And if we end up sneaking into the restricted section, I could look through their records on the plague. I've been wanting to get in since I returned from Enterea. Did you know the queen has denied my petition twice? Makes one wonder what they're hiding."

He glanced sidelong at Jayce, who forced herself to stare at the fire and not make eye contact.

Is this what he'd wanted all along? An excuse to break into the books and scrolls that the library caretakers and the rulers of the realm had deemed in need of protection? Would he use her to avoid getting caught?

"Now we're *planning* to break in?" Jayce asked. "How long have you been planning this?"

Sav raised his hands. "Hold on, now. I'm not planning to break into anything. But you need this information, right? About noxbrosia. So, you can stop more people from dying. Surely that's enough to convince you that we might need to bend the rules a little to get what we want. It wouldn't hurt anyone."

Jayce's hands curled into fists, her nails biting into her palms. "But that's exactly why this information is hidden. Because the people who have read it believe it to be harmful."

"Or valuable enough to be protected," Sav said, raising a finger. "We aren't going to steal any of it. Just take a peek and leave with more knowledge than before."

"Why do you care about the plague so much?" Jayce pressed.

"Why don't you?" Sav crossed his arms over his chest.

Jayce's jaw clenched. The wind swept a column of smoke in her direction, and she inhaled the choking ash scent, blinking against the stinging in her eyes.

"I care," Jayce said, voice breaking. "About people living and not dying."

"Who died, Jayce? Friends? Family? Your parents? Your brother?" Sav's voice grew quiet, unnerving. His gaze never wavered, and as the wind shifted again, Jayce found herself unable to tear her eyes away from him.

Her hands rubbed the smooth surface of her borrowed breeches, looking for their familiar handhold in her skirts and finding none.

A log in the fire broke, scattering copper-colored sparks into the sky.

In Jayce's minds' eye, five ages ago, another copper gleam flashed.

With copper you will slay the king.

"What was that?" Sav asked, suddenly sitting up straight. "About copper?"

Jayce startled. She hadn't realized she'd spoken out loud. She wiped her running nose and blinked away the mist forming in her eyes. She had to get away from him before he asked. Before her memories betrayed her.

"Nothing. I'm tired." Panic clung to her chest as she stood and headed for the tent, passing Sav as she went.

He grabbed her wrist and tugged her toward him as he stood to face her. "I know you're scared. Whatever you faced, it must have been horrible. But you need to talk about it. It's not healthy to lock things like that up inside of you."

Jayce yanked her hand away, and Sav let her take it. Her pulse roared in her ears, drowning out the sound of the crackling fire, the bird calls, and the wind in the trees.

She heard the thunder rumble in the trees. A gray sky and a promise of rain, the same as that cycle her brother headed out with his copper sword. A sword meant to slay a king.

Sav said something. His lips moved urgently.

Jayce stumbled back away from him. "Leave me alone!"

"Jayce!"

Her hearing rushed back, and cold droplets pricked her skin. She ran to the tent, ducked under the open flap, and pulled it closed behind her. She shoved her face into her bedroll and screamed as another rumble of thunder shook the sky.

CHAPTER SIXTEEN

The rain grew heavy on the canvas roof above Jayce, and after lighting a candle and setting up her bedroll, she wallowed in guilt. She was warm and dry while Sav was outside, putting out the fire, tending the horses, putting away their things, and getting thoroughly soaked.

Perhaps he'd already finished and stood outside, respecting her request that he leave her alone.

Her selfish, fear-driven request.

"Sav?" she called, her voice sounding thin and weak. She cleared her throat and tried again. "Sav?"

A head full of wet, blond curls ducked through the tent flap, and Sav glanced at her, but his eyes didn't linger. "Did I hear you call for me?"

"Yes," Jayce admitted.

"May I come in?" he asked, his tone flat and formal. "I'm getting rather wet out here."

Jayce closed her eyes and sighed. "Yes, come in."

Sav pushed his way into the tent, letting in a rush of cool air that smelled of damp earth. It swirled around Jayce's toes and made her curl in on herself to try to get warm.

Sav wrestled with his bedroll and several blankets. One of them hit Jayce in the face.

"Do you mind?" Jayce sputtered.

"That one is for you," Sav said. Then, under his breath, he muttered, "I'm soaked through. I need to change."

"What?" Jayce asked, her face heating. Change? He couldn't change with her in there! She had nowhere to go to give him privacy.

Sav sighed and rubbed his forehead. "I'm soaked through. I can't sleep in these clothes. You could face the wall. I trust you not to peek."

The teasing tone he often had crept back into his voice. Jayce rolled her eyes as she shifted to face the green tent wall, tugging the blanket he'd thrown at her up over her waist. She closed her eyes and tried to fall asleep, focusing on the sound of the rain rather than the rustlings she knew meant Sav was changing.

Was he muscular, like some of the men she'd seen working in the fields outside of the capital? He seemed broad, but she wondered if he might be softer toned given his profession of scholar.

She very nearly turned her head, then scolded herself. He'd trusted her not to look! She wouldn't invade his privacy. She sucked in a long breath.

"Nearly finished?" she asked in a choked voice.

Sav's breathless chuckle almost did her in. "Nearly." He cleared his throat a moment later. "All right, you can look."

Jayce turned to look at him, and her breath caught. Sav's damp curls gleamed in the warm glow of lantern light. His billowy white shirt settled over his broad frame, covering muscles she still couldn't be sure existed. He still had his back to her as he finished tucking his shirt into his breeches, but as he finished, he turned around and caught her staring.

"Do I have a bug in my hair or something?" He swiped at the back of his head, fingers combing through his curls.

Jayce licked her lips and shook her head.

"Good." Sav settled back onto his bedroll. He picked a wet leaf off it and flung it aside. He sat up again. "Can I turn off the lantern?"

Jayce nodded, not trusting herself to speak.

The tent plunged into darkness. Rain pattered on the tent canopy, beating a steady rhythm that she could fall asleep to in any circumstance other than the one where she shared a tent with a handsome man she'd met only the chant-cycle before.

Not to mention one she had argued with only moments before.

Outside, thunder broke the silence, rumbling loud and long. Jayce hadn't been able to see the lightning through the thick canvas. Hopefully that meant they'd stay dry as well.

"The rain smells nice," she said, when she could no longer stand the tension filling the tent.

"It's possibly my favorite scent. Aside from hot chocolate," Sav said. "We will have to make some in the morning."

His obvious joy at that thought made Jayce smile.

"What's it like in Enterea?" she asked, eager to shove past the discomfort lingering inside her from yelling at him earlier.

She heard a rustling and imagined Sav laying on his side, one arm propping up his head. She could almost see his outline, her eyes having adjusted to the darkness of the tent.

"Picture the palace, with its polished marble and wide windows. Now imagine it shorter, add a few pillars. Can you see it?"

"I think so," Jayce said, breathless with wonder.

"Now imagine that people from every part of the realm of Neldor, and many from the known continents around, walking through gardens, along pathways, weaving through trees, sitting on the grass with books sprawled about them. All races, all skin tones. And they all get along. Well, mostly," he said with a chuckle.

"That's... difficult to imagine. Here in the capital, we see a lot of people, especially during recording ages, but I'm usually in my shop or treating clients."

"You really need to get out more," Sav said, his tone joking.

The last time I left the capital, part of me didn't return. Jayce clamped down on the thought, holding it inside until she thought she would burst.

Sav cleared his throat. "You're doing a really brave thing, you know. Hunting down more information on this plant so you can find a murderer. That's truly noble. I'm not sure I've done a truly noble thing in my life. Not like that."

"You saved me from Dray!" Jayce insisted, sitting up. Above her, the sound of rain on the tent lessened.

"That was motivated by purely selfish reasons," Sav said.

"I don't believe it," Jayce said. "I don't expect you've done it purely out of the goodness of your heart, but you're not a bad person, Sav."

"Whew," Sav said, making an exaggerated sound. "Glad you cleared that up for me."

She could hear his smile, and the realization that she'd cheered him up, even a little bit after their fight, made her feel tingly inside.

She couldn't sleep. Despite the rain, it wasn't even dark out, and now she felt far too energized.

"I may not have traveled as much as you have," Jayce said, sitting up fully and tossing off her blankets. "But I'm certain I've seen some things you haven't. Come on. There's something I want to show you." She tugged on a pair of gloves and boots and unrolled her hooded cloak, clasping it on in the dark.

"In the rain? I just got dry," Sav complained.

"It's worth it," Jayce replied, leaving the tent.

Outside, she took a deep breath of crisp air. Rain drizzled down on the hood of her cloak as she bent to tie her boots.

Sav fumbled his way out of the tent, untangling his cloak to free his arms and straightening. He grimaced at the clouds, sticking his tongue out, and Jayce laughed.

"Come on, it's this way," Jayce said, leading the way through the woods beyond the clearing they'd set their tent up in.

Dark green leaves glistened wetly, crystal droplets falling from their edges onto the bark and grass-strewn ground.

Jayce kept her eyes on the ground, knowing that what she was looking for liked to hide. There—bright red fronds curled delicately against a large, moss-covered fallen tree. She crouched beside the plant and motioned Sav over.

"Listen," she said, then held her breath and stroked the red frond with her gloved finger.

The frond uncurled itself and revealed a pipe-like stem, which let out an ethereal tone.

Jayce stroked another shorter one, and it, too, opened and sang, this time a higher note.

"The thicker the stem, the lower the note. You try."

She leaned back, and Sav crouched beside her, reaching out a finger to touch one of the fronds. His eyes widened as it sang, the note lingering in the air for a long moment before fading.

"What are they?"

"Windferns. Some of the local folk call them Beggar's Pipes," Jayce said, gazing fondly at the dainty things as they curled back in on themselves.

"I didn't know plants could be so incredible. Are you going to show me one that can dance next?" Sav asked, teasing.

Jayce stood quickly, rubbing her gloves on her pants. "Well, it's not some vast city or a glorious landscape, but a plant could save your life some cycle."

Sav snorted. "I'll buy you all the hot chocolate you want the cycle that happens."

"Throw in some spapsas wool socks, and we'll call it even," Jayce replied.

A branch snagged her sleeve, and she stopped to undo it, noting the willowy branches filled with translucent white berries. They looked delightful, plump and dripping with dewy drops, and the leaf shape seemed right from the books Jayce had studied. But there was one easy way to be sure and save herself a stomach ache.

She slid her glove off her hand and touched one of the berries.

Moon currant. My succulent orbs delight the senses and refresh body and mind. Eat of me and—

Jayce removed her hand, cutting off the plant's vain ramblings. She put on her glove and grabbed a palmful then held them out to Sav. "Here, try these."

He took them reluctantly. "How do I know you're not trying to poison me?"

"Because if I were trying to poison you, I'd do it more subtly," Jayce replied, brushing the water off her gloves. She felt damp and irritable now, ready to go back to the warm, dry tent.

The sun had started to set, and now that the rain had nearly stopped, crickets were chirping their evening song. It was too quiet, and Jayce wondered for a moment why it unsettled her so much. Then she realized it was the first time in five ages that she hadn't watched the sun set to the tune of the queen's Evening Song.

"Those were delightful. You got them from this bush?" Sav asked, stepping closer.

"Yes. You know, plants save your life every cycle. You eat them, drink them, sometimes bathe in them," Jayce said, turning toward him.

Sav nodded, chewing a second mouthful of the moon currants. "You have me there."

"Good. You can deliver my socks in the morning," Jayce said teasingly, and she darted back to the camp, trying to shake the feeling of wrongness that seemed to permeate the otherwise peaceful woods.

CHAPTER SEVENTEEN

Jayce woke to the smell of dirt, smoke, and chocolate. She stretched her limbs, feeling remarkably well-rested for the circumstances, if a little stiff from sleeping on the ground. She sat up, stretching, and found her pack resting in the corner of the canvas tent by her feet.

Crawling to it, Jayce rummaged through until she found her hair oil and a brush. She had long, fine hair that got quite tangled when she didn't brush it, and she hadn't bothered to do a thorough combing since she'd left the capital.

First, she had her bandages to tend. Unwrapping the bandages covering her blisters, she was relieved to find her salve had worked, and the blisters had crusted over. Several of the larger ones still had fluid inside and felt sore, but she could manage well enough without bandages.

She set the bandages aside to be washed and reused, then turned her attention back to her hair.

Donning a pair of leather gloves she used specifically when handling plant oils, Jayce poured the slick oil into her covered palm and rubbed it into her hair. It smelled of rosemary and almonds.

She stared at the side of the tent, lost in thought and the rhythmic pull of the boar's hairbrush as she dragged it through her waist-length hair again and again, until all the tangles worked out and it shone a beautiful chestnut color.

Sav cleared his throat behind her, and Jayce shrieked and dropped the brush.

"Sorry. You seemed focused. I didn't want to disturb you. But, uh, breakfast is served." He did a little bow, more a bob of his head, and smiled apologetically.

Jayce's sharp reprimand melted on her tongue.

Sav's smile widened, and he ducked back out of the tent.

Jayce sat until her heart stopped racing, then carefully packed the brush, gloves, and hair oil away. She considered changing entirely but opted for just switching Sav's shirt for the one she'd worn before, a light wool blouse with an embroidered stay that she wore on the outside. After tying the ribbon in front, she tugged the bottom edge down and smoothed her hands over the olive-green fabric.

She felt naked wearing the form-fitting stay with pants, but they were so much more practical while riding a horse that she couldn't bring herself to change into her skirt. Not yet. After folding Sav's shirt and packing it with care, she crawled from the tent.

It had stopped raining sometime in the night, but the sky remained gray and sunless.

Sav bent over the fire, removing a pan from the rock nearest the flames. He glanced up as her footfalls drew closer and froze.

Jayce rubbed her lips together, unsure whether she should speak or not. "Breakfast smells good," she finally said, breaking whatever spell had come over Sav.

"Well, you did say I owed you last night." He fumbled with the pan and hissed before quickly setting it on the second flat rock nearby. He shook his hand and went to put it in his mouth.

"Oh no! Did you get burned? I have something for that." Jayce rushed back to the tent and dragged her pack out. She rummaged until she found her gloves and burn salve. It was the same ointment she'd put on the blister bee wounds the cycle before, a multi-purpose salve that was good for so many things.

She ran back, unscrewing the lid and taking a small amount on her gloved fingers. Stepping closer to Sav, she took his hand in hers and rubbed the salve on the spot near his thumb that had touched the hot pan.

His breath fluttered her hair, and Jayce realized just how close they stood, her holding his large hand in hers. Her fingers brushed against the callouses at the edges of several of his fingers.

"Archery?" she asked, stepping away from him.

Sav followed her with his eyes, hardly sparing a glance for the burn she'd just treated.

"Archery—oh, yes." He turned and dished food onto the two plates. "I thought it might be useful to have some means of defense, and I'm able to hunt as well."

"Where is your bow, then?" Jayce asked, glancing curiously over the baggage she could see and not finding it.

Sav flushed. "It broke. I haven't had a chance to replace it. I have some arrows around here somewhere, but they're not much good on their own."

He passed one of the plates to her, eyes lingering.

"Ah, well," Jayce said, flushing and taking the plate, nerves getting the better of her. "A bow would come in handy if we were traveling much farther. The moon stags are migrating toward the Hobhorn for the Blood Moon season."

"Are you worried about running into them?" Sav asked, sitting across from her.

Jayce pretended to admire the arrangement of food on her plate to avoid looking into his intense blue eyes. She didn't have to pretend hard. The presentation was incredible. Perfectly cooked eggs with glistening yokes, a golden-brown, slightly crumbly cheese sprinkled over the top, and of course the fresh white berries.

"I picked those currants this morning. You inspired me last night. I couldn't find the bush you picked from, but I found another bush by the riverbank," Sav said, popping several into his mouth.

Jayce studied one a bit closer. It seemed big for a currant, and it was missing the translucent quality the fruit usually had. Maybe it was a different variety?

She tugged off her glove and took a deep breath before touching one of the brilliant white fruits.

Nightlock.

Chill the blood. Empty the stomach. Cure indigestion. Stop the senses. I am Nightlock.

"Sav, no!" Jayce said, grabbing his hand before he tossed another palmful of berries into his mouth. "That's night-lock. It's poisonous!"

His eyes widened. He leaned away from her and made a string of horrible noises, spitting out gobs of red. "I ate quite a few from the bush while picking. Am I—will I—?" He couldn't seem to bring himself to say the words.

Hand trembling, Jayce touched the berry again, getting a sense of it, pushing through the freezing sensation in her fingertips. If she pressed on long enough, sometimes she got an image of the sister plant, a remedy that often grew nearby.

A common-looking green plant with broad, lobed leaves impressed itself on her mind. Jayce took it in for as long as she could bear the cold and the whispers of the nightlock.

"Wait right here," she insisted.

Sav looked pale but nodded.

Jayce got up and ran for the riverbank. Remedies to poisons often grew near their sister plant.

She looked for a shady spot not too near the water. Everything was green. How fast did nightlock work, again? Sav had been away for nearly a bell before her. Perhaps longer. She should have checked his fingertips. They would turn purple when the plant started cutting off his circulation.

Jayce collapsed on the ground, her mind filled only with Sav and his condition, listening to the insistent chant of the plants she ran beneath her hands. It wasn't here, it wasn't here.

She moved farther down the bank, getting so close she nearly rolled off the steep edge and into the water. Gripping the ground and shifting her weight, she stepped away from the river and under a birch tree that had a glorious spread of green carpet-like plants with wide, lobed leaves beneath it.

How many lobes did the cure-plant have? Jayce grasped one in her hand.

Please be the right one. She squeezed her eyes shut and listened to the plant speak.

Eveseed. I can do what you ask.

Jayce lifted her hand from the plant and crawled backward, shocked by the plant's speech, which was seemingly directed at her. Like the tree that had told her about the moribund on the road, this Eveseed had *spoken* to her. It had answered the thought in her mind.

A groan echoed through the trees, wretched and filled with pain.

Sav.

Either she could trust her magic, and this plant, or she could let him suffer while she second-guessed everything.

You can cure the effects of noxbrosia? Jayce thought, approaching the plant again and touching it. Coldness seeped through her, making her feel slow and sleepy despite the adrenaline pumping in her veins.

I can do what you ask.

Jayce ripped up a handful of it unceremoniously and stood, slipping on the muddy ground. The hand that gripped the Eveseed vines grew numb with cold. It raced up her arm.

She grabbed a mortar and pestle from her pack in the tent and started grinding as she walked toward Sav. A paste? Perhaps spread on a piece of bread for palatability? Or a potent drink of sorts?

"What are you doing?" Sav asked. His breakfast sat untouched. Was he sweating?

"How do you feel?" Jayce asked. "Give me every symptom. Don't leave anything out."

Sav laughed nervously, hands over his stomach. "Well, while you were gone, I had to take a break behind a tree. It was... unpleasant to say the least, and the cramping..." He squeezed his eyes shut a moment, his beautiful face distorted with discomfort.

"I feel clammy, too," he reported a moment later. "And my hands are cold." He lifted them up, showing her that the tips of his fingers were losing color.

She ground harder, adding a small bit of water from the pail Sav had filled that morning. She dumped out her hot chocolate, grimacing at the waste of the sweet drink, then scraped the contents of the mortar into the cup and added more water, just enough to make it liquid. It was an unappetizing black color, but it smelled of pine.

Breathing hard from the rush, she pushed it at Sav, whose face nearly turned green.

"I don't think I can—" he said, pushing it away.

"It's going to save your life," Jayce snapped.

Like a child, the man hunched over, refusing the cup, pressing his fist into his mouth.

Exasperated, Jayce shoved against Sav's shoulder, forcing him upright. She pinched his nose, pushed his head back, and thrust the cup against his mouth. Unable to breathe with her fingers on his nose, he opened his mouth and gasped. Jayce took the moment just after the breath to pour the eveseed concoction in, then released him and stepped back.

Sav gagged and moaned, twisting and bending from side to side.

"Augh! What did you give me? Why does it taste like boots? Au-oh no."

"If you need to retch, just let it happen. Some remedies work that way," Jayce said, tugging on a strand of hair stuck to her sweaty face.

A moment later, Sav raised his hand as if to say something, blanched, and bolted into a nearby copse of trees. Violent retching followed.

Jayce brushed off her pants and sat. She picked up her plate, knocked the nightlock berries onto the ground, and ground them with the heel of her boot. She sat, legs still shaking, and started eating her eggs. She tried to ignore the sounds of Sav being sick in the underbrush, her own stomach clenching but still empty and begging to be fed.

She'd started in on her tart by the time he came back, and she offered him the cup again, this time filled with fresh water.

Sav recoiled, a look of betrayal in his eyes. He sat on the rock across from her, his head in his hands.

"I rinsed it out," Jayce said quietly. "It's just water."

Sav raised his head. "Promise?"

She smiled. "Promise."

He took the cup and sipped hesitantly, swishing and spitting to the side, then took a bigger drink. He groaned again, moving to run off again, but then stopped, drawing in deep breaths.

"How are you feeling now?" Jayce asked, holding her breath.

Sav looked at her, eyes rimmed red and bloodshot. "I don't know what you gave me, but I think it made it worse." He held up his hands again, and the tips looked bruised as a black eye.

"No," Jayce whispered, running her finger around the rim of the cup to feel the eveseed liquid she'd made.

Eveseed. Common weed. Poor man's lettuce.

It had lied. And she had believed it. Like a fool, she had believed that the plant was telling her the truth.

"We have to get you to the monastery," Jayce said, bolting from her seat and gathering things, throwing them into a pile.

What was she doing? They didn't have time to pack.

"How far do we have to go?"

"What?" Sav asked, then retched again, moaning.

Jayce went to where the horses were tied. "Sorry, Elsa," she muttered, knowing the horse still wasn't well enough to ride. She approached Abigail, who side-stepped away from her.

"Whoa, easy girl. I need your help. Sav is sick. He needs a healer. Someone who isn't going to make stupid mistakes." Jayce's eyes welled with pity tears, and she sniffed them away. She grabbed Abigail's lead and untied it while the horse tossed her head and snorted with displeasure.

Freed from the tree, Abigail yanked against Jayce's grip. Jayce almost lost her hold, but she held on.

"Abigail, please!"

A heavy hand landed on her shoulder. She whirled around, coming face to face with Sav, who looked like death warmed over. His skin was pale and waxy, the purple tinge deepening under his eyes now. His breath seemed to rattle in his chest.

Rattling wasn't good.

"Can you mount?" she asked breathlessly, handing over Abigail's reins.

The horse instantly calmed.

Sav shook his head, licking his lips. "Take a knee, Abigail."

The horse obliged, lowering its front half. Sav leaned over the saddle, struggling to swing his leg over.

Jayce shoved against the back of his thigh, giving him a boost, and he slid into the center of the saddle.

Abigail rose before Jayce could mount.

"I have to come, too, Abigail! He'll never make it on his own," Jayce cried, looking for anything she could use as a lift.

Sav's hand descended in front of her. "You know horses… can't understand human speech, right?" he said haltingly, the ghost of a smile on his otherwise pale face. He jerked upright suddenly and leaned over the opposite side of the horse, vomit spattering the ground and making Abigail prance nervously.

Sav extended a hand to Jayce again. Not knowing whether he would fall off the horse at her weight or not, Jayce grabbed it and let Sav pull her up in front of him. It took some finagling, but she managed to get settled. Sav scooted back to give her more room.

"Please don't retch on me," Jayce said.

Sav didn't respond, and that, more than anything else, made Jayce's heart rate increase as she urged Abigail into a trot, and then into a full gallop.

The monastery had to be nearby. For Sav's sake, it had to.

CHAPTER EIGHTEEN

Morning birdsong startled to abrupt silence as they passed. Abigail ran hard, hooves kicking up water as she ran through puddles from the night before.

Sav's grip weakened, his hands slipping from around Jayce's waist. He leaned to one side, and Jayce reached back to grab him, tugging with all her strength. They would both fall off.

She scanned the trees ahead for any sign of the monastery, her breath coming in quick gasps even though the horse was doing all the running.

"Hang on!" she yelled as Abigail turned around the bend.

A cream-colored wall flashed through the tree trunks, and Jayce gritted her teeth, her arm aching from holding onto Sav behind her. She urged Abigail forward, faster, and when they finally broke into the vast clearing that held the monastery, she nearly cried with relief. But there wasn't time for that.

"Help!" she cried out, slowing Abigail to a stop in front of the monastery doors. She wriggled out from under Sav and slid off the horse. She turned to help him down, only to watch him slump over and fall to the ground on the opposite side.

"Sav!" She ran around Abigail, who pranced with nervous hooves, hooked her arms under Sav's armpits and dragged him away so he wouldn't get stepped on.

Robed figures poured from the monastery, a trickle of them at first, and then a swarm. All Jayce could see were waves of black and dark brown fabric as male and female monks gathered around.

"Alighieri!" One of the brown-robed monks gasped, crouching across from Jayce, who held Sav's head in her lap. "What happened?"

"He ate nightlock berries. I tried to cure him, but I… It was the wrong plant."

"What did you give him?" the monk asked, checking Sav's pulse at his throat and forcing his eyelids open.

"Eveseed. I've never heard of it, but it told me it could cure him." Jayce gulped past the lump in her throat and painfully swallowed the urge to cry.

"Eveseed isn't good for much more than salad," the monk said, the creases in his forehead deepening as he checked Sav's fingertips. He glanced up at the gathered monks. "Don't just stand there! Mel, fetch Mystri Prieta. Tell her there's a man here who has been poisoned."

A male monk in dark robes nodded and darted off.

"Did you say you *heard* the plant?" the monk asked.

Jayce nodded. "I've been able to do it since I was small. I've studied as an apothecary, and normally, I don't trust it because they don't always tell the truth. But I was in a rush." Guilt settled into Jayce's chest, thick and sludgy. She cleared her throat, trying to straighten out her leg beneath her, which had started to lose feeling.

"Never rush healing," the monk said, placing the back of his hand on Sav's forehead. "He's clammy. How long since the onset?"

"Hard to say. It's been a blur. Perhaps half a bell?"

"You were close, then. Praise the Three," the monk said, sitting back, fingers smoothing down his black goatee. "I am Elder Vambi, by the way. An old friend of the baron's. I completed my religious schooling at Enterea before taking up residence here at the Draigh." Elder Vambi bowed his head low, hands together in front of him.

"Jayce Keenstone, apothecary of Neldor," Jayce said. She didn't feel much like an apothecary at the moment. She'd harmed someone she'd meant to heal, hastily reaching for the first plant that had promised to help without checking. If she hadn't been in such a rush, she might have found the real remedy, which she assumed must be a close look-alike.

Elder Vambi's hand clasped hers. "I know that look on your face well. You didn't fail him. He's here, isn't he?"

Jayce bit her lip as a tide of emotion rose into her throat, choking her. She nodded, unable to speak.

A white robe broke through the sea of brown and black, and an elderly woman shuffled forward, carrying a basket of bottles that clinked.

“What do you have here, Vambi dear?” The female monk spoke warmly, and her entire face seemed alight with affection.

“Only our favorite patron,” Elder Vambi said, moving out of the way as several black-robed monks helped the female monk to kneel. “Jayce, this is Mystri Prieta. She’s head healer here at the Draigh monastery. Mystri, Jayce is an apothecary.”

“Then she can assist me. Open this,” Mystri Prieta said, holding out a brown bottle.

Jayce took it and yanked the cork out of the top. “What is it?”

“Sunpetal tonic. The sister plant to nightlock is sunpetal. Where did you study?”

Jayce flushed. “My mother taught me many things. I apprenticed with a local apothecary for an age, then spent some time in the palace.”

Mystri Prieta grunted, tilting the tonic into Sav’s mouth. “That explains this gap in your knowledge, at least. Local remedies should always be emphasized. Those fancy apothecaries and alchemists at the palace always want the most exotic and complicated remedies. Simple is best. Most poisons have a sister plant, and it almost always grows nearby.”

“I know that!” Jayce said, then bit her lip when she realized her tone had been disrespectful.

Mystri Prieta raised her eyebrows at her but didn’t chastise. Instead, she took a salve jar from the basket and passed it to Jayce, who unscrewed it for her.

The salve had a familiar, pungent smell. Peppermint and goatsmure? Her eyebrows furrowed.

"Are you going to sniff it all cycle or pass it to me?" Mystri Prieta asked, holding out her wizened hand. "Remove his socks."

Jayce handed over the salve and scooted out from under Sav, laying him gently on the ground. Since he'd taken the tonic, his color had improved, the pink returning to his face and the purple fading from his fingertips. But he hadn't stirred.

At his feet, Jayce loosened his boots and slid them off, then peeled off his socks.

Mystri Prieta came up beside her with the salve, holding it out to her. "You can apply this, right?"

Jayce gritted her teeth. She wasn't totally inept. She'd made one mistake, one time! But she eyed the salve, hesitating.

"I-I don't have my gloves," Jayce finally said.

They were back at the camp with her things. And the two horses. Someone needed to fetch them.

"What do you need gloves for? It's just salve. It washes off." Mystri Prieta's eyebrows furrowed until they met in the middle of her forehead.

"No—it's—I hear the plants. Their whispers… they're maddening. And cold." Jayce shuddered.

Mystri Prieta frowned, crouching beside Jayce, her knees cracking. She took a scoop of the sun-colored salve on her fingers and vigorously massaged it into both of Sav's feet.

"You need more exposure, not less. I've seen abilities like yours. Powerful. More powerful than most. But if you're afraid to use it, it will continue to be a weakness. Things like this will happen more and more. The plants will rule your mind, manipulate and terrorize you."

Mystri Prieta sat back, handing the salve to Elder Vambi, who sealed it. She sighed and glanced from Sav to Jayce. "You were lucky this time. He'll be well again, make a full recovery, even. Within hours, you'll hardly know he was near death. But next time… next time it might not go so well. An inexperienced healer is a danger to everyone."

"I'm not inexperienced! I've been healing people for ages. I've even worked on the plague cure," Jayce insisted, her voice rising.

"Have you created it yet, then? My monks are dying. My friends. I get letters about family passing. Don't brag about almost finding a cure. It means nothing to those suffering."

Jayce shot to her feet, hands closing into fists. "No one has suffered more than me to find a cure," Jayce snapped.

Mystri Prieta didn't rise with anger. Instead, her face seemed to age before Jayce's eyes, and the monk sighed heavily, holding her arms out to the silent, black-robed monks nearby to help her up.

"If I had time at the moment to ask your story, I would hear it. Your suffering is valid, and yet, I can guarantee I've heard dozens like it in my time, and worse. Yes, worse. I do not mean to insult you but warn you. Lean into your powers, not away from them, or you will lose everything."

Jayce watched Mystri Prieta hobble away. A black-robed monk collected her basket for her.

As much as Jayce's heart hurt at the elderly monk's words, they rang with a truth that disturbed her. She'd avoided contact with her powers as much as she could over the ages, frightened as a child that she would die from the cold they inflicted, warned by her mother of the potential for madness from their words, not to mention the danger of their lies.

A danger she had forgotten and paid for. And this woman wanted her to listen to them *more*? Touch them more, feel their cold and decipher their whispers? She'd used her powers more in the last few cycles than she had in ages, and in every instance, things had gotten worse, not better.

"Do not worry. She has that effect on everyone. Especially those she admires," Elder Vambi said from where he sat on the ground next to Sav. He motioned to the handful of black-robed monks that remained. None of them spoke, but they gathered around Sav and lifted him from the ground.

Elder Vambi tucked his hands into his robes and approached Jayce. "I will make sure he is settled in a room and looked after. Would you like a room to rest in as well?"

"Yes. But I have to return and get our things first. It may take me some time. Abigail won't let me ride her without him," Jayce said, feeling miserable at the thought. She looked around for the horse and realized that at some point she had disappeared. "Where is Abigail?"

"The mare has been led to the stables where she will be properly cooled down, brushed, and fed. If you'd like, our acolytes will return to your camp and aid in retrieving your things." Elder Vambi bowed.

Jayce nodded, not sure if she should bow back or not. "Thank you. I accept."

By the time Jayce had returned to the camp, put out the fire, and repacked their things with the help of three black-robed acolytes—whom she found out had taken oaths of silence and did not speak—the bells had struck well past mid-cycle, and her stomach clenched hungrily.

She took her lunch in the dining hall at the monastery, enjoying a hearty meal of cold-cut chicken with a goat-milk yogurt dip and hard-boiled eggs.

Sav still hadn't fully woken when she checked, so she found her room—which Elder Vambi had arranged to be next to Sav's—and took out her journal.

The leatherbound book smelled of the apothecary; oils from the plants she had worked with seeped into its surface. She unwound the leather strand holding it closed and opened the book to a random page in the middle. She smoothed it out with her now-gloved hand, running her fingers over the sketch of brindleweed, a meadow plant that, when dried, made a flavorful seasoning.

She'd recorded every plant she had ever learned of or encountered in this book. Drawing the best representation she could manage, writing out a description of all parts of the plant, and writing the locations it grew in as well as anything she'd heard them say and their medicinal properties.

She had a few plants to add to it.

Nightlock already had an entry, though it was far from complete. She recorded what she'd learned, taking a sketch from the branch taken from the campsite when she'd returned, noting the spiky leaves and smooth branches.

She noted the remedy, sunpetal. She would have to bite back her pride and visit Mystri Prieta to inquire about it. Perhaps the old healer would show her what it looked like, at least. Jayce made her own note that sunpetal shouldn't be confused with eveseed.

She hesitated at the top of the next page, wondering whether to give eveseed its own entry. A useless plant, Elder Vambi had said, but harmless. It had still spoken to her. Why had it lied? Why did the plants lie at all? Was it what Mystri Prieta had said, that she feared them, so they took advantage of her?

Jayce sat in her room as the sunlight outside turned golden, setting earlier and earlier each day. Bells rang, but she missed the queen's Evening Song, sung each night as the sun slipped below the horizon in Lothian.

She closed her eyes, wondering if she'd wrongly come to believe that her powers were a danger and what she could possibly do about it, until Elder Vambi knocked on her door and informed her that the baron had awakened.

CHAPTER NINETEEN

Sav looked to be the peak of health when Jayce knocked on the door and entered. He sat on the edge of the bed, struggling with one of his boots.

"You're supposed to be resting," Jayce said sternly.

"I've been resting... for hours," Sav said, grunting as he finally got his boot on. He tied the laces then moved on to the next boot. "We came here on a mission, and I'm not going to keep you from it."

"I can research it on my own," Jayce replied, crossing her arms over her chest.

Beside her, Elder Vambi chuckled. "That's Al for you. Can't keep the man down. Last time he was here, he came down with a terrible head cold. I found him reading late into the night by candlelight, a hot water bottle on his head, and a blanket around his shoulders."

Sav grinned, pausing with the second boot half-on. “Jayce, have you met Vambi? Friend of mine from school. Had to become a monk instead of... What else were you considering?”

“My past life has no bearing on my service to the Three,” Elder Vambi said, rolling his eyes.

Sav rolled his eyes. “You even talk like a monk now. He could have been a performer, you know. Maybe even for royalty. The man is so bendy, I think he’s missing bones.”

“He exaggerates,” Elder Vambi said, crossing the room to close the curtains against the pale blue evening outside.

“Are you on your second goddess blessing yet, Elder?” Sav said, teasing.

Elder Vambi’s smile vanished. “I do wish you wouldn’t mock my position simply because I didn’t choose the path you would have chosen in my stead. We can only live the lives we are given, no matter how much we may wish to live the life of another.”

Sav glanced down at his half-booted foot. “Sorry. I didn’t mean to make light of something sacred to you.”

“I forgive you, my friend. Now, is what you came to research so important that you must risk your health? The books will still be there tomorrow.”

Sav glanced at Jayce, half-heartedly tugging on his boot. “It’s up to her. This is her mission, after all.”

Elder Vambi faked a swoon. “Not here for your own research? I’m in shock. I wonder what else could have captured his attention.” He looked at Jayce, who flushed.

“Sav agreed to help me. He said he had friends at the library.”

"You know we don't favor any patron over another," Elder Vambi said sternly in Sav's direction. "You get the same treatment regardless of whether—"

"I'll of course make a generous donation. I know the Patron is eager to repair the tower bells and expand the gardens," Sav said.

The offer seemed to render Elder Vambi speechless, and Jayce surged ahead.

"The reason we are here, Elder, is to research a particular plant."

"In that case, we have an extensive herblore section. I will show you to it."

Sav got up from the bed, groaning as he stood and keeping one hand pressed to the mattress for support.

"Sit and eat, Alighieri. You'll need your strength to keep up with your lady friend, I'm sure." Elder Vambi's eyes twinkled, and he put a hand on Jayce's back to lead her from the room.

"If I didn't know you were planning a life of celibacy, I would assume you were trying to steal her attention from me," Sav said, groaning and leaning back on the pillows with a mug of broth in his hand. He gestured at Jayce with the mug. "Don't let him trick you into only looking at the boring books, Jayce."

Jayce recalled what Sav had said about the restricted section, and she nodded. If she could convince the Elder to let her have even a peek at a volume containing more information about noxbrosia, it could allow her to pinpoint where the maker of the noxbrosia remedy had gotten the rare plant to begin with and potentially give her more leads to discover who was behind it all.

"Enjoy your broth," she said aloud, turning to leave the room.

Sav muttered something behind her, and his obviously sullen attitude at being left out made Jayce laugh under her breath.

Elder Vambi followed behind her, closing the door to Sav's room and moving ahead of her in the hall. "Have you seen the library?" he asked.

"Not yet," Jayce admitted, following him to the stairs. All the rooms were on a second floor overlooking a large communal study area filled with desks. She caught a glimpse of the edges of the room, which were lined with bookcases.

At the bottom of the stairs, they turned left and entered the communal study area where a large desk guarded the entrance to the library.

Jayce gasped. The room was lit by the sunset outside through a massive stained-glass window that took up the entire west wall of the monastery.

The stained-glass window depicted three ethereal women, the patterns of their faces and dresses casting rainbows across the marble floor. They were known as the Three Sisters, goddesses who had once saved the realm with their power and sacrifice.

The Draigh monastery was quite possibly the most beautiful building Jayce had ever entered, and the number of books alone made it by far the most interesting. Pillars arched around the room in a circle, and beyond them stood shelves. Rows upon rows of books. She had heard there was a library near the capital containing all the realm's most important volumes, but she had never thought to go herself.

Looking at the collection before her, regret plagued her. This treasure trove of knowledge lay a mere three cycles from her home on horseback, and she'd never been.

"It's incredible," Jayce said in a hushed voice, spinning in a circle to take it all in.

Elder Vambi smiled. "I judge a person's character by whether they hold appropriate awe for this sight. You've passed. Now, what can I help you find today?"

Jayce twisted her hands together anxiously. "There's a particular plant I wish to study. Do you have any volumes containing information on noxbrosia?"

Elder Vambi frowned, creases deepening between his eyebrows. "You'll have to forgive me, I'm not familiar with all the notable plants of the realm, though it does sound familiar… What area is it native to? Or perhaps you can tell me some of its properties?"

"I know very little about it, but I do know it is a poison and quite rare due to it being against the law to buy, trade, or grow. I think it grows in the north?"

Elder Vambi snapped his fingers. "Yes, I do know it! I'm afraid your research will not be as complete as you might like. All volumes containing extensive information on the plant have been sent to the restricted section. You'll find mentions of it in a few of the books on these shelves, but only what is currently allowed as per the limitations of the ban. Unless you happen to have a writ from the queen with permission to see the banned documents?"

"I don't. I wasn't able to see her before I came. It's critical that I complete my research and return with proof that someone is using it for ill purposes," Jayce said, her voice rising.

Elder Vambi glanced around, lowering his voice to almost a whisper when he replied, "Perhaps that is something better left up to proper authorities?"

Jayce shook her head, her throat tightening.

Elder Vambi cleared his throat. "It is upsetting, I'm sure, to travel here only to be turned away. If you'd like, one of our messengers can send a message to the castle requesting permission for you to access the restricted records?"

Jayce considered the option. The danger in waiting as long as four or five days for a letter to return was that the poison remedy would be distributed further and more people would perish. Even if she did feel confident the queen would approve her request, could she risk so many lives?

"Is there anything else you can do? Perhaps I can speak to the Patron? Surely he can give permission in special circumstances like these," Jayce pleaded.

Elder Vambi seemed to consider her for a moment. "No, I'm afraid not. But you will find that we have many volumes with such a variety of information, you may find something helpful after all. I can show you where we keep our books on medicinal herbs, if you wish to try to glean something from them."

Jayce nodded, and Elder Vambi led her between the towering shelves. He gave fellow monks a silent bow as they passed. Eventually, they wound around toward a section containing volumes where many bore titles related to botany and medicine.

Jayce itched to pull out numerous volumes and curl up in a corner to read them. But she had to remain focused. She had to think of a way to get access to the books that surely contained the information she needed.

Elder Vambi halted suddenly, and Jayce stumbled into him.

"Sorry," she said, flustered.

Elder Vambi's fingers fluttered over the spines of books lining the shelves until he paused on one and tugged it out.

The Botanist's Curative Compendium stood out in gleaming gold foil on the dark leather. Elder Vambi held it out toward Jayce, and she took it, staggering under the unexpected weight.

Elder Vambi scanned the shelves again, taking out *Leech's Book of Balms, Tonics, and Infusions* and *The Alchemist's Botanical Formula Encyclopedia.*

Both were massive volumes, and Jayce nearly tripped over her own feet as she tried to keep all three volumes in her arms.

"Those are the ones I know of. I will also discuss with Mystri Prieta about your subject matter. She might have further insight."

"Thank you," Jayce managed, huffing as Elder Vambi showed her to a table in the study area.

She leaned forward, dropping the books the last inch or so onto the desk. The thud echoed loudly in the vast and silent room. Eyes glanced up from their texts at the disruption.

Jayce slid into her chair and slid the volumes to one side, taking *The Alchemist's Encyclopedia* from the top first. She flipped through the alphabetical volume to the 'N' section and ran her finger down the columns.

Some encyclopedia. The entry for noxbrosia contained barely anything for her to go off of.

Umbraflorae noxbrosia vespera, commonly known as duskshade or nightbloom, is a rare botanical. This flowering plant is found in frigid mountain regions and is best known for its iridescent indigo blossoms, which bloom only at night. The compounds within the noxbrosia plant contain a poison so deadly it was made illegal to cultivate or obtain in any manner by His Highness King Alaric *Donovanu.*

The description ended by detailing the decree and the date it was sent out. Jayce flipped to the front of the book, checking the volume's date. Sure enough, this was an updated edition. No doubt the original contained full details of noxbrosia, details which would have been excluded from this otherwise impressive book.

She set the book on the floor, her desk running out of space with the huge volumes, and checked the dates on the other two books. She rejected *Leech's Book of Balms* immediately after noticing it, too, had been amended since the ban on noxbrosia, but the *Botanist's Compendium* didn't have a date of recording, and the cover seemed far more worn.

Jayce parted the cover and flipped through. The entries were grouped by genus and species. Using what she'd learned from the *Alchemist's Encyclopedia*, Jayce found the noxbrosia entry and read eagerly, skimming past information that was similar to what she'd already read until her eyes landed on a name she had never heard before.

The alchemist, Dagric Wortcunning, made the first notable discovery of a cure for noxbrosia when Queen Lyadne *was poisoned with a wine infused with the flower prior to King Alaric Donovanu's ban.*

The rest of the entry didn't contain anything of note, but Jayce went back to that name, searching her memory for any recollection of it from her studies. If this alchemist was so famous that he'd cured the queen before Queen Lyra of poisoning, why hadn't she been taught about him in her studies at the palace?

She spent the next two bells pouring over the three volumes, looking for further mention of the alchemist, but by the time the light outside turned golden, all she had to show for her efforts were three mentions in other plants, one of which he'd discovered.

Growing hungry and frustrated by the lack of information, Jayce hauled the massive books to the front desk, where Elder Vambi stood talking to the other brown-robed monk on duty there.

"Can I help you?" the monk asked.

"Did you find anything of interest?" Elder Vambi added.

"Possibly," Jayce said, huffing as she lifted the books onto the desk's edge and slid them toward the seated monk. "I'm finished with these, but I would like to read more about the alchemist Dagric Wortcunning."

The female monk gasped. "Wortcunning? He was denounced, and all information pertaining to him sent to the restricted—"

"The restricted section," Jayce finished, rubbing the smooth spot in one eyebrow. "I should have guessed."

"It would seem you share the same interest in arcane and forbidden knowledge as our mutual friend," Elder Vambi said in a wry tone.

"It's not my fault all the interesting subjects get banned from the public eye," Sav said from behind.

Jayce startled, whirling around. "Should you be out of bed?"

"I finished my broth and held it down, and Mystri Prieta declared me fit enough to leave her monastery. As if she doesn't love having me here." Sav rolled his eyes and crossed his arms. "I told her I would leave as soon as you finished your research, but judging by the sound of it, you haven't gotten what you came for."

"I have a lead," Jayce said. "This alchemist, Dagric Wortcunning, seems like he could be a valuable resource, but I don't know where he lives or if he's even still alive, and they've locked up everything on him."

Sav leaned against the desk, somehow managing to look both casual and earnest at the same time. "Vambi, my friend, isn't there something you can do for this young lady? I wouldn't ask if it were passing curiosity, but lives are at stake."

Elder Vambi shrugged his shoulders, looking uncomfortable. "I do not have authority to grant access to restricted records. None here do. If you wish to research further, I suggest you make an appointment with Her Majesty in Lothian and return once you have a writ of permission."

Sav said something about spapsos dung that made Jayce's ears heat up.

"Sorry, I don't think I heard you correctly. This woman, this skilled apothecary, needs access to a volume about her colleague to conduct research on a deadly plant that may be at large again in the realm. Obstructing her research could lead to more deaths. Do you want to be held responsible for that?" Sav asked, clenching his teeth.

Elder Vambi's expression twisted with conflict. He took a deep breath in. "You know my hands are tied, Alighieri. I am pained by the trouble this will cause, but I cannot break the rules."

Sav snorted, and Elder Vambi's expression grew concerned.

"As your friend, I feel compelled to remind you that banishment from the monastery and imprisonment await you if you choose to ignore my warning and enter the restricted section. Go through the proper channels. Get permission. Or go somewhere else to find the information you seek."

The monk beside him looked a little helpless as she watched the two men stare each other down, a silent argument happening between them.

"Then you will do nothing?" Sav asked.

"I do not break the rules of my order for anyone. I am sorry we could not be more assistance. If you'll excuse me, the dinner bell will ring soon, and I am assigned to serving duty." Elder Vambi bowed and walked away.

Sav pushed away from the counter with a sigh. "I'm not entirely sure he wasn't mind-wiped when he joined this religion."

"Is there anything else I can help you with?" the female monk asked sharply, giving Sav a disapproving stare.

Jayce shook herself from her stunned stupor. "Not at the moment, thank you." She hurried after Sav. "What was that about?"

Sav stared straight forward, headed for the front door, his arms swinging in fists at his sides.

"That was the culmination of over a year of my attempts to see if my friend still existed beneath that proper monk exterior. Apparently, he's gone for good. Given all the parts of him that I remember to the service of the Three. The old Vambi would have snuck us in the moment he heard of your cause. This new version has a stick up his—" Sav cut off as the door in front of him opened of its own accord and a red-robed monk strode through, freezing as soon as he saw Sav.

"Why, Baron Alighieri. You're back so soon?" The monk did not sound pleased to see Sav, judging by the pinched look on his face, as if he'd just bitten into a sour grape.

"Master Chalu," Sav said, bowing slightly. "How could I stay away from your gracious hospitality?"

Jayce followed Sav's example and bowed, unsure what the proper protocol was.

Master Chalu's eyes glanced over Jayce with passing interest. "Who is your delightful companion?"

"This is Miss Jayce Keenstone, apothecary of Lothian."

Master Chalu's eyebrows shot up. "An apothecary? Have you come to study with our Mystri?"

"Not at this time, but perhaps someday," Jayce said, trying not to rub the creeping feeling off her arms.

"Well then, you may want to choose your companions more wisely. Those things are taken into consideration where apprenticeships are concerned. Mystri Prieta only takes the best." Master Chalu's eyes locked on Sav, and he smiled, but the smile had a sly twist to it.

"Have a good day, Master Chalu," Sav said coldly, putting an arm around Jayce and steering her toward the doors.

They were outside before Master Chalu responded, if he did.

They strolled the gardens in silence, Jayce glancing over at Sav. What was he thinking? And why did all the monks here seem to have a problem with him? Perhaps she should have chosen her traveling companion more wisely.

"I'm sorry I couldn't be more useful to you," Sav said as they passed a series of rose bushes in their end-of-season bloom.

The roses' heavy perfume permeated Jayce's senses, making her head swim a little. "It isn't your fault. I understand their rules, even if I don't like them. You didn't have to put your reputation on the line for my sake."

Sav laughed. "It was in tatters before you met me. I'm surprised they haven't banned me yet, but I suspect they appreciate my generous donations. My question is, what are you going to do now?"

Jayce paused at the bend in the path, gloved hands fidgeting behind her back. "It sounds like my only option is to return to Lothian and request an audience with the queen."

She bit her lip. She could likely get an audience if she returned, especially if she mentioned the name she'd been too afraid to use before. But back at The Silver Gardner, Dray had threatened that if she returned to the capital, he would be waiting. Did she dare risk returning without solid evidence to convict whoever had made the noxbrosia remedy?

On the other hand, if she could find out where this alchemist, Dagric Wortcunning, lived, she could consult with him about the remedy. Perhaps she was wrong and noxbrosia had some hidden healing properties when prepared a certain way. But her gut told her that someone had used the poison intentionally, and she suspected they would use their remedy for personal gain that could do far more harm than good.

Jayce looked up at Sav. "I need to know where Dagric Wortcunning lives. I have to speak with him about the poison being used in this remedy, and he might know where someone obtained the noxbrosia to put in it."

"Is there anyone here we can ask? Mystri Prieta might know."

"Here I thought you'd jump straight to breaking into the restricted section," Jayce said, a bit taken back by Sav's thoughtful response.

Sav laughed. "I'm all for rebel causes if they're necessary. But if we can get the same information with a simple conversation, I'm not about to risk jail."

"Then I'll talk to the Mystri," Jayce said, her gut twisting as she thought about approaching the elderly healer who had criticized her faulty methodology and accused her of being afraid of her own magic.

She might prefer risking imprisonment over talking to the Mystri.

CHAPTER TWENTY

Jayce knocked on the door to Mystri Prieta's private office on the third floor of the monastery, her armpits damp with sweat.

The door swung wide within a moment of her knock, and Jayce stood there gaping, all the words she'd prepared to introduce her dilemma vanishing under the glare of the white-haired Mystri in her white robes.

"I wondered when you'd make your way to my door," Mystri Prieta said, gesturing for Jayce to enter. "I know hunger for knowledge when I see it."

"Thank you for seeing me; I know it's late," Jayce said, entering the room and circling a little helplessly. A desk by the window, a cot by the corner, and shelves of remedies adorned the small room.

Mystri Prieta opened a closet door that practically blended into the white-washed wall and took out a second chair. "Please sit."

Jayce obliged, hands clasping and unclasping in her lap. "I'm here because—"

"You want to know about the remedy I used on the young baron," Mystri Prieta said, plucking a bottle off her desk and handing it to Jayce. "Go on, open it. I want to see your magic in action."

Jayce eyed the bottle, then Mystri Prieta. "You want me to use my magic?"

"Tell me what's in it." Mystri Prieta leaned back and closed her eyes, the light from the lantern on her desk illuminating the cracks in her wizened face.

"I try not to use my powers, in favor of strengthening my intellect—"

Mystri Prieta's eyes shot open. "And where has that gotten you today? Hm? Perhaps if you had more confidence in your abilities, you might have been the one saving Savage instead of me. Now, tell me what's in the remedy. Everything you hear, I want you to tell me."

"This isn't why I—" Jayce tried again.

"Enough excuses," Mystri Prieta said abruptly. "I am offering you a chance few get, my dear. A free lesson. Now proceed."

Jayce took a deep breath and set the bottle on the desk, then removed one of her gloves. She touched the rim of the brown bottle where a bit of liquid gleamed.

Sunpetal.

The plant's whispers sighed into Jayce's mind, light and breathy. She gripped the bottle in her other hand as the cold burned at her fingertips. She resisted the urge to wipe the tonic off to get rid of the discomfort and gritted her teeth, forcing herself to listen to the plant speak.

I wander the forest in search of sunlight to imbue its light into my veins. I flush the bloodstream and ease cramping. I can sense your distress. Let me ease your mind...

Jayce gasped and nearly dropped the bottle, fumbling with it until she managed to get it on the desk. She wiped her finger on her borrowed pants, trembling.

"So? What did it say?"

"Sunpetal in a suspension of alcohol," Jayce said, shaking out her hand, which still felt cold.

Mystri Prieta narrowed her eyes. "And? What did you hear? What did you feel?"

"I felt cold. Like I always do," Jayce snapped, rubbing her finger. "And it lied, like every other plant I've ever heard."

"I wonder why the Three would give the gift of plant-speech if the plants were only going to lie to you. What use is that?" Mystri wondered aloud, reaching for a cup on her desk and sipping at the contents. "Perhaps they wish to test you."

"Or maybe it's useless, like you said," Jayce said, finally settling her hands into her lap again.

"No, I don't believe that," Mystri Prieta said, tapping her chin. "What did the sunpetal say? Its exact words?"

Jayce repeated them, despite her growing frustration that she still hadn't been given a moment to say why she had really sought the Mystri's company.

"Sense your distress? How very aware. I had no idea even dead plants could maintain such awareness. When they're attached to their roots, that I understand. They are as sentient as you or I. But dead? Preserved? It's truly a wonder, this gift of yours. Tell me, why do you think it mentioned your distress?"

Jayce gritted her teeth. "Because plants lie. They manipulate, distract, and tell outright falsehoods. That's how I made that mistake earlier when the eveseed told me it could help."

"Did you ask it how it could help?" Mystri Prieta asked.

Jayce furrowed her brow. "No."

"Perhaps it knew where to find the sunpetal. I think you've been led to misinterpret your gift your entire life. You were taught to fear it and told you had to gain knowledge to prevent being deceived by it. But if you don't trust your gift, or the plants themselves, and they can sense your distrust, perhaps you have created your reality."

"I didn't come to talk about my magic," Jayce said, eager to move on from the uncomfortable thoughts that Mystri Prieta's words dragged to the surface of her mind. "I'm here to ask about Dagric Wortcunning."

The air in the small room seemed to thicken. The light in the lantern flickered, casting dancing shadows across the walls.

Mystri Prieta put a hand over her mouth, then took it away again. Her lips trembled. "Dagric? Wortcunning, you said?"

Jayce nodded. "The famous alchemist? Did you know him? Do you know where he is now?"

"Oh my," Mystri Prieta said, taking a handkerchief from her pocket and using it to dab at her eyes. "It has been a while since anyone dared speak that name."

Jayce tilted her head. "Why?"

"I knew Dagric. We apprenticed together at the Ivory Guilds many years ago." Mystri Prieta got a far-off look in her eyes as she gazed out the window at the growing dark reaching over the garden.

"He held such promise, even when he was young. Became the favorite of all our professors. Then became one of the instructors. We worked together for a time. Some of the happiest years of my life..." Mystri Prieta trailed off, glancing down and sniffing loudly. "That was before he ruined everything and lost it all. His tenure at the Guilds, his reputation with King Alaric, and my trust." The healer's eyes flashed with anger.

"What happened?" Jayce asked hesitantly.

"He was caught working with banned plants, replicating poisons, and that led to him being framed for the murder of several notable dignitaries at the time. They had no other suspects, and Dagric had not spoken kindly of these men and women. He disagreed with their political opinions. Never mix healing and politics."

"Did he go to prison, then?" Jayce asked, twisting her fingers together.

"No, shockingly. The service he'd done the king by saving his wife's life years prior led to him being exonerated but stripped of his titles, cast into obscurity, and forbidden from practicing alchemy ever again," Mystri Prieta said, emphasizing each punishment as she gazed at Jayce. "Why would you ask about him?"

"I need to ask him about noxbrosia," Jayce said, emboldened by Mystri Prieta's response. She had known him. She might know where he was now, and Jayce was determined to get the answer.

"Noxbrosia is one of the plants that was his downfall. You don't want anything to do with him or it," Mystri Prieta insisted.

"Someone created a remedy they said could cure the plague, but it has noxbrosia in it, and it killed one of my clients. I have to find out who made it and how they got hold of noxbrosia before it kills too many others," Jayce said.

Mystri Prieta closed her eyes and sighed. "Do you know how I became Mystri of the Draigh monastery?"

Jayce shook her head.

"I avoided everything exotic and conspiratorial. I learned the common ailments and their cures, inside and out. And I worked every day to become the best healer I could become. When I expressed an interest in joining the Order, Patron Vircoz told me he had seen my work, and he wanted me to become the Mystri here.

"When I look at you, I see a young woman eager to prove herself as a valuable asset to her community. You wish to be seen for your wisdom and the services you provide, but you have not earned it yet. You will earn the respect of your community through hard work and staying humble enough to continue learning, not chasing down potential murderers and illegal substances. Leave that to the soldiers and spies. The queen employs them for a reason."

Jayce closed her eyes, fighting against the tears that threatened to fill her eyes. Being told again that she wasn't good for anything, that she needed to stay in her place and let others do the important work, filled her with despair. But the despair felt different this time. It carried a tinge of something stronger, something bolder.

"If you suggest I should learn more, why not refer me to your old colleague? He's recorded in these books as having made vastly important discoveries. He sounds like just the kind of person I should apprentice with," Jayce insisted.

"Dagric is the last person you should study with," Mystri Prieta snapped. Then she sighed, running her hands through her white hair. "What I mean is, his reputation would ruin yours. Even being seen with him could be grounds for arrest. He's been denounced and cast into obscurity, forbidden from practicing alchemy. His being alive isn't even a guarantee, and even if I could be certain of that, I do not know where he lives now. He could be anywhere."

The older woman stared out the window for a long moment.

Jayce stood. "Thank you for your time, then," she said stiffly, then turned to leave.

Mystri Prieta reached out and grabbed Jayce's arm. "I see that gleam of determination in your eyes, Miss Keenstone. Do not do something you would regret."

"I will do my best," Jayce replied.

The woman let go of her hand like it had suddenly burned her. Jayce smoothed her expression over, trying to rid it of any evidence of her rebellious thoughts. She'd had enough regrets already in her twenty-six years. Giving up on finding the creator of the noxbrosia remedy wouldn't be one of them.

She found herself knocking on Sav's door as the ninth bell rang and the lights in the library at the center of the monastery turned down low, signaling it was time for bed.

The door creaked open just enough for Sav to look out, and Jayce gave him a little wave.

"How did it go with the Mystri?" Sav asked, widening the door slightly.

"No good. She just wanted to lecture me on earning the respect of my community the proper way. Which I assume means not hanging out with riff raff like you." She gave him a sideways grin.

Sav snorted. "She didn't give you anything else? Did she know him?"

"Oh, she knew him. Worked with him. I think they might have been more than colleagues, but she didn't confirm that. Even worse, she doesn't know where he is now or whether he's still alive."

"I'll bet that isn't true," Sav added.

"I agree. But what she did tell me was that in his prime, Dagric was the realm's leading expert on rare plants and, in particular, poisons. He experimented so much that he had a cure for every known poisonous compound in not only our realm but also several others. If I'm going to find out who managed to get their hands on a banned poisonous plant, he's the one I need to talk to. But we have to find out if he's alive first and where he might live, and the only place I can think of to get that information—"

"Is in the restricted section," Sav finished for her. He crossed his arms over his chest. "And you expect me to risk everything and break in with you."

Jayce stammered. "I, well, I mean—"

Sav shook his head, grinning at her. "It's all right. I know what I'm good for. I'm the one who brought it up in the first place, aren't I?"

Jayce gave him an exasperated expression. "I'm sure it's locked up tight. I don't know anything about sneaking around and getting through locks."

Sav's expression morphed into one of mischief. "Locks are one man's deterrent and another man's challenge," he said with a wink.

It didn't take long for Jayce to guess which category Sav fell under.

CHAPTER TWENTY-ONE

Jayce clutched a pillow, laying fully clothed under the thin blanket she'd been provided. She found the firm mattress pressing into her back barely better than the forest floor she'd slept on the night before.

A rapid staccato penetrated the otherwise still night.

Jayce sat up, setting the pillow aside, and walked across the room in stockings. Shoes would create too much noise. She'd also decided against changing into a skirt in favor of the breeches she had yet to return to Sav. They were big on her, but the belt held them in place, and they were much easier to move around in than her skirts when she had to be stealthy.

She turned the knob and tugged her door open. Moonlight from her window spilled across Sav's freckled face. He motioned for her to follow him.

They'd decided to wait until nightfall to attempt to break into the restricted section. Jayce had walked past the area on her way to her rooms to pretend to go to bed. Literal locked bars separated them from the restricted materials. How did Sav plan to get in?

He'd assured her it would be a cinch. Finding information to help them without getting caught... Well, that would be much more difficult.

"I've been watching the area near the restricted section for a little over an hour. I was able to confirm that not much has changed since I was last here. They have an elder making rounds on each floor. We're allowed to be out of bed, but if we're found in or around the restricted section, we'll be put in the monastery's equivalent of jail—a locked, empty room—until they can gather the Elders and the Patron to pass judgment on us."

Jayce had to jog slightly to catch up with Sav's longer strides. Her breath already came in heavier gasps.

"Judgment that could include prison, right?" Jayce asked.

"If what we're caught reading is deemed bad enough," Sav replied. His tone came off nonchalant, but Jayce thought she caught a hint of strain.

Losing access to a library like this would affect Sav heavily. Jayce hadn't known him for long, but from what she did know, he practically lived in libraries. Not to mention the jail time that neither of them wanted.

"After you," Sav said, his voice hushed, gesturing in a gentlemanly manner.

Jayce stepped ahead of him. They'd discussed briefly what it would take to get from their rooms to the restricted section, after which neither of them knew what awaited. Jayce felt awkward making her way along the wall and wished she could walk down the stairs normally. She watched her feet, trying not to fall, until she heard a shuffling sound.

A robed figure walked across the landing at the bottom of the staircase, and Sav pushed her gently against a pillar, standing close as if to hide her.

"I thought we could be out of bed," Jayce whispered.

"We can. But a man and woman out of bed together will be suspicious."

A bright, cinnamon scent wafted into Jayce's nose, and underneath it the unmistakable scent of ink and parchment. She squirmed a little against Sav's arms on her shoulders, but he didn't budge, and she wondered if he realized that being caught smashed together like this would be far more suspicious than if they were walking down the stairs. But she bit her tongue to keep from blowing their cover.

Eventually, Sav moved away, taking his parchment and cinnamon scent with him. Jayce moved ahead of him on the stairs, crouching as low as she could against the short wall that looped down toward the first floor.

Shuffling steps came from the hall ahead of them, indicating the way the monk had gone.

Sav touched her shoulder, motioning with his hands that he would go first through the center of the library, and Jayce let him take the lead, not wanting to mess up this part. They would have to pass through the communal study hall at the center of the library, lit up almost as bright as day by the full Purple Bell Moon shining through the rainbow stained-glass of the Three goddesses.

Before Jayce was ready, Sav hooked left, dashing into the center of the library and sliding down the surface of the large, front desk where they'd spoken to Elder Vambi earlier that morning.

Jayce slid across the slick granite floor and sat beside him.

Fractured moonlight filtered through the colored glass, falling on the white floor like jeweled pools. Jayce's sock took on a violet hue, Sav's bare feet a pink one. Weren't his feet cold on the marble?

Jayce shuddered thinking about it. She stared at the back of Sav's head as he craned it around the desk, looking for the monk's location.

Sav's hushed whisper broke the silence. "In a few moments, he'll pass behind that big pillar there. On three, we each take one of those desks over there. One, two, three!"

Sav crawled to a desk about ten feet away and ducked under. He looked back, motioning frantically for Jayce to do the same.

She scooted a few feet, then flipped over and crawled, trying to place her hands so they didn't slap on the stone.

Once she made it under the shadow of the desk, Sav made a "wait" motion with his hands. He watched the monk, his head turning slowly as the monk passed the entrance to the restricted section. According to Sav, it was in the older, lower level of the monastery, where confusing, twisted halls wound beneath the floor on which they currently stood.

Sav motioned again with his hands, pointing to the monk. He swirled his hands around to indicate the monk's guard rotation, and then pointed back at the stairs.

Jayce thought she understood. Once the monk got near the landing of the stairs they'd just come down, they would make a break for the pillar closest to the barred door to the lower level.

No—Sav pointed at himself, held up one finger, then pointed at her and held up a second finger.

He wanted to go first, to unlock the door, she assumed. And that way, if he got caught, she could sneak back to her room without being implicated.

She kept her response to a nod and waited.

The monk's shadow passed over the moonlight's reflection from the stained-glass mural of the goddesses. He stopped, perhaps gazing up at the three glorious figures bathed in full moonlight.

Time stretched. Jayce's back ached from remaining hunched under the writing desk. She wiggled, trying to relieve her screaming muscles.

Suddenly, Sav bolted from under his desk, running in a crouch, his feet barely making a sound.

Jayce spotted the monk at the stairs turning around, a spear suddenly in his hand. Where had he gotten the spear? And what did a monk need with a weapon like that in a library?

Her heart pounded. She looked for Sav, but she didn't see him. Had he made it to the pillar?

It had to be a good sign that she didn't see him. That meant the monk couldn't see him either.

Seconds dragged on before the monk turned away, continuing his rounds. Jayce waited for Sav's signal.

In the shadows near the barred door, something moved. Sav had made it to the door.

Jayce glanced from him to the monk on guard and back again, her blood rushing in her ears. The monk would round the curve again and be on Sav in a moment. Jayce didn't have time to dash over to him without getting seen. She hunkered down, her breath heavy and hot against her face as she tucked it into her knees, afraid to look.

When she glanced up again, Sav was gone. The barred door remained shut. Had he found another place to hide?

A flash of white caught her attention, just inside the staircase leading to the lower levels. He'd gone inside and hidden in the stairwell. Hopefully, the monk wouldn't look down as he passed.

The monk gave the door a passing glance, then his shadow appeared in front of the window again. He didn't stop this time, and Jayce moved, readying herself for the dash across the floor.

NOW.

Jayce ran, her covered feet slipping a little as she pushed off, but she made it without incident, ducking behind the pillar, then slithering across the floor on her stomach to the barred door.

Sav opened it for her, the well-oiled hinges hardly making a sound.

Together, they descended the dusty steps, heading for the treasure trove of knowledge that waited in the depths of the Draigh monastery.

CHAPTER TWENTY-TWO

Sav breathed loudly in Jayce's ear as they pressed themselves against the wall and waited for the monk to pass the barred door at the top. She could only see ahead to a wall, where a hallway intersected in two directions.

A dark shadow passed, and fortunately, he did not look their way. Jayce's shoulders relaxed when the sound of the monk's footsteps trailed away from them.

Once the monk had gone on, Sav descended the steps quickly, his light steps barely making a shuffling sound on the stone.

Jayce eased her way down, gripping the wall, still worried the monk might hear them and return, but there was no sound of the monk's steps in the corridor.

Sav grabbed an unlit torch, removing it from its sconce. He fumbled with a flint, and Jayce took the torch from him so he could strike the flint properly to create a spark. The oil-soaked rag on the torch caught, and a small flame sputtered, then lengthened.

He gestured toward the left-hand hall. "If I recall correctly, the books we want lie this way."

They walked silently in the corridor. It forced them to turn right, then left again, until they came to a row of barred doors lining both sides of the narrow hall.

"This was once all prison cells, before the monks turned this building into a monastery," Sav explained. "They're not in use anymore."

He stopped outside a much larger cell, one that looked like it had once been several smaller cells before the walls had been broken down between them.

Jayce tried the first cell door—it was locked.

Sav pulled several thin instruments out of his pocket. He struggled to juggle both them and the torch, so Jayce took the light from him, her hand brushing his clammy skin.

The torch wavered in her grip. She gripped it with both hands, angling it so the flickering flames cast light on Sav.

"What are you doing?" she asked, her voice, even at a whisper, seeming to carry through the basement passageways.

"Picking the locks. Something useful I learned at the university." He grinned cheekily at her, his hands manipulating the skinny sticks of metal in the massive iron lock.

Moments later, Sav gave a grunt, and the lock clunked open into his hand. He unhooked the chain holding the door and pulled the door open slowly.

The metal hinges creaked so loudly Jayce was sure they'd wake the entire monastery. She held her breath, waiting to hear the clatter of footsteps down the stairs.

Sav entered, gesturing for her to join him.

Jayce walked into the barred room. It wasn't wide, but long, with tables and shelves lining the walls and jutting into the room. Stacks of bound and loose-leaf parchment stood in piles on some of the tables, along with rolled documents, maps, and more.

She found a sconce in the wall and slid the torch inside, then faced Sav, who gazed at the heaped documents.

"What is all of this?" Jayce asked, astounded at the volume.

"Banned books. Documents. The stuff on the tables has yet to be sorted into its proper place, I assume. Or someone is currently studying." Sav picked up a document, eyebrows furrowing, then dropped it and moved around the table to one of the shelves. "Remind me what we're looking for, exactly?"

"Books that look like they're about plants, herbology, alchemy. We're looking for mentions of noxbrosia, specifically more about where it grows and its properties. Also the name Dagric Wortcunning," Jayce said, emphasizing each syllable as she ran her fingers along the books on the shelf in front of her.

Many of the books didn't have title or author on the spine, and she had to slide them out to see what they might be about.

"*Preparations and Prescriptions from the Abbey Garden?*" Sav asked, head bent over a sage green volume.

It didn't sound like the kind of book that contained illegal information. Unless one of the monks had brought it down here and left it by accident, it must have some cause to reside in these shelves.

"Start a pile," Jayce said. She moved down the shelf systematically, adding both large and small volumes to the pile Sav had started after clearing a spot on the table's surface.

Jayce got three-fourths of the way through the final shelf on her side of the room, when Sav made an interested sound.

"Huh. Listen to this. 'noxbrosia was discovered by Orath Wortcunning on a trading expedition to the Norwast, when one of their party succumbed to death by its poison, contained in the darts of the Norvastir people when they attacked after being offended by the offered trades. His son, Dagric Wortcunning, later discovered the cure in time to heal Queen Lyadne.'"

"It's interesting, but not particularly helpful," Jayce said, bringing a final stack of books to the table. She added them to the wobbling pile and sighed as she took one off the top and flipped through.

The torch flickered while they browsed through book after book, each one offering snippets or containing concoctions with noxbrosia among the ingredients. They were either trying to kill people, as in *Merclede's Tome of Curses and Poisons*, or utterly ignorant to the effects of what they suggested.

Jayce's eyes ached as she flipped through the last several pages of the third book she'd picked up, and she closed it, then rubbed them.

"You all right?" Sav asked, making a note on a piece of blank parchment beside him.

Only a few meager words were scratched on the paper, and Jayce recognized all of them as things she already knew.

"Just tired. I'm not used to staying up all night." She breathed out heavily and stood, moving her chair carefully backward so it wouldn't scrape on the stone floor.

She stretched her neck, arms, and back as she paced the cell. Every time she headed back for the table to take another book off the stack, she grew restless and uneasy.

As if something inside her was telling her the answer wasn't contained in any of those volumes.

Then where? They'd found little of any use, and it had already been hours. They'd had to light several more torches to increase the light in the room for reading and replace the torches burning down. How long until dawn? And what if they found nothing?

Jayce stopped in front of the last bookcase she'd searched, scanning the volumes. She'd gone through them hastily, eager to get on with her research. Perhaps she'd missed something.

A thin black volume with no text on the spine caught her eye, and Jayce felt a strong pull toward the book. She tugged it out from where it was sandwiched between two fat, gilded volumes, and flipped it over in her hands, looking for any writing.

"If you're going to take a break, so am I," Sav said, his chair scraping loud enough to make Jayce wince.

"I'm not taking a break," she said, opening the book to the first page. It contained only one line, handwritten in faded, dark brown ink.

The studies, formulas, and musings of D. Wortcunning.

Jayce's breath caught, and she licked her lips to moisten them. D. Wortcunning had to be Dagric. This was his formula book, like Jayce's journal, where he put his experiments and observations and things that worked and hadn't worked. Considering he'd specialized in poisons, there had to be information on noxbrosia, perhaps even the cure, and she might get some hint about his current whereabouts by studying it.

"Sav," Jayce whispered, slowly standing, using the bookshelf to give her cramped legs some balance.

Sav didn't respond, and Jayce tore her eyes away from the journal in her hand to see what he was doing.

A massive volume, among the thickest in the room, sat on the table before Sav. He ran a finger down paragraphs of miniscule, handwritten text, muttering to himself.

"Sav? What are you looking at?" Jayce asked, moving closer to the table. Close enough to catch a glimpse of some of the words.

In the year King Reginald Donovanu went up to battle with Enrich the Enlightened of Eyd...

"That's what you stopped looking through the plant books for?" Jayce asked.

"It's nothing," Sav said, barely glancing up. "I just thought, since you seemed to have found something, I would take a peek inside and see if it mentions..."

The last part came out too quiet for Jayce to hear.

"What was that?" she asked.

"The Plague King," Sav said, watching her cautiously.

Jayce's vision tunneled. She heard Sav saying her name but couldn't bring herself out of the dark hole her mind had thrown her into. All she could see was the cave in the Hobhorn mountains, her brother gazing at her with sightless, black irises and telling her to run.

Just as quickly, the scene zoomed away, and she landed back in her body, in the present moment, Sav shaking her shoulders.

She blinked and looked at him, and he dropped his arms, an expression of relief on his handsome face.

"I thought I'd lost you for good there. You always do this whenever someone mentions... I just wanted to see if there was anything that could help in my research."

Jayce glanced at the floor, her fingers running along the edge of the little black book she still held. He hadn't said it to make her feel guilty, but she felt guilty all the same. She swallowed hard.

"If I could tell you, I would. But I—"

"You don't have to explain yourself," Sav said sharply, his footsteps moving away from her. Pages rustled. "I've seen what it does to you, and I'm not inclined to torment you. But if you ever do find yourself able to talk about it..."

Sav's voice trailed off, and after a long moment, Jayce glanced up to find him staring wide-eyed and frozen at the page before him.

She opened her mouth to break him from his stupor, but a clacking sound echoed down the corridor, and she shut her mouth.

Footsteps, and not very careful ones.

Someone had heard them. Someone was coming.

CHAPTER TWENTY-THREE

Jayce grabbed Sav's sleeve and tugged him toward the door, tucking the black book into the waistband of the breeches she wore.

"They heard us. Come on. Is there another way out of here?" She looked both ways down the corridor. They had moments until the sentry found them.

Sav blinked back to alertness and jerked his sleeve out of Jayce's fingers.

"Do you know how long I've tried to get access to this room?" His eyes had a red-rimmed desperation to them as he held her gaze.

"And you won't ever get access again if we get caught," Jayce said, exasperated, her blood rushing to her ears as fear rose inside her.

She couldn't hear the footsteps anymore. Had they abandoned their pursuit or were they trying to sneak up on the intruders in the restricted section? Jayce imagined the monk with the spear coming around the next corner. They would be on them in a moment.

Jayce stepped out of the room, glancing down the corridor and shoving the little book farther into her waistband to ensure it wouldn't fall out if she had to make a run for it.

Paper tore loudly from inside the cell.

"Sav!"

He was tearing pages out of the book seemingly at random, folding them in great wads and shoving them into his pockets.

"Even if we get out, they'll know it's me regardless," Sav said, turning on her, his expression burning with a ferocity Jayce hadn't known he felt, and she wondered what would make him go so mad as to deface a record like he had. "I might never get another chance to look inside this book. I'm not leaving without something."

"Is it worth ending up in prison?" Jayce asked through clenched teeth. If they got caught, the book she had would certainly be confiscated and she'd lose the only lead she had on Dagric and the noxbrosia.

Sav stared down at the book. He rubbed his hand down the front cover.

"I'm leaving," Jayce announced. Her breathing hitched, and her throat tightened. "Stay and get caught if you want."

She turned and walked swiftly from the room. She didn't know if he would follow, but she wouldn't risk everything she'd come to this monastery to find for him, especially when he was being so utterly unreasonable.

Jayce felt her way along the wall, heading down the opposite way down the hall they'd come in the dark—she'd left the torch with Sav.

Her hands hooked around a corner, and she breathed a sigh of relief, curving around the wall on the other side. She had to keep moving or the monk sentry would find her, but she felt safer now being out of sight.

She scooted along, listening for any sound indicating Sav had been caught—a loud protestation, sounds of fighting, but nothing came.

And then, a gentle huffing sound came from her left, and her left shoulder was bumped by something big and warm.

"Sav?" Jayce whispered, voice barely audible to her own ears.

His curls tickled the side of Jayce's face as he leaned in. "If we want to get away, we'd better run," he replied.

"Run where?" Jayce hissed.

He leaned in farther, pushing against her shoulder as if urging her to move faster.

"There's an exit—a sort of trap door leading into the gardens. I found it last time I was here. I failed to get into the restricted section, but I did find this exit. They know where it is as well, so we'll have to hide once we're out, but if we're fast, they won't find us."

Jayce sped up, careful to not let her feet slap on the pavement, hoping the monk would give up pursuit or head in another direction.

Ahead, a thin lavender sliver of the late Purple Bell Moon appeared through wooden slats in the ceiling. Jayce ducked under, squinting into the bright light.

Sav came up behind her and lifted his arms, pushing up on the trap door. It landed on the ground outside with a soft *thump*.

Sav bent down, propping one knee up and motioning for Jayce to step up.

She complied, grabbing the lip of the narrow exit above her and straightening until her head popped up above ground. She strained with everything she had and made such slow progress it was embarrassing until Sav pushed on her knees from below and she surged onto a patch of grass.

Jayce rolled away from the entrance, gripping Dagric's black book to keep it close, barely catching the whispers of the grass as its feathery tops brushed her bare cheek.

Sav followed her out, his movements much more coordinated than hers had been. He stood, brushed off his pants, held a hand out to her, and she took it.

Together, they ran to where the willow tree drooped over the edge of the pond. Jayce arrived first, parting the willow fronds. A long one escaped her hands and swung down, resting against her face.

Hide here, it said in a hushed tone.

The words almost made Jayce turn back and run the other direction, regardless of the danger that lay behind her. Could she trust the willow? She'd been lied to so many times, her time wasted by senseless plants that gossiped and manipulative ones that had nearly cost the life of her new friend.

But the birch hadn't lied about the moribund on the road, and she couldn't help but think that it had intended to warn her.

Sav turned, motioning for her to come farther under the tree's cover.

Jayce stayed where she was, yanking off her glove and sticking it between her teeth. With her bare hand, she grabbed one of the willow's swaying tendrils, letting the cold wash through her, embracing the words that came.

Willow, the protective mother.

Are you lying? Jayce thought to the tree. She felt foolish, but she had to try something. Mystri Prieta had been right about her fear of her powers. It would continue to cripple her if she didn't try to move past it. *Please, don't deceive me now. We can't be found.*

My branches are a refuge. Hide here.

Jayce shivered and dropped the willow branch. She had a sense of something closing around them, an invisible force that pressed in on her. Sav yanked her behind the tree's trunk, pinning her against its rough bark.

Jayce almost protested, but stopped herself as she looked up at Sav's earnest face, which she could barely make out in the dappled moonlight filtering through the trees. Occasionally, Sav looked away from her and leaned around the tree's trunk.

Jayce tried to duck under Sav's arm and look around the tree as well, but Sav's hand gripped her shoulder, holding her in place.

"What do you see?" she whispered, her voice barely audible to her own ears. She clutched her glove in her hand, having not had a moment to put it back on.

Sav didn't respond, but with his proximity, Jayce felt his breath catch as his chest stilled for a brief moment. She wanted to know what was going on. She clenched her fingers, then spread them wide and slid her hand against the smooth willow bark behind her.

What do you see? She asked.

I do not see. I feel. I feel vibrations. Your vibrations. The one with you. And another.

The willow sent her an image through her fingertips. Not something she could actually see but an impression of things. For a moment, she sensed what the tree sensed, from the tiniest bug digging at its roots to the birds nesting in its branches above.

Her mind filled so quickly with the multitude of sensations from the tree that the cold pierced to her core and she thought she'd go mad. Her breath quickened, and she tried to pull her fingers from the tree's surface, but she couldn't move them.

"Sav," Jayce said, her lips forming his name soundlessly.

His eyes remained fixed on whatever he saw through the willow's swaying branches.

Jayce squeezed her eyes shut, the cold starting to hurt as it pulsed through her chest. She focused on breathing and sending the message to her hand that it needed to move.

"Sav," she tried again.

By some miracle, Sav glanced at her. He took in her wide, frightened eyes and stepped back, silently scanning her body, then caught sight of her bare hand on the tree's trunk. He grabbed her shoulders and tugged her away from the tree and into him.

Her hand left the willow trunk, and immediate relief washed through her, so strong she collapsed against Sav, tucking her hand between her body and his to bring feeling back into it. She shook like an autumn leaf on the wind, and Sav's arms gripped her, comfortingly solid.

The pressure Jayce had felt when she first stepped under the willow increased, and Jayce stiffened, stepping back from Sav.

"What is that?" she whispered.

His grip loosened, but his arms didn't drop from around her.

"The monks receive blessings from the Three," Sav said, leaning in until his lips moved against Jayce's ear. "Enhanced sight, hearing, smell, physical abilities. The sentry is still hunting. They're on their third rotation of the gardens. I think they would have heard us by now. My guess is they have advanced smell or strength."

Jayce shifted only her eyes, looking for any movement beyond the willow branches, which tousled like hair on the wind.

A strong, pleasant floral scent wafted past, like magnolias or lilacs, but those bloomed in the Sprouting Moon season, not at the end of the Purple Bell Moon. What flower smelled so fragrant this late in the age?

Jayce tried to step farther away from Sav, to put more appropriate space between them, but Sav's arm remained wrapped around her back. She stopped trying to move away. She couldn't say she disliked it. In fact, his proximity calmed her. She wanted to rest her head on his chest and stay, content and safe in his warmth and solidity.

Jayce might have dozed, the scent of spring flowers still coming with each gust of the breeze, somehow making her feel safe.

When Sav moved next, glancing around the tree slowly, her head had indeed fallen onto his chest, and she sheepishly wiped a bit of drool off the corner of her mouth.

Sav's arm slid away, and his hands grasped her arms, pushing her gently, but firmly, away from him. "They're gone," Sav said in the barest whisper, glancing back at her with a relieved smile.

Jayce adjusted the book in her waistband again, reassuring herself it was still there.

Sav pointed at it. "You found something."

"So did you," she said pointedly.

Sav looked away from her, his hand going to the pocket of his embroidered vest, where a thick wad of folded papers poked over the top.

Jayce sighed. "We should talk about it later. For now, we have to get back inside without anyone suspecting us." Goosebumps rose on her skin from the late-night chill.

Somewhere in the night, a bullfrog sang.

"I still don't understand how that sentry missed finding us," Sav said.

The faintest whiff of magnolia and lilacs caught Jayce's nose again. She sniffed in wonder, wishing she had a way to confirm it. Had the willow somehow created that extra strong scent to hide them from the sentry?

"In any case," Sav continued. "I don't think we can get back inside, not without running into that sentry, and there's no way they won't hold us for questioning. And if they do that, they're sure to find what we both took from the restricted section and confiscate it."

Jayce licked her lips and rubbed her hands on the bumpy stone seat of the bench. “You’re suggesting we sleep out here?”

“Ground’s a bit bumpy, but it’s not too bad under here,” Sav said, looking up into the boughs of the willow. “At the very least, it’s unlikely to rain.”

A night on the ground, where grass and leaves and moss could whisper to her all night long if she turned the wrong direction... Jayce shivered. “I-I don’t know if I can do it.”

“You can have the bench. Roll up my vest; you can use it as a pillow,” Sav said, removing the folded papers he’d taken and shrugging out of his embroidered vest. He held it out toward her.

“All I need is your shirt, and I’ll have a complete set,” Jayce murmured, placing the bundle on the bench where her head would rest.

Sav chuckled quietly, rolling onto his back and folding his arms beneath his head, staring upward.

Jayce turned on her side, then on her back, trying to find the most comfortable position. She settled for her side, gazing at Sav’s face, illuminated by a dappled patch of lavender moonlight coming through the top of the willow.

“You did something with the tree. I saw you talking to it. You took off your glove,” Sav said, shifting his head to look at her.

Jayce glanced upward. “I just... asked it to hide us.”

Sav propped himself up on one elbow. “And it did what you asked? You really can talk to plants, can’t you?”

“I always thought it only went one way. They talked to me. Well, told me things. But lately...” Jayce trailed off, glancing over at Sav. "I'm beginning to realize that I barely understand my own magic."

"Well, I think it's incredible. And thank you," he said, his eyes shining with sincerity.

Jayce shook her head, swallowing the lump in her throat. "Don't thank me. Thank the tree."

"I still feel like I owe you something," Sav said after a long moment.

Jayce stared at the swaying curtain of willow branches, her hand gripping the black journal, which she'd pulled out of her waistband and laid on the bench beside her.

"You can make it up to me later," Jayce said.

"How?" Sav asked.

Jayce smiled to herself. "Hot chocolate, of course."

CHAPTER TWENTY-FOUR

Morning came swift and vengeful, a bright sunbeam shooting straight into Jayce's eyes from a crack in the willow's foliage.

She sat up, alarmed to find herself outside, her back complaining from hours of sleeping on the hard stone bench, and Sav a few paces away, quietly snoring.

The book. It wasn't on the bench where she'd left it.

Jayce jumped up, scanning the bench even though the surface remained empty, and then her gaze drifted to the side and spotted the black rectangle. She snatched it from the ground, wiping the dew off the worn leather cover, and sat back on the bench, breathing deeply to calm the shaking in her limbs, either from the cold or the fear she'd experienced at the thought of losing the book they'd risked so much to find.

She brushed across the cover and opened the book, turning past the first page that indicated it had belonged to the alchemist Dagric Wortcunning, to the first entry written in a scrawled, almost unreadable handwriting.

Jayce squinted. She rubbed her eyes. No, the letters hadn't gotten any clearer. In fact, the more she looked, flipping through the book, the more her heart sank.

The journal wasn't written in the common script. Either Dagric had known another language, or he'd developed a sort of shorthand to keep his findings from prying eyes.

Jayce hugged the journal to her chest and tried not to cry, the tightness in her chest growing almost unbearable. All that trouble the night before, and everything she'd done to get to this point, and the journal was unreadable.

By her, at least. She could only read the common script.

Her gaze landed on Sav, still sleeping, his chest rising and falling rhythmically.

Sav was a historian. He'd gone to an elite school across the Atean Sea. Surely, he'd learned multiple languages during his studies.

Unable to wait a moment longer, Jayce knelt beside him. "Sav?" she said, softly, trying not to choke on the tightness in her throat.

After a moment without response, she nudged his shoulder.

Sav opened his blue eyes and gasped, sitting straight up. He glanced frantically around as if looking for a fight, and then his gaze landed on her, and his shoulders relaxed. "Oh, Jayce. It's you." He wiped a hand across his eyes, blowing air between his lips. "I thought you were a dagwere or one of the monks or..."

"Sorry," Jayce said.

Sav brushed his hands down his shirt. "I am in a state. I need a bath. Do you need a bath?" He moved to stand.

Jayce reached a hand toward him. "Please, wait a moment? I need to know if you can read this." She held the book out.

Sav took it from her, opening it to a random page. His eyebrows raised. "This is what you found in there? The whole thing is in Fimbulvintr, the Cold Tongue. Do you know how many people speak or write this outside of the Norvastir tribes? I know one."

"Looks like Dagric is another," Jayce said, her heart sinking. She held her hand out for the book. "I knew it wouldn't be this easy."

"Now hold on," Sav said, holding the book out of reach and scanning another page. He pointed to a section. "See that word?"

Jayce leaned in, holding her breath. The word *Musport* stood out in plain common script, a stark contrast to the symbols of the Cold Tongue.

"Musport? That's the next city over to the east. What does it say?"

Sav licked his lips and rubbed his chin, which Jayce noticed had a fine stubble growing across it. He must typically shave.

"It could take me some time to decipher. I've studied Fimbulvintr, but I'm nowhere near proficient. It would be far better if we could take it to my mentor, Ionsa."

His voice changed pitch at the mention of his mentor.

"She's in Enterea, isn't she?" Jay said. "Not easy to get to."

Sav tightened his lips and closed his eyes, shaking his head. "No, she's not in Enterea. She's dead."

"Oh," Jayce said, her hand going to her lips. "I'm so sorry."

"One of the only known translators of Fimbulvintr and a brilliant historian and friend. I still wish I knew how it happened. But that's not important now. What's important is we get this translated and find out where Dagric is living now so you can talk to him."

Jayce didn't miss his hand trailing toward his breeches pocket, where he'd shoved the papers he'd found the night before. What had he found?

"Do you think the book can tell us that? Mystri Prieta said he was banished ages ago."

"But this book was only confiscated two ages ago," Sav said, showing her the last entry in the book. "And he mentioned Musport a few pages before. I'll scan for mention of any other locations and try to translate the surrounding words. After all, mere mention of a place doesn't mean he lives there. But before I can translate, I need breakfast."

Sav heaved himself off the ground and held a hand out to Jayce. "Miss Keenstone, will you join me for first meal?"

Jayce smiled up at him, sliding her hand into his palm. "So dignified, even after spending a night on the ground."

Sav inclined his head, then smiled at her, and Jayce had the sudden, unbidden thought that he looked particularly beautiful with his curls fluffed up and springing wildly from his head. The reflection of the morning sun off the lake illuminated the sparkle in his eyes, and even more, the hopeful expression was clear on his face.

His hope was infectious, and she felt it all the way back into the monastery and up to her rooms, where she was able to wash and change her clothes before heading down to the common area for breakfast.

Sav was waiting for her at an otherwise empty table, an extra plate loaded with food beside him. When he saw her, he stood and pulled out a chair for her, and Jayce graciously took it.

"It's been a few days since I saw you in skirts. I have to say it's a nice change," Sav said, sitting back down.

Jayce flushed, picking up her utensils to cut the ham slice on her plate. "Are you saying breeches don't suit me?"

"No, not at all," Sav stammered, dabbing at his mouth with a napkin, a bit of color coming to his cheeks. "It's just... You look lovely. That's all I'm trying to say."

Jayce didn't know what to say. She fought the blush rising to her own cheeks as she took a pat of butter from a nearby dish and spread it on the dark brown bread on her tray. From the corner of her eyes she caught sight of the black book beside Sav.

"Is that wise?" she asked, nodding toward the book. "Having it in the open like that?"

Sav put a hand over it protectively and cleared his throat, glancing everywhere but at her. "I figured I could work on it while we eat. We need to know for sure where we're headed next, and I assume you'll want to talk to this Dagric fellow."

Jayce frowned, but didn't comment further as she dug into her breakfast. She kept glancing around, paranoid that one of the monks would identify the book as having been stolen, even though several others also read at the table and there was certainly no way anyone would recognize *this* book on sight.

The whispers from the rye bread irritated her mind like the itching on her arms from the mostly healed blister bee stings.

She choked it down for the nutrients and moved on to the cheese and meat on her plate.

The doors to the dining hall opened, and a man in red robes strode in. Jayce recognized him from the day before—Master Chalu.

Sav glanced up from his food, then quickly wiped his hands and face on his napkin and slid the little black book off the table into his lap.

Master Chalu went to the front of the hall and stepped up on a raised platform. He lifted his hands to the sparse crowd of mostly monks interspersed with a few visitors. "I am sorry to interrupt your meal this morning, friends and comrades. We have a most urgent message to deliver this morning." He cleared his throat. "Last night, an intruder, or intruders, were discovered to have been in the restricted section of the library. Books were carelessly taken from their places. A book was found desecrated, and another is believed to be missing." Master Chalu scanned the crowd, their bent heads whispering, and their faces wide with abject horror.

Jayce tried to look horrified as well, and she glanced at Sav from the corner of her eye. He had paled significantly, and his eyes were blank. She nudged him with her elbow, and he startled, then glanced down at the book in his lap.

The stolen book. The book they were forbidden to have.

"We are conducting a thorough investigation and assure you that all will be put to rights and the perpetrators will be caught," Master Chalu said, emphasizing each word and staring out at the crowd with a fierce expression.

Jayce forced herself to meet his gaze rather than drop it, hoping neither she nor Sav appeared too suspicious.

"The investigation will include all rooms. We apologize in advance for the intrusion. Your cooperation is most appreciated. All acolytes are requested to meet in the Patron's antechamber for your assignment to help with the search. All guests are requested to move outdoors and remain there until the search has concluded. We politely request that you do not leave the premises, unless you wish to be immediately added to the list of suspects who will be summoned for questioning shortly."

Master Chalu's eyes drifted to where Jayce and Sav sat, and this time, Jayce couldn't hold the monk's gaze.

Her heart squeezed. They wouldn't find anything in her room but the books they'd left out in the chamber the night before. They were all books on alchemy and herbology, plus Sav's book on the history of the plague.

It wouldn't take the monks long to put two and two together and bring Jayce and Sav in for questioning, and she had no doubt they would be arrested the moment that happened. Even if they did manage to hide the black book and Sav's pages somewhere, everything pointed to them as the most likely suspects.

"What do we do?" she whispered, squeezing her gloved hands together.

Everyone around them had stood, acolytes moving to their assigned location and the few remaining visitors heading for the doors outside as directed.

"How quickly could you get your things together and meet me at the stables?" Sav asked, leaning so far over his hair brushed against her cheek.

"But they said—"

"I know what they said," Sav said, his eyes flashing. "And you know that they're going to realize it was us. Our only chance is getting out of here before they apprehend us."

Resolve flooded Jayce, drowning out her fear, and she nodded. "I'm mostly packed."

"Good. There's a bush below my window. We'll sneak upstairs, and then you'll come over to my room and we'll drop our things into the bushes, then collect them on our way out."

Jayce glanced at a brown-robed monk headed straight for them and quickly stood from the bench.

"What if someone stops us?" Jayce asked as Sav joined her.

"Are you willing to leave without your pack?" he asked.

Jayce's heart clenched at the thought of losing her herb vials, her journal, and supplies. Much of it was replaceable, but her journal filled with all her painstaking findings would take ages to recreate.

"Keep walking." Sav nudged her from behind.

She stumbled forward. "Are they following us?" Jayce murmured, resisting the urge to glance over her shoulder.

"Yes."

Jayce quickened her pace and mingled with the small crowd moving toward the front doors. They passed through the main entrance hall then split from the crowd to dart up the stairs.

A man in a brown robe stepped gracefully in front of them, hands clasped together, a calm expression on his face.

"No access to private quarters, I'm afraid."

"Vambi, you have to let us through," Sav pleaded, one arm behind his back, holding the black book.

Jayce stepped slightly behind him, using his body as a shield as she slid the book from his grasp and shoved it under her shirt, then tucked it back in and put her arms over her stomach.

"Doing so could jeopardize my position with the Patron. I could be reduced to the position of acolyte if betrayal is discovered. Do you realize what you've done, Sav?" Elder Vambi said, his expression urgent.

"In the pursuit of truth, Vambi. Isn't that something we both value?" Sav asked, spreading his hands before him.

The small crowd had nearly dispersed, with only a few stragglers remaining. Jayce glanced around, her hackles raised at the thought that at any moment Elder Vambi could take them into custody or another monk could see them.

"Please," she said, stepping forward, keeping both hands tight over her midsection. "I'm not feeling well, and—"

Elder Vambi shook his head. "Lying will not get you anywhere. I can hear the minute changes to your tone when you lie. My hearing is a gift from Damaris, praise be the Three. What could convince me is you telling me what could possibly be so important you would risk imprisonment."

"We don't have time!" Sav said, licking his lips. He grabbed Elder Vambi's hands in his. "Please, dear friend. Trust me when I say our cause is critical, and we cannot afford the delay of imprisonment. Lives are at stake. Let our past friendship be enough for you to aid me, just this once."

"We will return and absolve our crimes with the Draigh when we are finished," Jayce said quietly, gazing at the monk with as much sincerity as she could muster.

Sav turned on her, blinking with surprise. "We will?"

"Yes, we will. I vow it." She held her gaze steady, and she could see the Elder considering, and then he slowly started to nod.

"I know you are a man of integrity, Sav. And while this young woman is a stranger to me, I can hear the sincerity in her voice. If you both vow to return and receive your punishment, I will allow you to leave. I will aid you no further than letting you up these stairs. You will be on your own after that," Elder Vambi warned.

Sav pressed his lips together until they appeared white, then sighed and relented. "I vow to return and admit all of my wrongdoings to receive proper judgment that the Patron deems I deserve."

Elder Vambi nodded and looked to Jayce, who repeated the words Sav had spoken. They sank deep in her gut, the oath settling there with a finality she knew would haunt her until the day she returned to fulfill her end.

"Then may the Three guide your journey, and let the next time I see you be a happy occasion," Elder Vambi said.

Sav clapped him on the shoulder, then gestured for Jayce to go past. "I do not see how that could be, given our vow here today, but I thank you for the thought all the same."

Jayce ran up the stairs without looking back. Sav's footsteps echoed behind her until she got to her door, and he passed her on his way to the room next door.

"See you in a few moments. Hurry," Sav said.

Jayce pulled her door open and rushed around, gathering the few things she'd left out. Her hairbrush and oils, a spare pair of gloves, a dirty pair of stockings from the night before. They were grass-stained and filthy, but she rolled them up and packed them anyway, wondering when she'd have time to rinse them.

Shouldering her pack, she took one last look around the small, simply furnished room before slipping into the hall and into Sav's room.

He stood by the window, sleeves rolled up and an urgent expression on his face. He gestured for her pack. "Quickly," he said.

Jayce handed it over, and Sav immediately pushed it out the window.

She winced as it crashed into the large, flowering bushes below, grateful she'd thought to wrap her vial pouch in her cloak, hoping without hope that nothing had been damaged in the fall.

She took a deep breath. "Now we go back downstairs and claim... what? That we got lost?"

"Unless you have a better idea," Sav said, striding for the door.

"Separate. I'll claim I was using the lavatory. You could say you were reading in your room?"

"They saw us both in the mess hall," Sav said, his hand on the doorknob. "Come on. Elder Vambi will likely be the one at the bottom of the stairs."

Jayce moved past him, clutching the book in her shirt and muttering a prayer to the Three that they could pull this off.

CHAPTER TWENTY-FIVE

Jayce and Sav were not stopped all the way to the stables. They had retrieved their packs without incident, most of the visitors being on the other side of the gardens close to the willow tree and the lake where they had hid the night before.

Jayce gripped the strap of her pack tightly as she stepped into the stables. Warm, dust-ridden air swirled around her in Sav's wake as he moved to where Abigail, Elsa, and the donkey Maggie were being held.

Sav bridled and saddled Abigail, then skipped over Elsa's stall with only a pat on her eager nose.

The black and white horse still had paste spread across her body over each of the nasty blister bee wounds she had received, but Jayce was relieved to note that the weeping blisters had crusted over, indicating they were healing.

“We’re not taking her with us?” Jayce asked.

Sav clipped a lead on Maggie. “She will be miserable on the road, and the stress of travel will slow her healing. I may be a wanted criminal after this, but my horse isn’t. They’ll care for her until I return.”

Maggie brayed, and Jayce jumped, whirling around to face the donkey, startled. She glanced toward the stable doorway, watching for anyone that might come investigate the noise. Her insides clenched, and her shoulders crept up. She forced them to relax.

“Maggie feels ignored, I think.”

Sav scratched the donkey’s head. “Don’t worry, girl, we couldn’t do this without you.” He strapped his and Jayce’s belongings on the donkey’s back, and then he mounted Abigail in the narrow space between stalls. He held a hand out to Jayce.

Jayce reached for Sav’s extended hand, her callouses catching on his. His hands were soft otherwise, the hands of a scholar, but he had callouses marking him proficient at shooting a bow. Her brother Javin had possessed the same ones.

She settled behind Sav, arms around his waist, his blond curls blowing against her face with the breeze. She spat them out, shaking her head to get away from the tickling strands.

“Maybe you should borrow a tie from Vambi before we depart,” Jayce said, still sputtering.

Sav laughed and moved Abigail forward, Maggie following behind on her lead.

The moment they emerged from the stables, Sav turned to Jayce. “Hold on!”

He urged Abigail forward, and the horse leapt into a gallop, Maggie braying behind them. All eyes in the garden turned on them, including a few black-robed acolytes that began running and silently waving their hands, asking them to stop.

No *chance*, Jayce thought, grinning at the thrill that surged through her at their escape. They'd done it. They'd gotten away before anyone could bring them in for questioning. Now they just had to get far enough down the road that no one would follow them.

Sav let Abigail run until she started to slow down on her own, a couple of miles down the road. He kept her going at a steady pace, and neither Jayce nor Sav spoke.

The adrenaline wore off, leaving Jayce feeling irritable and hungry, as she hadn't eaten much of her breakfast before the announcement by Master Chalu. In an attempt to ignore her aching stomach—which was made worse by the horse's galloping—Jayce leaned in closer to Sav.

"You never told me what you found in that book you ripped up last night," she said.

Sav flinched away from her voice in his ear. "You make it sound so violent."

"It looked violent."

"I wish I'd been able to take the entire book. It looked like it contained more of the specific information on the plague's beginning—and the war that preceded it—than anything I've read before. It might have even had your story in it," Sav said, sounding regretful.

"I haven't told anyone the full story," Jayce murmured, pulling away from him slightly. She'd left so much out of what she'd told the queen's recorder. And she hadn't told the truth, hadn't been able to bring herself to say what actually happened…

"Hey," Sav said softly, twisting in the saddle and reaching a hand back to grip her arm. "Don't go there. It's okay. I'm not asking you to tell me."

Jayce shook her head, dragging herself out of the undertow of emotions that had tried to pull her under.

"Thank you." She shook her head again to clear it. "Did you pull the pages at random, or because you saw something important?" She swallowed, licking her lips and trying to get rid of the cotton feeling in her mouth.

"I saw a language I haven't seen anywhere except the library at the Ivory Guilds. It's all in Erish."

"And… you can't read it?" Jayce asked.

"I'm a historian, not a linguist," Sav said, dropping his hand away from hers. The absence of his warmth felt cold, similar to the way she felt when touching plants.

"It isn't an easy language to learn, I'm afraid. Both of the people I know of who can read it are in Enterea at the Ivory Guilds," Sav continued.

"Can you write them?" Jayce asked.

Sav shook his head. "I wouldn't. Not with something as sensitive as this. If the mail gets searched and this information falls into the wrong hands, I'd never forgive myself. I have reason to believe that somewhere in these papers could be the prophecy of the Plague King. Few people have heard it in its entirety. No, we'll have to go in person, get passage on a ship."

Jayce's spine shivered at the mention of the prophecy that had gotten her brother as good as killed, but she wasn't about to mention it.

"A ship?" Jayce asked. She'd rarely traveled outside Neldor, and if they were going so Sav could pursue more about the prophecy, she wasn't sure she wanted to go.

"I intend to go to Crotos post haste and book passage. I haven't felt this excited since... well, since I met you for the first time."

"But what about the translation of Dagric's book? What about Musport? Finding the creator of the poison?" Jayce asked urgently.

"In the grand scheme of things, it really isn't that important, is it? Compared with stopping the Plague King entirely—imagine if I translated the prophecy and figured out what it meant, and we stopped him together? We'd make history. I could write it all down. We'd be known by everyone—"

Jayce's hearing and vision tunneled. She wouldn't let the emotions drag her under again. She had to stay awake for this, to stop letting it pull her into a panic. She couldn't let fear rule her life forever.

"He can't be stopped!" she screamed out.

Abigail startled, side-stepping toward the edge of the road. Birds fluttered out of the trees.

Sav reigned Abigail in and leaned over her neck to pat it and calm her.

Jayce slid off the horse, landing hard enough that the heels of her feet stung. She crossed her arms over her chest and faced the forest, afraid to look Sav in the eyes and lose her composure completely. What little she had left.

"What do you mean?" Sav asked quietly. His feet landed on the ground with a *thud* behind Jayce.

Jayce took a shaky breath in and let it out slowly before responding. “I can’t… I can’t go through that again.”

“I get that you don’t want to relive what happened in the past, but you’re the only one I know who’s been there who hasn’t been paid off by the queen to keep quiet. I need your expertise.”

Jayce squeezed her eyes shut. The queen had offered to pay her. Insisted on it, in fact. With a title and enough money that she never would have gone into debt. But it had felt too much like blood money. A cheap consolation prize to pay her to never again talk about what had happened to her brother.

“They knew the prophecy. Queen Lyra. Her counselors. The people who trained us. They knew it, and we still failed.” Jayce gripped her hands and turned around to face Sav. “It doesn't matter what you know—you can’t kill the Plague King. And I won’t watch another person I care about be destroyed!”

Her chest burned and heaved, as if she couldn’t get enough air. Spots danced in her vision, but she held steady and didn’t sink under the red panic blazing behind her eyes, threatening to swallow her. Because she had to get him to understand, had to say enough for him to realize that what he wanted was a hopeless waste of his time.

For a brief moment, Jayce thought she had succeeded. Sav’s eyes locked on hers, blue and filled with a passionate fierceness that Jayce had come to admire. But those strengths would be the end of him.

“I’m going to Enterea to get these pages translated. They might be nothing more than… shipping records, for all I know. But it’s the only lead I have since you won’t get over this fear you have of whatever happened before. Discovering the key to destroy the Plague King and writing the history is my only chance to—"

Sav cut himself off, his expression darkening as he glanced away. "Never mind. You wouldn't understand. You're too caught up in your own problems."

"My own problems? Finding the creator of the noxbrosia remedy isn't my problem, but I'm trying to solve it anyway. Because I'm an apothecary. I help people," Jayce insisted, her vision clearing a little as the conversation steered away from the topic she hated most. Anger surged inside of her. "People are dying from this remedy. I have to talk to Dagric and see if he knows the cure and where someone might have gotten the noxbrosia. Either you're coming with me and saving lives, or you can leave on your fool's errand alone."

Jayce's crossed arms felt so tight and her head so light she thought her circulation might be getting cut off, but she didn't adjust, and she didn't take her eyes from Sav. He had to know she meant what she'd said.

"Fine," Sav said, hands curling into fists. "I've paid hundreds of thousands of djwels to find you and free you from your debt in the hopes that you could share some of your story with me, and it has gotten me nowhere. I know a failed investment when I see one."

Jayce gaped at him, her chest clenching so hard she could barely take a full breath. "How dare you reduce me to... to... a business transaction!"

"That's all this ever was," Sav said coldly, turning back to Abigail and mounting her. He didn't glance at Jayce as he held a hand out to her. "I'll drop you off in Musport. I'll be passing through, regardless. You can find Dagric on your own from there."

Jayce stepped back, sputtering. "I am not getting on that horse with you after—"

Sav clenched his jaw, still not looking at her. "And I'm not leaving a young woman alone this far into the Oakmist. It would take you days to walk to Musport. The least I can do is give you a ride there."

Jayce bit the inside of her lip and furiously rubbed the bald spot on her right eyebrow. She paced one direction, then the other, until her boot rammed into a rock, sending a throbbing pain through her toe. She sucked air in sharply and stopped, flexing her fingers and breathing through the pain.

"You're a pain in the—" she started.

"The only ass here is Maggie," Sav said wryly, staring at her again with those infuriatingly beautiful eyes that somehow managed to look calm despite the storm that had just raged through them. "Don't say something you'll regret later."

Jayce pressed her lips together, holding the words inside. He was right that he was her best option for getting to Musport. Unless she wanted to walk back to the monastery and commit another crime by stealing a horse, the only way she would get there was with Sav. She almost couldn't bear the thought of sitting behind him after the way he'd just dismissed her and the importance of what she'd given up everything to accomplish, but she'd done harder things before. She could do this.

She gritted her teeth and stomped up to the horse. She grasped Sav's hand and pulled herself over the back of the horse.

"How sure are you that Dagric's book says he still lives in Musport?" Jayce reluctantly asked.

Sav clicked his tongue, and Abigail started moving again. "Fairly. Musport is mentioned rather often, including mention of his apothecary. It seems likely he would have remained there, despite his livelihood being stripped from him." Sav's words had taken on a distant tone, and he sounded more like a scholar than a friend.

It rubbed Jayce the wrong way to hear him talk so distantly. All the charm and humor was gone from his voice. She clamped her mouth shut, avoiding asking any of the questions or telling him any of the theories she had as they made their way farther down the road toward the city of Musport.

CHAPTER TWENTY-SIX

Around midday, they shared a cold, wordless, torturous meal on the side of the road before mounting the horse again and continuing on their way. Jayce grew sore and tired of the silence, but she refused to be the first one to break it. At least until Sav apologized for what he'd said to her.

He didn't even have to agree to help her find Dagric. If they could at least clear the air between them before they parted ways, she could deal with the disappointment that had plunged its way into her heart from the moment he'd said he was leaving Neldor without her.

They had different goals. They'd always had. So why did it feel like such a dagger wound to think of Sav departing, possibly never to see him again?

Jayce squirmed on Abigail's back as the horse passed under a twisted pair of trees that had grown so tall their canopies covered the road.

She frowned. The road had narrowed at some point, looking more overgrown now.

"Did you turn off the main road?" she asked Sav, breaking her resolve to not be the first one to speak.

A cool breeze brushed past her, rattling the leaves on the trees. A lone bird sang a strange song, not one of the cheery tunes Jayce recognized, but a sort of dirge-like melody that brought to mind haunted tales of men and women lost in the woods turning into specters and haunting those who entered thereafter.

"No. This is the main road. Musport used to be a lively thoroughfare on the way to Crotos, but after the plague started and roads were initially shut down, the city itself nearly collapsed. I passed through when I came back from Enterea. Dismal place." He clipped his words short, as if he'd meant to say more but stopped himself, then cleared his throat. "We'll be coming up on the former baron's estate soon, and you'll see what I mean."

Jayce straightened, searching through the trees for the first sign of the estate, wondering why Sav had sounded almost frightened when he'd spoken of it.

She couldn't even see the sun through the trees now, and the road was so overgrown that Abigail wound her way through clumps of grass to find the smoothest ground. Behind them, Maggie snorted. The cool breeze from before had vanished, leaving a stifling, humid afternoon heat that made Jayce's head and eyes droop drowsily.

She woke some time later, her cheek pressed against Sav's back, drool trailing down his vest.

Jayce sat upright quickly, wiping her mouth and feeling disoriented. It seemed darker than it should have been, even beneath the trees. Through them, Jayce caught glimpses of puffy gray clouds and groaned.

"I don't think it'll rain until later tonight," Sav predicted.

Sure enough, the clouds held.

What seemed like ages and miles down the road later, Jayce still hadn't seen any sign of the estate Sav had mentioned.

"Are we going to get to Musport tonight?" she finally asked, reaching for the waterskin they'd filled up at the last creek they'd come across. The waterskin was nearly empty, but she resisted finishing it off, instead, handing it to Sav. Not as a peace offering. He still needed to apologize. But kindness and respect for all beings had been bred into Jayce by her parents, and she wouldn't stoop to rudeness, no matter how upset she was with him.

"We could. Not until after sundown. Are you all right with getting in late, or do you want to set up camp?"

Between the threat of rain and their earlier argument, Jayce couldn't imagine spending a night in close quarters with Sav. Sleeping next to him, sharing at least two more meals with him... What had been one of the greatest pleasures of human company she had enjoyed now seemed unbearable.

"Let's push through. I don't want to waste any time in my search."

"Most of the city will be asleep. You likely won't be able to do any searching until morning. And I'd highly recommend staying off the streets until the sun rises. Musport isn't kind to strangers after dark. I vote for making camp."

"Don't the moon stag herds come through here this time of year? We'll be at greater risk if we stop and light a fire," Jayce argued, her arms tightening unconsciously around Sav's waist.

"So, we don't light a fire. We'll be more at risk riding through."

"It's early in the season yet. The moon hasn't turned red yet. It's barely pink. The herds don't start moving until it's red," Jayce said, trying to reassure herself.

"Are you sure about that?" Sav said, sounding unconvinced.

"Sure, I'm sure," Jayce said, with far more confidence than she felt. She admitted to herself that she'd rather face the minimal risk of the moon stags to avoid being shut within the cozy confines of a one-man tent with the infuriating man beside her. Even though, by her own measure, that made her an utter fool.

"As the lady wishes," Sav said, and he urged Abigail onward again, renewing her trot to bring them closer to their destination more quickly.

Despite the trot, Jayce's eyelids weighed heavy, and she caught herself jerking awake on more than one occasion. In an attempt to stay awake, she played a game with herself of spotting plants in the underbrush that she could name on sight.

Wood sorrel. Meadowsweet. Beech. Is that ground ivy or purple deadnettle?

Her gaze jumped and skimmed, examining leaves, stems, and flowers from afar. The nut trees were easy to spot, loaded with their undropped fruit. In a week or so, those loads would litter the road and forest floor. Not too long until the season of the Blood Moon.

The forest road only had so much diversity to offer, and Jayce switched to scientific names and medicinal properties, adjusting her seat on Abigail to find a more comfortable position to no avail.

Her gaze skipped over a wild rosebush dropping fragrant yellow petals and landed on a broken wooden gate. She squinted at the overgrown path beyond it, which was still defined enough she could see where it led deeper into the woods. Barely visible between the trees were the tips of two pointed turrets.

Jayce tapped Sav's shoulder. "Is that the previous baron's mansion, just there?"

Sav glanced the direction she pointed. "It's in the right place. I suppose it is. No one lives there now."

"This must be some kind of servant's access to the woods, for foraging," Jayce said, excitement creeping into her voice and energizing her lethargic mind. Quite suddenly, her legs begged for a stretch, aching unbearably no matter how she moved them.

"Could we stop for a moment? Stretch our legs? We've been on this horse all day, and my legs are killing me," Jayce said.

"We ought to be getting on toward Musport," Sav insisted. "It's nearly evening."

Jayce glanced around and up at the small bits of sky she could see through the canopy above. Sure enough, it had grown darker again, the shadows deepening between the tree trunks and crickets beginning their songs.

Jayce slid her leg around behind her and down to the ground.

"Jayce, we don't have a torch," Sav said, exasperated.

"A quick jaunt. I'll be right back," Jayce said, swinging her arms at her sides as she strode into the woods. She stepped over the wooden gate and onto a thick carpet of various woodland ground cover. She tugged her leather gloves more tightly onto her hands and stepped over a fallen limb, picking up her skirts to keep them from snagging and wishing she'd had a moment to change into breeches, which were far more convenient for traveling on overgrown woodland paths.

"Wait," Sav shouted. "I have to hobble the horses. They could use a graze anyway."

Jayce paused, breathing in the sweet scent of the woods and noticing the thousand signs of life all within a few stretches. The mansion she made her way toward might have been abandoned, but the woods still teemed with life, and somewhere ahead, she could make out the sound of a creek.

Sav jogged breathlessly down the path, his blond curls tied back from his face. He motioned her forward. "Carry on. Pretend I'm not here."

Jayce rolled her eyes. "You didn't have to come."

"Once again, I'm not leaving you alone in these woods. This close to the city, you could run into vagabonds of various natures, none of them pleasant. You could eat a bad mushroom. You could trip and fall into that creek," Sav said.

Ahead, a wide creek burbled loudly over a rocky bed. The bridge looked to be barely hanging on, with many of its boards missing and the handrail broken completely—probably by the thick fallen branch now partially submerged in the creek.

"Far enough. My legs feel stretched, don't yours?" Sav said.

Jayce looked back at him. "It's not that bad. I'll hold your hand if you're scared."

"It's not a matter of being scared but having poor balance and feeling a strong sense that if we don't get back to Maggie and Abigail soon, those vagabonds I told you about might decide they like the idea of a free horse."

Jayce rolled her eyes. "It's about to rain. No vagabond in their right mind would be out here in poor weather." She put her foot on the sturdiest-looking bit of wood and leaned her weight onto it, looking for bowing. It held firm, if a teensy bit wobbly.

"They aren't in their right mind. They are desperate, and money is nice to have, and Abigail is a nice-looking horse..." Sav said as he climbed down the bank toward the burbling creek.

"What are you doing now?" Jayce asked, standing at the edge of the bridge, hands on her hips.

"Filling our waterskin," Sav called back.

Jayce kept her discontented response to herself and focused on placing one foot in front of the other, walking swiftly with her arms out for balance. With two pieces of wood next to each other, she found the walk across the bridge easy, and landed on the other side with a little bounce. She turned back to find Sav still eyeing the bridge warily.

"Come on, we're almost there!" Jayce said, pointing to the much-larger turrets in the distance.

"If I fall in, you have to give me back my breeches," Sav said, stepping sideways onto the planks.

"If you go like that, you will fall in."

"I really want my pants back," Sav joked.

Jayce crossed her arms, shaking her head at his teasing. It was all nerves, she knew. So why did it make her heart flutter to be bantering with him again?

"You can have the pants back. I wasn't planning to steal them. I ought to buy myself a pair once I'm able," Jayce said as Sav made it to her side of the bank, breathless and red-faced.

"Keep them," he finally said. Without another word, he turned and started up the inclined path ahead.

Jayce followed him, confusion and regret pricking her heart. Their light-hearted banter had somehow vanished, replaced by a heaviness in the air that even birdsong couldn't permeate. She walked behind Sav, her gaze on the ground to watch for fallen roots and rocks she could trip over. After a while they broke through the trees at the top of a grassy hill, which overlooked the overgrown estate of a long-dead baron.

Sav made his way over to a large rock with a flat, jutting top and sat down. He closed his eyes and breathed deep.

Jayce held her arms against her chest, taking in the stunning, cloud-filled sky and the drooping, charred building in front of her. "It must have been magnificent once," she said, glancing at Sav.

Sav patted the rock beside him, and Jayce reluctantly moved toward him. She perched on the rock's edge, trying to make sure her arm didn't brush against his. If banter confused her, touching would be much worse.

"Baron Oliver Armand. The people loved him. He taxed fairly, threw plenty of parties, and took care of those less fortunate with the abundance of his land. One of the rare, good ones," Sav said.

Thunder rumbled faintly in the distance, and the still air held the scent of rain, though Jayce hadn't felt a single drop yet.

"You sound like you knew him. Did you meet him?"

Sav laughed. "No, I talk like that about all the people I study. My books are my friends. The people in them sometimes feel so real I forget there is distance between us. I saw the baron once, I think, but I was young. My guardians didn't take me out to socialize much. They were instructed to raise me as much like a normal child as possible, with exception in regard to my education." His brow furrowed, and he abruptly stopped talking.

Jayce stared at the side of his face, watching his expression, wondering about his childhood. She hadn't known he'd been raised outside of the realm of nobility by people other than his parents. It struck her in the moment how little she knew of Sav, aside from his schooling in Enterea at the Ivory Guilds and his claim to the title of baron. He'd told her as little of himself as she'd told him of herself, a fact that was likely her fault.

Jayce glanced away at the streak of dirt she'd scuffed in the grass with her boot. "What happened to it? There was a fire?" she asked, changing the subject.

Sav took a deep breath in and straightened. "Yes, there was. Baron Armand died of the plague and turned into moribund, as did a number of his staff, and everyone inside was killed. The townspeople were fortunately warned in time and barricaded the moribund inside the manor and lit it on fire. Local legends have grown quite a life of their own—stories of seeing figures in the windows and wandering the grounds, ghostly flames flickering on the walls."

The sadness of the story settled in Jayce's gut, and combined with the heaviness in the air, she felt an urgent need to leave this place.

She put her hands on her legs and stood. "I think I've had enough of this place. I'm all creeped out now."

"Sorry. It isn't a pretty story. Perhaps I shouldn't have told it."

"No, I asked you," Jayce reminded him, watching her steps closely as she re-entered the sloping forest path.

"I didn't mean to frighten you, truly," Sav said, and Jayce could hear the concern in his voice.

"I know," she said, glancing over her shoulder with a quick smile to reassure him. Her glance cost her her balance as she struck a small, jutting rock and stumbled, then fell and skidded several feet down the incline.

Jayce hissed with pain. She tugged her skirt up past her knee to get a good look at a wide scrape that took up the entire side of her leg. She could barely see it in the dark of the late evening.

Sav half-slid down the slope and stopped next to her. He crouched down and reached a hand out toward her leg before stopping just shy of her skin. His eyes were wide, and he seemed breathless.

From the sight of the wound or the sight of so much of her leg? Jayce pulled her skirt down. "It's shallow. Nothing to worry about. Just burns a little. Help me up."

Sav snapped to attention and stood, catching Jayce's hand and bringing her with him. "Do you need to lean on me?"

"I can walk," Jayce snapped, suddenly irritated by his attention, but more so by her foolishness. They approached the bridge, almost invisible against the dark water below. How had it gotten dark so fast?

Lightning flashed above, lighting the wood planks just long enough for Jayce to be sure of her footing. She ignored the pain in her leg and stepped quickly across the bridge. Rain pattered around her, turning quickly from a few drops to a downpour.

Sav jumped the last length of the bridge. "Go!" he said, moving fast but not passing her, his hand touching the small of her back.

Jayce rushed forward, tripping over every root and rock she'd been able to avoid before. The trip through the woods the first time hadn't been so long, had it? Surely any moment they would reach the road.

Lightning crashed again, and Jayce ran straight into a low-hanging branch.

Sav fumbled, trying to catch her, his hand grabbing her elbow but failing to pull her to him. Instead, he fell with her.

His weight knocked the air from her lungs, and she gasped as he scrambled off.

"I'm sorry, terribly sorry," Sav said, sitting up off her.

Jayce propped herself up, taking a moment to catch her breath. The woods lit up with lightning again, and just off the trail, a pair of glowing silver orbs beamed back at Jayce.

Her breath caught. She grabbed Sav's bicep, squeezing the muscle there, trying to find courage in his warm bulk beside her.

"Sav? What's that?"

Sav turned his head sideways, slowly, and his muscle under her hand tightened. "Moon stag," he whispered. "Get up slowly."

"No, don't move," Jayce whispered back, tightening her grip as she stared at the glowing eyes of the carnivorous deer. She'd seen drawings of their sharp teeth and hooves in books, and she had never desired to meet one in person.

"We can't lay in the mud all night," Sav said, lightning illuminating his face.

Thunder followed with a crash that echoed through the woods, and the moon stag startled, bugling with fright.

More orbs blinked to life. Dozens filled the forest as the rest of the herd turned their heads toward the young deer that had sounded the fear call.

"Now we should run!" Jayce cried, scrambling to her feet. She let Sav help her up and push her ahead of him. Eyes lit up on the path in front of them, the round, moon-like orbs of more moon stags.

Jayce screamed and pulled Sav's arm, yanking him off the path. They crashed into the wet underbrush, leaves slapping their faces, branches scratching their arms. Jayce ignored the cascade of voices washing over her, too focused on running away to let herself hear what they said. She raced to get ahead of the moon stags that leapt behind her, sounding a different call.

A hunting call.

CHAPTER TWENTY-SEVEN

Breath burning in her lungs, Jayce ran for her life. Her mind reeled, searching for an escape, a way out of the danger that galloped on their heels, the hooves blending with the thunder.

The willow tree had hid them from the monk the night before. Could the trees in this forest do the same?

Jayce ripped off her glove and slapped it onto the nearest tree. Cold flooded her hand as she sent her frightened pleading into the tree, imagining her thoughts connecting with the underground network of the tree's roots.

Hide us. Protect us. Do something!

The tree—an oak—remained silent.

Jayce glanced over her shoulder at the approaching stags, their massive antlered heads tossing as they bugled triumphantly.

A hand grasped her, yanking her away from the tree.

"Are you trying to get gored?" Sav shouted breathlessly, dragging her along behind him.

Jayce closed her eyes against the rain-soaked tree trunks that were lit by lightning. She ran behind Sav by feel rather than sight and tried not to think about what it would feel like when the moon stag's antlers pierced her back and tossed her into the air.

Sav jerked on her arm and slammed her into a tree. Her eyes shot open. She stared into the dark where his face had to be, heart racing. Why had he...

The tree seemed to fold around them, its hollowed-out trunk oddly smooth and almost comfortable against her back. Her head ached, but the pounding eased, and Jayce realized Sav almost fit inside the tree trunk with her. Her bare hand rested on his arm, quivering with adrenaline and fear.

Outside, the trees creaked and groaned as if a great wind had suddenly come up. Branches snapped, and Sav pressed himself farther into the tree, his hands sliding around to grip her, holding her tight against him. Jayce rested her face on his damp shirt, his heartbeat making its way into her ears.

She listened as the moon stags' bugles faded, and the only sound left was the gentle roll of thunder.

She couldn't have said how long they stood there, embraced by the tree and each other. She could have stood there far longer, her fingers tracing slow circles on his back, her breath shallow, hardly daring to move for fear of it ending.

Once the sound of hooves had long gone, and the moon stags' calls could no longer be heard, Sav stepped away so fast Jayce almost fell over.

"You all right? I know I pushed you too hard; you must have hit your head," Sav said in a quiet rush.

Jayce couldn't see his face, but the urgent tone of his voice warmed her core. "I'm all right. Not hurt, except my leg. Are you hurt?"

"No," Sav said, his voice breaking. He cleared his throat. "You're certain you're all right? I could carry you."

Tempted though she was, Jayce shook her head, then realized he probably couldn't see her. "I can walk, thank you. Though your arm would be nice."

Sav immediately reached for her, guiding her hand to his arm in the dark, and she took it shyly, grateful he couldn't see the blush rising to her cheeks.

She could almost forget their earlier argument, until she thought of it, and the tangled knot of feelings rose again, disrupting the light, almost floating feeling. She leaned on him a little more than she needed, perhaps, until they reached the road, which was now slick with mud and littered with fallen branches.

Jayce glanced both ways, her brow furrowing. "Where are Maggie and Abigail?"

"We ran quite a ways. I'm certain they're just up the road," Sav said, reaching over to squeeze her hand.

Sure enough, the horse and donkey waited for them beneath a large tree. Maggie brayed when she saw Sav, and Sav left Jayce to look the two animals over. He rubbed his hands over their faces, legs, and backs, checking for injuries as best he could in the dark.

"They're all right," he said, relief palpable in his voice.

Jayce swallowed the lump in her throat. They were too tired and beat up to continue to Musport tonight. She would have to push through the churning in her stomach and the hurt that sat in her chest like an unwelcome guest and face another night in the tent with Sav.

"We should try to get some rest," she said at last, clearing her throat.

"Yes, that would be wise."

The clouds above slowly parted, and a beam of pale pink moonlight illuminated the glistening forest. It had been more purple the night before, Jayce was certain. How quickly things changed, and how much had happened in such a short time.

Sav held up his hand, catching the moonlight. "The rain stopped."

So it had. Damp and aching, Jayce helped Sav lead the animals off the road and into a cramped clearing.

"Do you think the moon stags will be back?" Jayce asked, shivering in her wet clothes as Sav unloaded their packs and the tent gear from Maggie.

"After what you did to scare them away? I think they'll steer clear from this part of the woods for a while," Sav said, flashing a grin at her. "What did you tell those trees?"

"What are you talking about?" Jayce asked. She'd talked to the oak, but it hadn't responded. "I didn't do anything."

"I saw you talking to that tree. Your glove is still off," Sav pointed out. "After you did that, that tree hollowed itself out for us, and after we were inside... you didn't see or hear anything strange?"

"You found the hollow tree—that's not unusual in a forest like this," Jayce argued, pulling her vial holder from her cloak and shaking the thick material out before wrapping it around herself.

Sav made a disbelieving sound. "You really don't know? The trees came *alive*, Jayce. Waving all around, scattering the deer away from where we hid. And it wasn't the wind. Their branches were like whips, flexible, bendy like a willow's branches."

"That was just the storm," Jayce stammered, her lips quivering as her teeth chattered. She was cold, colder than she had any right to be. She ran her hands along her arms and neck, feeling for any errant leaves that might have stuck to her, but she didn't hear any whispering. Why was she so cold?

"We need to get you inside," Sav said. "I think we can chance a fire, a small one at least. Can you get that started?"

Jayce forced herself to move. She dug a pit in the damp ground with her hands, turning over mats of wet leaves to find dry twigs underneath.

Fortunately, Sav had a flint, and a few sparks later, a tiny fire sputtered to life, the damp wood popping and cracking and reluctantly burning.

Jayce warmed her hands and tried to get some warmth back in the rest of her while Sav made quick work with the tent.

When he joined her some time later, blowing on his hands and holding them out to the fire, Jayce had a hard time looking at him. What must he think of her? Taking off into the woods at sundown with a storm on the way, all for a curiosity.

She glanced up at him several times, each time finding him looking at her ponderously. Each time unable to bring herself to apologize, shame stopping her throat. He could have died tonight because of her. They both could have.

Wordlessly, Sav handed the waterskin out to her, raising his eyebrows.

Jayce took it gratefully and drank large gulps of the cold creek water. She handed it back to him, and their fingers brushed, sending another shiver through her.

"I'm sorry," she blurted, hunching in on herself.

"Sorry for what?" Sav asked after several gulps of his own. He screwed the waterskin cap on with deft fingers and set it down beside him.

Abigail nickered in the distance.

Jayce bit her lip. "The walk in the forest—it was a terrible idea. It's my fault—"

"Look, of all people, I can understand the urge to discover the history of a place. It's a pull unlike almost anything I've felt," Sav said, resting his forearms on his raised knees and gazing into the fire. "There's only one thing it compares to. For me, that is."

"And what's that?" Jayce asked, her breath hitching.

"Falling in love." His eyes met hers for the briefest of moments, then he glanced away.

Jayce's heart rate increased with a crescendo, her breath coming in shallow gasps. She licked her lips, staring intently at Sav until he looked up at her again, rubbing the back of his head.

Jayce glanced away, but she felt Sav's eyes on her long enough to make her skin prickle with heat.

"You're staring," Jayce finally said, shifting her seat on the ground.

"I'm sorry, it's just...The way the fire hits your face... You look... you look wild. Beautifully wild." He blinked rapidly and shook his head.

Jayce stared back at him, her mind blank as she tried to internalize why he had used that word. *Beautiful.*

She could use the same word to describe him.

The way his blond curls trailed past his face each time he lowered his head. The bow-like curve of his lips as he smiled. Her gaze wandered down his broad shoulders. The loose-fitting white shirt, tucked in by a green brocade vest with faint yellow swirls, seemed to glow in the firelight.

She had been fortunate he'd followed her to The Silver Gardener that night Dray hunted her down. That he'd been looking for her, prepared to pay her debts and bring her on this adventure with him. Despite their disagreements, she had to admit that she rather liked him, and everything they'd been through only made their inevitable parting that much harder to face.

"Now you're the one who's staring," Sav said with a throaty chuckle that sent a thrill through Jayce, straight to her core.

Jayce shook her head, words catching in her throat. "It's nothing. I'm tired. I think I'll turn in."

Fumbling with her cloak, Jayce managed to stand and hobbled toward the tent, stiffness in her limbs and the bruised scrape on her leg complaining. She'd have to get some salve on it before she fell asleep, not to mention changing into dry clothes.

"I'll sleep out here," Sav called after her.

Jayce turned and glared at him. "No, you won't. Not with the moon stags out there. And what if it rains again?"

"I'll be fine. I'm not worried about the deer, and I set up an extra part of the tent, see? It will keep the rain off, for the most part. I just... I think we both need some space tonight." He looked away from her, his Adam's apple bobbing as he swallowed.

Jayce stared at him a moment longer, then looked back toward the tent, which had an awning-like attachment coming off one side. Sav's bedroll and pillow were already spread out beneath it.

The sight made her throat close, and she tried to swallow past it as she ducked inside the tent. With only one bedroll, it was quite roomy. She changed out of her damp clothes and into the dry breeches and a blouse, then brushed out her hair, braided it, and crawled into bed.

Staring up at the tent ceiling while listening to the sounds of the forest and Sav soothing the horse and donkey did nothing to help her sleep.

She crossed her arms and rolled onto her side, forcing her eyes to close and deepening her breath.

Sav's voice trickled through the trees, singing an old Lothian folk melody in a lovely baritone that made Jayce's heart ache for her father, who had loved to sing and often did as he worked.

No, no tears. She sniffed and rubbed at her eyes and pulled the thin blanket up tighter around her neck, but she couldn't block out Sav's singing.

Her mind drifted from one thought to another. The way the trees had reacted so oddly, as if protecting her and Sav from the moon stag stampede. She had been desperate for some way to protect them at the time, but she hadn't done anything—had she?

She fell asleep to Sav's humming, the wind in the trees, and a tight sensation twinging in her chest.

CHAPTER TWENTY-EIGHT

Jayce woke the next morning to birdsong. She sat up and stretched, then rolled up her bedding and repacked her things before crawling out of the tent.

"Good morning," Sav greeted her, crouched by a newly started fire. His tousled curls fell over his face. He brushed them away reflexively.

Jayce smiled. "Good morning." She crouched next to him, warming her now-gloved hands. "What were you singing last night? I recognized the song but couldn't think of what it was called."

Sav flushed, the color making the freckles stand out on his cheeks. *The Miner's Daughter*, followed by *A Little Laurel Bird* and *In the Shadow of the Hob*. I like folk tunes. Might have gone into music if history hadn't caught me by the lapels and shoved me against a wall."

Jayce gave an appreciative laugh, but it felt fake and hollow after their argument and Sav's insistence that he sleep outside. There was a distance between them, where there had once been a blooming friendship.

That thought sank in her stomach like a stone in a lake, taking some of her cheer with it. She stared at the deep red-purple of the flames, entering into a sort of depressed trance that she didn't come out of until she smelled ham and heard eggs hit hot oil.

Sav had started breakfast, whistling a jaunty, random tune as he cracked four eggs and laid down thin strips of cooked ham. "You have any herbs you want to add to this, mistress of the forest?" His eyes gleamed.

Jayce snorted. "I have herbs, but if you call me that again, you might want to start sleeping with one eye open."

"Why? Because you'll sick your pet trees on me?" Sav said, his tone light and friendly.

The idea she had more power that she hadn't discovered made her feel unsettled. Even joking about it sent tremors through her, and rather than laughing it off, she found herself clenching her fists and her jaw.

"I told you, I didn't tell the trees to do anything. I barely touched one. They reacted on their own," Jayce said, using as calm of a tone as she could muster.

Sav pursed his lips, using a fork to flip the ham over in the pan. "Hm. Have you ever heard of that happening? Because I haven't. And I've read and traveled a lot."

"There are a lot of rumors about magic in the Oakmist. Ask anyone who lives near these woods or travels through them, and you'll hear all kinds of stories." She waved a hand dismissively, then crossed her arms, trying to ignore the troubling thoughts her mind provided as evidence in Sav's favor.

The birch tree, warning her of the moribund on the road. The gardens at the monastery covering their scent with one of flowers, so the monk gifted with super-strong scent couldn't discover them hiding beneath the willow.

She wanted to brush them off as coincidences, but she had to admit the evidence was mounting.

Sav eyed her for a moment before returning his attention to cooking breakfast.

The satisfaction Jayce felt at having disarmed his arguments was short-lived. She eventually got up and retrieved her plant vials from the tent and pulled out a packet of herbs that were especially good with eggs. Parsley, chives, dill, and goatsmure. Savory, with a pungent, smoky punch from the goatsmure.

She passed the packet to Sav as something of a peace offering.

"Smell it," she instructed.

Sav leaned in to sniff the spices, and his eyes went wide. "What is that?"

"That's the goatsmure," Jayce said.

Sav's nose wrinkled. "You want to put that on our food?"

"I promise it tastes amazing," Jayce said, sprinkling just a pinch across the bubbling yellow egg yolks.

Sav took the pan off the fire and scooped everything onto their plates, which Jayce realized he'd had to clean by himself the night before. She had gone to bed like a grumpy child without offering to help clean up.

She put the first bite of egg and ham into her mouth and immediately melted at the perfectly cooked yoke and the salty, browned crunch of the ham. She would do all the dishes after breakfast this morning.

Sav might be nosy, privileged, and infuriatingly handsome, but he was also kind and an incredible cook, and Jayce wasn't about to bite the hand that fed her.

She kept her word to herself, going so far as to pull Sav's plate from him the moment he scooped up the last of his eggs and ham, running from his protests about chivalry. She scrubbed the two plates, the utensils, and the pan with a handful of sand and water from the river.

She returned to the camp, knees muddy and her front wet, but a satisfied smile on her face.

"You don't have to look so smug just because you beat me to the dishes," Sav grumbled.

"I wanted to repay you for your amazing cooking. It's almost unfair how good you are without even trying," Jayce replied.

Sav tried to look offended and failed. "Without trying? I'll have you know that I received instruction from one of the best cooks in all the realms, who is currently in residence at the Ivory Guilds. One of these cycles, gods willing, you'll meet him. And you'll learn just how poor of a cook you've been putting up with."

Jayce laughed at his impassioned glare and started packing the dishes. "Maybe I should cook for a few cycles. Cold cuts or simple soups with no between. I can't even bake bread." She struggled with the strap on Abigail, who shifted impatiently beneath her attempts to secure the pack.

"Nonsense. My cooking might mimic something gourmet, but I'll bet yours is like cozy home cooking. Filling, simple, good," Sav said. He stood, and to her shock, his arms reached around her shoulders, stilling her fumbling fingers. His hands ran along the strap to where it twisted under the pack, preventing it from cinching tighter.

Jayce let Sav guide her hands, trying not to feel whatever emotion she was feeling. That impossible lump in her throat, the tingle traveling down her hands and arms and into her chest, the pit opening in her stomach, filling with a warmth she hadn't known before.

He was leaving. She had to remember that.

Sav's hands dropped away too soon. He looked toward the sky, where gray clouds hunted across the blue sky on the horizon. "If we hurry, we might beat the rain."

If anything attested to the change of seasons from the Purple Bell Moon to the Blood Moon, it was the arrival of the incessant rain. Jayce helped Sav smother the fire before they both mounted Abigail.

The chestnut horse side-stepped as Jayce climbed on, using a rock and Sav's outstretched hand to boost herself up. She slid into the saddle behind Sav, settling into her place and sliding her hands around his middle with practiced ease. Her breath, however, betrayed her by hitching. Blood roared in her ears and climbed her neck toward her cheeks with a prickly sort of heat.

Thank the Three he couldn't see her just then. What had come over her? They'd fought. He'd said horrible things, and so had she. And in a few hours, they would reach Musport and part ways, possibly forever.

She tensed, steeling herself against the flood of regret and the feelings she had for this man, which she didn't want to face. No sense getting caught up in it now.

"Everything all right?" Sav asked.

"I'm fine," Jayce said, the words sounding like they came from someone else.

She resisted the urge to bury her face in his shoulder and drink in his scent—like parchment and cinnamon. She glanced around the clearing instead, the scene jolting as Sav clicked Abigail forward. Maggie followed behind, tossing her head and straining against her lead for the juicy plants on the side of the road, despite the fact that she'd had plenty of opportunity to graze since the evening before.

The donkey had been surprisingly cooperative until now, Jayce realized. Not balking once, not kicking. Not even a bray. She simply carried her pack and accepted scratches and carrots from Sav. A nice, good-tempered donkey. So why was she acting so agitated?

Jayce heard the hard *clack* of the donkey's teeth and twisted around to catch a glimpse of the naughty donkey playfully nipping at the long hairs on Abigail's tail.

"You'd better stop that if you know what's good for you," Jayce warned.

"What is Maggie up to?" Sav asked, turning, but he couldn't look back as far with Jayce sitting behind him.

"She's just playing. I'm sure it's no—"

A rude bray interrupted Jayce mid-sentence, and Abigail's smooth gait jerked to a halt.

Jayce glanced back again, this time finding Maggie stubbornly planted on her haunches, reaching her dark, shaggy head over to the sweet, long meadowsweet on the side of the road. Her lips barely caught the tips of the plants, so she dug her front legs into the dirt road and scooted herself closer.

"Oh, no," Sav said with a groan. He lowered his head until it rested on Abigail's neck.

Jayce felt his heavy sigh through his back.

"Can't you get her going again?"

"She rarely does this, but when Maggie decides to stop, you're stuck." Sav sat up and dismounted. He walked past where Jayce still sat on Abigail and approached Maggie.

The donkey seemed entirely disinterested in him, now vigorously ripping at the grass.

Sav put his hands on his hips. He untied Maggie's lead and clicked his tongue. "Hup, Maggie," he encouraged.

The donkey faced him, still chewing, a bored look in her eyes. She blinked slowly, as if she might fall asleep, then turned away.

Sav glanced at Jayce. "She's probably upset about how I left her last night. And the moon stags might have scared her."

He tried tugging next, his muscles straining and his face going red as he tried to drag the beastly mammal onto all fours.

She tossed her head, nearly yanking Sav off his feet. He stopped, panting, then walked right up to Maggie and stuck his finger in her face. "Look here, Maggie. Now isn't the time for this nonsense."

Maggie seemed entirely uninspired. She went right back to ripping up grass.

Sav stalked around behind the donkey. He leaned over to put his hands on her back. He pushed with a grunt.

"Musport is a nice place, where we can find a nice stable"—he shoved—"with clean straw and"—he shoved again—"more carrots."

The donkey's ears perked at the mention of carrots, and she stood, making Sav stumble. He straightened, brushing off his hands, and grinned at Jayce, who had watched the entire exchange trying tremendously not to laugh.

"Sav, look out!" Jayce cried.

Maggie's ears flattened with agitation, and she brayed.

Sav dove out of the way as Maggie's hind leg kicked back with bone-breaking force. He scrambled to his feet, flustered and covered in dirt and grass stains.

"That ass nearly killed me!" Sav shouted as he stomped toward Jayce and Abigail. The indignation in his voice and his flushed and disheveled state was too much for Jayce's self-control. She burst into laughter.

Maggie joined her, braying with great guffaws.

Sav clenched his jaw, folded his arms, and looked up at Jayce with disbelief. "Do you have to encourage her?"

Jayce laughed harder, her hand over her mouth as if she could stop the tide of laughter at will, but she was too far gone. The stress of the last few cycles had her wound as tight as a metal coil, and now that she'd let it loose, she could only ride it out.

Sav stalked to Abigail's head, where he stood stroking her and muttering something about the horse being his only friend left in the world, which only made Jayce laugh harder.

When Jayce's howls had quieted to occasional chortles and sighing laughs, and she'd started to work the soreness out of her cheeks and jaw from smiling so hard, Sav finally spoke.

"Are you finished?"

"I think so," Jayce said, breathing fast to keep from bursting out again.

He clicked his tongue, and Abigail walked on.

"Did I really look so foolish?" he asked after a long moment.

Jayce glanced behind, noticing Maggie was watching them. Would the donkey follow? Or did Sav intend to leave her behind? All their things were tied to Maggie's back. Her clothes and herbs, their dishes and food.

Jayce scooted up in the saddle, wondering what she should hold on to without Sav in front of her. She tried to rock with the horse's gait so she didn't slide off.

"You did look pretty silly arguing with a donkey," Jayce admitted. "But not as much as my laughter made it seem. I'm sorry if you were hurt by it. I guess the past few cycles have gotten me a bit wound up."

"I didn't realize monasteries and horseback rides were so stressful," Sav said, his tone teasing.

"Har har," Jayce replied. "We only met, what, four cycles ago? While fighting off an abusive debt collector, mind you. Then we got run down by a carriage, and I got stung by blister bees, and then we broke into restricted records at the monastery where we almost got caught and sent to prison, and then—" Jayce drew a breath, and Sav's chuckle reached her ears. "Finally, we got chased by stampeding moon stags, and the trees came to life. How are you so calm about all of this?"

"Is that all?" Sav said, still laughing. "In light of new evidence, your behavior is excused, milady."

Jayce laughed, shaking her head, and she caught a glimpse of something moving out of the corner of her eye.

It was Maggie, sneaking along the road behind them, glancing up every so often and seeming to realize they were getting ahead of her, then trotting a few steps to catch up before putting her head in the meadowsweet again like she didn't care if they left her.

"I do believe Maggie is still hoping for those carrots you promised," Jayce said.

Sav glanced back over his shoulder, then snorted and faced forward. "She's getting tied up outside in the rain with a patch of weeds for dinner. That's what she's getting."

Jayce only smiled, knowing by now that Sav had a soft spot for most creatures, and even a stubborn donkey wouldn't keep him from showing kindness.

Maggie trotted up behind Sav and bumped against his back, making Sav start a curse. He cut it off with a look at Jayce. He grumbled but rubbed between the donkey's long ears, declaring exactly what he would do to her once they got to Musport. Maggie just lipped his shirtsleeve as if she knew he didn't mean a word of it.

Watching the two of them with a flutter blooming in her stomach, Jayce was forced to admit that she quite liked the handsome historian herself, and she would miss him when he left.

CHAPTER TWENTY-NINE

Jayce was grateful for the moment of mirth Maggie had provided that distracted her from the impending separation, but it wasn't long before they arrived on the outskirts of the city of Musport, and the depressing surroundings were enough to plunge her back into wallowing.

The farms leading up to the city had been derelict, with pinched-faced, weary people working the land. Even the animals at pasture seemed miserable, fighting over hay tossed carelessly into their pastures, their coats mud-spattered and dull.

Jayce felt sorry for the animals, but even more so for the people. Musport was nearly as crowded as the capital but not managed nearly so well. Refuse lined the streets. Dirty water ran in open ditches, and the faces she passed were filthy.

The few people that looked up from their path and made brief eye contact had wide-eyed, haunted gazes and deep shadows beneath their eyes. What had they seen? What had they been forced to do to survive the plague and the undead that followed in its wake?

A faded red X on the door of what looked like an abandoned home caught Jayce's eye. The windows were filmed with filth, the flowers in the window planter were dead, and one of the upper windows was shattered. The red X burned itself into her vision, and the farther they rode into the town, the more frequent the X marks became.

"What are the Xs for?" Sav asked, turning his head so Jayce could hear him in the crowded main street.

Jayce swallowed hard before answering. "Most likely they marked the homes of the sick."

Sav shifted in front of her, twisting in the saddle to glance at the doors on both sides of the street. Every two or three doors were marked now with those faded red Xs.

"There are so many," he said with hushed, horrified wonder.

Jayce shivered and leaned in closer to him.

How could Musport be like this, when the capital thrived nearby with clean streets and healthy, vibrant, content people? Surely the queen was aware and would do something?

If Queen Lyra visited and sang the Dawn and Evening Chants for a few cycles, it would make a measurable difference. But the queen hadn't left Lothian since the war, and the land and its people were suffering without the queen's magic.

If she ever got to speak with the queen, she would put in a word for Musport. The people deserved more than this.

Up ahead, a broken fountain took over the city center square. Shouts from buyers and merchants echoed up the street toward them, the most lively part of the city they'd seen so far.

"That's a good place to drop me off," Jayce said into Sav's ear.

Sav steered Abigail and Maggie to the fountain, where he dismounted first, then reached his arms out to help Jayce down.

She almost refused. Looking him in the face now made a lump form in her chest, and her breathing became restricted. She glanced at the ground, suddenly dizzy, and was forced to brace her hands against his shoulders and let him guide her down from the horse by her waist.

As soon as her feet touched the ground, his hands were off her waist as if they'd been burned. He rubbed the back of his head, his mass of curls looking a bit tangled and worse for the wear, but no less handsome.

Sav glanced around the square and cleared his throat. "Do you need help finding Dagric? I could stay for a little while, make certain you find him."

Jayce shook her head, her throat closing at the thought of spending any more time with him. It would only delay the inevitable.

"It's a long road to Crotos. You might as well get started now," Jayce said. She gestured to the market. "Besides, you need to stock up on supplies. While you do that, I'll ask around about the alchemist."

Sav's mouth opened and closed a few times, as if he had something to say, but either thought better of it or chickened out.

Jayce stood, frozen by indecision. Should she shake his hand? Simply say goodbye and walk away?

Market chatter filled the awkward space between them, and people flowed past, occasionally glancing at the horse and donkey and two people who stared at each other without speaking.

Finally, Sav took a deep breath and shoved his hands into his pockets. "I guess this is really happening. I'm going my way, and you're going yours."

Jayce nodded firmly. "It's for the best."

"Sure, sure," Sav said, bouncing on his heels. He held up a finger. "Before you go—" He stepped around her and dug into his pack on Maggie's back. He pulled out a small pouch. He tossed it to Jayce, and it clinked as she caught it.

"What's this?" she asked, brow furrowing.

"I know you don't have much, if anything. I can't, in good conscience, leave you without means to purchase a night at an inn, food, anything you might need for your trip back to the capital."

"Sav, I can't take this. I still owe you—goddesses, I'm still wearing your pants." She held the pouch back toward him, but he stopped it with a flat palm, his other hand coming to rest on her shoulder.

"Please accept it." Sav licked his lips. "And keep the pants. For now. They look better on you anyway."

Jayce rolled her eyes but brought the pouch in closer to her chest. She nodded, unable to speak for a moment. "Thank you."

Sav's shoulders relaxed, and a wide smile spread on his face. "You're something else, Jayce Keenstone."

"You, too, Savage Alighieri," Jayce said, and then she held her breath because if she didn't, she might cry.

Sav turned away from her and closed the pack on Maggie's back, then undid the ropes and unloaded Jayce's things. Her vial holder, her cloak and pack. All of it piled up neatly on the cobblestones at Jayce's feet.

Once he finished, he re-tied his packs and patted Maggie's white nose. "Guess it's time to find you a carrot or two," he said, and then he swung himself onto Abigail's back. He glanced down at Jayce and fidgeting with the reins.

"I'll see you again," he said.

"Write to me from Enterea. You can send post to the apothecary," Jayce said. She wouldn't make any promises. She waived, taking a shaky breath that almost undid all her work to hold the tears at bay, and Sav finally urged Abigail onward, Maggie following behind as he led the animals toward a nearby hitching post.

He would be in town for another hour or so, and then he'd be gone. Jayce planned to stay clear of him as long as she could, to avoid another awkward attempt at goodbye. She needed to find Dagric as quickly as possible, then.

She shouldered her pack awkwardly and crossed the square to the nearest vendor, who was selling some kind of buns and cakes. He finished speaking to a customer, who shot Jayce an odd look before they left quickly.

The bearded man crossed his thick arms over his chest and eyed her warily. "Hello, traveler. I assume you are hungry?"

"Two of those buns please," Jayce said, pointing.

"Eight chips," the vendor said with a grunt, holding out one hand.

The price seemed high for the little buns, but Jayce wasn't there to haggle. She counted out the chips and gave them to the man, who counted them twice and even bit one as if to check for authenticity.

Apparently satisfied, he took a paper bag from behind his stall and reached for a bun. Now was her chance. Jayce took a deep breath.

"Do you happen to know if Dagric Wortcunning still lives here? In Musport?"

The man froze, the bun in his hand nearly to the edge of the bag. His dark eyes studied her beneath a fringe of black hair. He narrowed his gaze.

"Get out of my sight, and don't go mentioning that name around here if you know what's good for you." The man dropped the bun into the bag, folded over the top, and handed it toward her.

"Y-you only gave me one bun," Jayce stammered, perplexed by the man's sudden change of demeanor.

"Consider it payment for a tip that could save your life," the man growled, shoving the bag toward her again.

Jayce swallowed, took the bag, and fled back to the fountain. She ate the bun, which had a rather good savory flavor, but it was too small to really fill her. She glanced around the square after finishing, wondering if she dared try another vendor or if she was better off asking at a tavern.

Her gaze wandered, skipping over Sav's back when she saw him standing at a food stall, apparently haggling over rations for his trip.

Her gaze stopped on a stall a few down that was covered with plants, bottles, jars, and pouches. Dried bundles hung from the awning, and a hand-painted sign on the front of the stall read *Mistress Grella's Herbs and Tonics*.

It was as if the woman's stall was invisible to the people milling around the market. They visited the one right before and right after, not even sparing a glance for the rotund woman sitting behind the table.

If anyone had known Dagric, it would be a fellow apothecary. Jayce squared her shoulders and cut a line straight for the herbalist's stall, scanning the plants and offerings the woman had spread out on her table.

Except for a few bottles labeled things like *love*, *clarity*, *baldness*, and similar—which seemed more like *spells* used to entice curious passers-by but were unlikely to deliver whatever they promised—the woman seemed to know what she was doing.

Jayce cleared her throat.

The woman, Mistress Grella if her sign was to be believed, had apparently been busy crushing plants with a mortar and pestle, but she gave Jayce the side-eye the entire time she approached the booth.

She ground the plant dust a few more times before brushing her hands off on her apron and turning to face Jayce with a broad grin. "What can I get for you, my dear? My admiration tonic is popular among young ladies your age. Or perhaps you would like an oil for that lovely hair of yours?"

"No, thank you," Jayce said firmly. "I'm not here for any remedies, Mistress Grella. We share the same trade, and I was hoping you would be willing to give me some information."

The woman's eyes narrowed. "You seem awfully young to be an herbalist."

"I prefer the title of apothecary, and yes, I am young but skilled. I've been employed by the queen in Lothian," Jayce added, hoping it would lend credibility that her youth did not.

"Well, well." Mistress Grella chuckled, bowing slightly. "I'd go down on one knee, but old joints, you know. What brings such a royal visitor to my humble stall?"

Apparently the queen card had been the wrong card to pull. Jayce blinked rapidly, trying to collect her thoughts, wondering if she ought to be direct or start over and try to get into the woman's good graces. In the end, she went with direct.

"I'm looking for the alchemist Dagric Wortcunning. I read in his book that he lived here once, and I was hoping you could direct me to his current residence."

The woman tapped her plump chin, considering Jayce. "Even talking about that man could get us both drawn and quartered by the occupants in this town. The only reason they haven't come for me is because half of them need my potions, and the other half are terrified I'll curse them." The woman chuckled. "Even as a cushy royal apothecary, you must be familiar with the way people see us purveyors of the plant arts."

"I'm not a royal apothecary," Jayce blurted. "I was hired once, for a specific job. Yes, I understand how people can be sometimes. Does that—I mean, did they—" Jayce glanced over at the two stalls on either side of them.

"You mean, did they kill ol' Dagric?" The woman practically said the words in a loud whisper, then broke into howling laughter, drawing all the eyes from the next stall over.

Jayce winced and curled in on herself slightly, almost wishing she hadn't approached Mistress Grella's stall.

"They're more scared of 'im than the Three themselves, I can tell ya that. As for whether he's dead or not..." Mistress Grella shrugged. "Couldn't say. Haven't seen him myself in years. Far as I know, he's rotted alone in that shack he's got on the edge of town, and no one is ever going to know it, since they're all cowards that refuse to even check on the man. Kids and youth dare one another to go inside, but none are ever brave enough to actually do it."

The woman cackled again, rocking on her stool and returning to grinding dried plants into a fine dust. After a few strokes, she picked up a bottle of golden oil and poured some into the mortar, stirring the mixture into a thick paste.

"So... he's not dead?" Jayce said, furrowing her brow. She readjusted her grip on the strap of her pack, sweat prickling her brow as the afternoon sun beat down and the strong scents of the market made her feel light-headed. Perhaps she should eat more before seeking out the alchemist.

"Don't you listen, girl?" Mistress Grella snapped, turning to face her with a grimace. "I don't know. No one knows."

Jayce leaned back from the angry woman. "But you do know where he lives."

The woman made a dismissive gesture. "Head that way, to the far edge of the city. You can't miss it. It's the most run down, overgrown shack. The very last house on Beacon Street."

Beacon Street. Beacon Street.

"Thank you for the directions."

The woman grunted in response, scooping the mixture up with a stick and scraping it into a little pot.

Jayce turned away from the stall and, without meaning to, scanned the crowd for Sav.

He was gone. Abigail and Maggie weren't tied up at the stocks anymore. Had he really bought his supplies so quickly and moved on?

Jayce shook herself. She hadn't wanted another goodbye. The first one had been hard enough. But it was difficult to believe that after a week of traveling together, sharing meals and even a tent, that he was really, truly gone. Gone to get his documents translated at the Ivory Guilds of Enterea.

Jayce's feet dragged on the dusty ground as she made her way across the square toward a tavern. She could get out of the sun, get a good meal, perhaps get a room and take a nap before she found out where Beacon Street was and tracked down the realm's most notorious alchemist to ask him for a cure for noxbrosia.

CHAPTER THIRTY

The darkened streets of Musport were worse than in the daytime. At night, all Jayce could make out were leering eyes, the flash of a dirty grin. Several times shadowy forms peeled away from the walls, following her for a stretch before disappearing without a sound.

She wished Sav were there. He'd lighten things up with a joke or let her loop her arm through his and reassure her. She missed his positive outlook and his enthusiasm. Even her food back at the tavern hadn't tasted right, and she'd slept, albeit fitfully, for far too long. She'd intended to go out before dark, but her body had had other ideas.

As she turned onto Beacon Street—the sign faded but visible in the pale, pinkish moonlight—Jayce questioned her judgment. The street stretched before her, completely dark, the lanterns on the more populated streets too far away to light this one. The houses leaned against each other like tipped statues that would topple the moment one of them got bumped.

She walked down the middle of the street, jumping at the squeak of a rat and what sounded like the scuff of a shoe. She gripped her pack straps so tightly her hands ached.

She should turn around, run back to the pools of light and the crowd of the tavern. She could come back at the first morning bell, in broad daylight.

Her neck itched, the fine hairs rising, and Jayce wheeled around, only to be greeted by an empty stretch of cobblestones. She had almost finished turning around, almost convinced herself to head straight back to the tavern she was staying at, when a loud groan echoed down the street.

She froze mid-step, straining for any other sounds.

The groan came again, this time softer, and Jayce forced herself to face the far end of the derelict street again, heart thudding.

Her feet moved forward of their own accord, driven by a curiosity she couldn't shake. Could the groans be coming from the shack at the end of the row? She could just make it out, surrounded by a crumbling stone border and a massive mound of what appeared to be broken furniture and trash in the field that met the end of the street.

The shack slumped so far over it might fall down the grassy slope on the other side. Jayce stood in front of the bent iron gate that hung half-off its hinges. It squeaked as a breeze blew past, and she put her hand on it to stop the sound, watching the house intently.

Jayce couldn't shake the watched sensation of being watched that had the hairs on the back of her neck still rising. A cat slipped across the street ahead, the only sign of life. No lantern light even showed through the windows of the other buildings, most of which were boarded up so no one could see in or out. None of the shadows moved, at least.

No more moans came from within the house.

Jayce took a deep, slow breath, then let it out gradually. She'd come this far. If the alchemist still lived inside, at worse she'd be disturbing his retirement. If he'd died, she'd find a body in an empty house.

She'd dealt with bodies before. She could handle a body, couldn't she?

She tried not to think about the pained groaning she'd heard, and what it could mean, as she stepped over the weed-strewn front path, up the front steps, and raised her hand to knock on the door. It moved under her hand, creaking open slightly the moment she touched it. The door hadn't been latched.

A third groan answered the creak of the door, and Jayce jumped back, her heart racing.

"Dagric?" she called, gathering her wits and leaning in through the door.

A groan responded, and Jayce lunged through the door, dashing through the front room and into a tiny kitchen area. She glanced around for any sign of the man moaning in the dark house.

Jayce's thoughts raced with her pulse. He could be hurt, he could be sick. Herbs raced through her mind, each one presenting itself as a possible solution for she didn't even know what, yet.

"Dagric? Can you hear me?" Jayce called again, starting down the pitch-black hallway. Her foot kicked something solid, and she stumbled back, the image of a bloated, dead body vivid in her mind.

Not *dead. He made a sound.* Jayce knelt on the floor, reaching forward until her hands brushed clothing. She recoiled from the body, but recovered quickly and patted her way up what she discovered was an arm, then a shoulder, until she found the neck.

Thick and stubble-covered as it was, she figured it was a man, though she wouldn't know for certain it was Dagric unless he said something.

Blood pulsed beneath Jayce's fingers where they pressed into the man's neck. Alive.

"He's alive," she breathed aloud to herself. "We need light."

She slid her pack off her shoulders and darted back to the kitchen, using her hands as her eyes tried to adjust to the dim moonlight filtering through the grimy windows. Was Dagric ill? How long had he been on the floor?

Her searching hands bumped into a lantern, the gas kind that she could light if she found flint and steel. Fortunately, she found some beside the lantern on the kitchen counter. She turned the key in the lantern's base to open the gas access and struck the steel and flint together, creating a spark that whooshed to life as a steady blueish-orange flame.

Back in the hallway, Jayce leaned over the unconscious man, putting her hand over his mouth and gaining more reassurance as warm breath touched her palm. She pressed her ear to his chest. An irregular rhythm met her ears, and she frowned, putting her fingers back on his neck and counting.

She sat up and sniffed the air. No metallic blood smell, so she didn't think he'd been wounded. Poisoned?

She put her palm to his forehead. Slightly warm, clammy. She listened to his chest again, this time evaluating his breath. Yes, there it was, a slight wheeze.

She brought the lantern closer to his face. gray lips. More sweat. He moaned, turning his head. No paralysis of the muscles, then. Not demon lily, thank the Three. She didn't know how to cure that. No one did.

Jayce sat back on her heels, careful not to touch her hand to her own face. Some poisons passed through the skin, and she didn't want to risk it until she could be sure she had identified this one correctly. She ticked off the options she could think of, her voice loud in the otherwise quiet house.

"It's either musgava, tendrondil, or dusk ivy. Of the three, musgava and dusk ivy are local and more likely to be used. Tendrondil grows in the Norwast." Jayce shook out her hands, resisting the urge to tap her chin or rub them on her skirts. She bit her bottom lip, observing the man again, scanning him for any other symptoms that might point her to the remedy.

She considered Dagric's gray face again, and realized she hadn't ruled out the most likely cause—not poisoning at all, but the plague. She adjusted her gloves and risked opening his eyelids, fairly certain if it were a poison that it wasn't the kind that could move through the skin.

He moved his head away at her touch, but she managed to glimpse his eyes. Not bloodshot at all. And not feverish. The plague most often came with both symptoms. Besides, the gray on his face wasn't patchy, and he didn't have a cough or a rattle in his lungs, just a slight wheezing.

"Who poisoned you, and how long ago?" Jayce wondered out loud. She glanced around, noting the picture frame broken on the floor beyond Dagric, and the door ajar at the end of the hall. Would she find a clue in there?

Jayce stepped carefully over Dagric's legs and moved toward the room. The bed made her think it was where the man slept, but the rest of the room was crowded with tables and desks. Every surface, including the walls, was plastered with papers filled with scrawled notes, and the last thing she'd expected to find in the man's house: an alchemy set. Several, in fact. The tubing looped and twisted; glass and metal beakers alike were filled with liquid, some of it bubbling over still-lit flames.

Despite his lifetime ban from ever doing alchemy again, Dagric Wortcunning was still working on something.

The alchemist in Jayce wanted desperately to find out what, to not let Dagric's efforts go to waste, but she wasn't here for his illegal experiments. She needed to find out what he'd been poisoned by so she could ask him about noxbrosia.

She scanned the documents spread across the tables, swinging her lantern carefully over them. She turned off the burners on the alchemy sets, not wanting the house to get set on fire and not knowing how long they'd already been burning unsupervised.

The papers were written in the same language as the journal, a language Dagric was clearly fluent in but Jayce couldn't read any more than she could read the stars in the sky. She rifled through a final stack on the table nearest to the bed, then a familiar type of parchment caught her eye.

Picking it up, feeling the smooth, unblemished surface, Jayce recognized the parchment as the kind she got when her quarterly debt statement had arrived. Few could afford the same quality of parchment as the palace. Her eyes skimmed the missive to the bottom, where she spotted a familiar signature.

Sir Dray Wilhelm, on behalf of L.A.

Sir Dray had contacted the alchemist? When? Why? Jayce noted the date at the top of the letter from just two turns prior. The letter requested, among other ingredients, several drams of noxbrosia and promised due compensation upon delivery.

Dray had ordered the noxbrosia. Had he created the poison remedy and distributed it among the people of Lothian? Why? She scanned the letter once more, her gaze landing this time on the second half of Sir Dray's signature.

On behalf of L.A.

Who was L.A.? Was he working with Dray, or was Dray working for him? Jayce couldn't imagine Dray coming up with the noxbrosia remedy on his own or the plan to distribute it to those afflicted by the plague. She could see him taking credit for ridding the city of the threat of the moribund and using the accolades to get a new title. She could also see him being bribed into being the front for the operation, to protect whoever was really behind it in case things went south.

Or someone like Jayce discovered the truth.

He'd warned her. Dray had. When he'd threatened her at The Silver Gardner and beaten her. If Sav hadn't been there, would Dray have killed her? Was Sav the only reason he hadn't?

A chill went up Jayce's spine. She'd shouted at Dray. Defied him. Without ever realizing the full extent of how dangerous he was. Perhaps some pity on his part had caused him to leave without killing her, assuming the threat would be enough to keep her from returning to Lothian. But he had underestimated her determination to get to the bottom of the noxbrosia remedy and find a cure before too many more innocent people were needlessly killed.

He'd had no such reservations about killing Dagric, however. And given the evidence before her, she had little doubt that Dray, or at least the mysterious L.A. he worked with, was behind Dagric's poison, and it must have happened recently. That day. Perhaps hours or even moments before she'd arrived, the poisoner barely missing her arrival.

Jayce snapped her fingers. "That's it. It's slow-moving. With musgava, he'd be dead in moments. It has to be dusk ivy!" She ran back into the hallway, careful to avoid stepping on the man's fingers.

She leaned over the man, taking note of the deeper wheeze in his chest.

"Dagric, can you hear me?"

The man's head moved, and he moaned, sliding his hand from the floor to his stomach.

"You've been poisoned, but I know the cure. I just have to find some..." Jayce trailed off.

An alchemist and apothecary like Dagric no doubt had a garden where he grew all the essential plants, especially cures for the poisons he typically worked with.

Carrying the lantern back outside, she glanced around the yard. Under its light, she saw that weeds and dirt had taken over the front yard; nothing that seemed useful grew there. She made her way around the side of the house, through a wooden gate, and under a broken arch covered in dead vines. She stopped dead at the sight that awaited her.

The back garden was nothing but ash and dirt. It had been burned, and recently. Not even weeds grew.

Who would have done such a thing? Her own apothecary garden was the result of generations of her family planting and tending. If it were burned, she would be devastated. Had it been part of the banned alchemist's punishment, having his garden destroyed so nothing would grow?

The ashes on the ground were cold, but her face felt hot as fury built inside her. Fury over Dagric's loss and the way he'd been treated. Though perhaps he didn't deserve her righteous anger or her pity, if he worked with men like Dray.

Jayce shook herself and turned away from the ashen garden. She wouldn't find anything to help her there. Where had Dagric gotten any ingredients for the experiments he seemed to be running on the sly? Had Dray offered them as part of Dagric's payment for supplying him with noxbrosia?

She considered her options. There was a dying man inside the house. She already had enough evidence that Dray had played some part in creating and distributing the noxbrosia remedy. What she didn't have was a cure. She would need to wake Dagric and get that information from him. If she saved his life, surely that would be enough payment for one cure.

But where to find the plant she needed for the cure?

Honey pilewort was a fortunately common plant that grew anywhere the ground was disturbed. It creeped along the ground with curling tendrils and had tiny waxy leaves that children liked to chew on for their sweet taste.

She passed back through the wooden gate and made her way to the junk pile stacked high with old furniture, stone, and anything else the people in this town had decided to throw out and let nature reclaim at the edge of town.

She scanned the ground around the junk pile, but even with the lantern, it was too dark and too much ground to cover in a short amount of time. She crouched down, putting out her hand and running it over anything that looked plant-like.

Fabric. Sow thistle. Goatsmure. Something wooden.

Jayce's pulse increased, and her hands numbed with cold. She pressed on, occasionally lifting her hand from the plants to stop the maddening whispers in her head, breathing on her hands to warm them before shifting her attention to another area.

She eventually stood and walked around the pile, crossing part of the field to the nearest tree and ran her hands around the ground. Barm nuts had fallen recently, littering the ground with their hard shells. That was all she could feel, and she grew discouraged. She slid down the trunk and glared at the surrounding field with frustration, knowing that every moment she wasted, Dagric grew closer to death. Dusk ivy worked slowly, but he already showed advanced signs of the poisoning. He had moments, not entire bells.

Honey pilewort grew everywhere, though it was more of a summer plant and might be mostly withered by the few cold nights they'd had recently. But she should have been able to find some, if even a small amount.

She rubbed the heel of her ungloved hand in her eyes, willing the tears to stop coming so she could think. She couldn't fail now, not with this man's life at stake.

In her desperation, she considered asking the tree to help her. She felt like a fool for even thinking it. Just because some odd things had happened recently didn't mean that plants actually talked to her about anything other than themselves.

Jayce lifted her hand all the same, considering. It couldn't hurt, could it? Not more than the shock of cold and the whispers already in her mind.

She leaned forward, pressing her palm against the rough bark of the barm nut tree.

Barm gives all, sees all, is all. Barm sustains life. Barm—

Please, Jayce thought, squeezing her eyes shut. *Is there any honey pilewort growing nearby?*

Barm gives all, the tree repeated.

Jayce sighed, all her breath going out of her in a rush. She pressed her lips together, trying not to cry out in frustration.

A man is dying. Please! She threw the plea out knowing it wouldn't work. Either the tree couldn't hear her or the obvious, trees didn't care about anything but themselves.

The barm tree prattled on about its own properties, and Jayce felt so sick in her gut she had to move her hand. If she heard *Barm gives all,* one more time, she'd hurl. It gave nothing but nuts that were so hard only the squirrels could crack them without breaking their teeth.

Her hand fell away from the tree's trunk and brushed the hard ground. Something tickled her fingertips, a tiny whisper that Jayce barely heard in her despair.

Could she bear to go back inside and watch the man die while she looked helplessly on?

Something tugged on her pointer finger, and the whisper grew louder. Jayce glanced down, but in the dark of nightfall and the deeper shadows beneath the tree, she still couldn't see anything. So she felt, reaching farther down to grasp the tendrils of the plant that was climbing out of the ground as if striving to reach her.

Honey pilewort.

She didn't listen to the rest of what the plant had to say but withdrew her hand, then put it back, feeling the waxy, circular leaves. More and more grew beneath her fingers impossibly fast, and where a sprout had once been, long tendrils now crept along the ground, bumping into her leg and nudging her hand, almost insistent.

More tears sprang to her eyes, but for a different reason now. The plant had grown for her. Whether the tree had done something despite its useless chatter or whether dormant roots of the plant itself had heard and responded to her plea.

She could no longer deny that when she'd spoken just now, the plants had responded.

She snatched up a fistful of the honey pilewort, sending words of gratitude to the plant and the earth and even the barm nut tree. She took as much as she could manage and sprinted back toward the house, holding the alchemist's life in her freezing cold hands.

CHAPTER THIRTY-ONE

Jayce ripped the leaves and put a few under Dagric's tongue. She crushed the rest of the leaves into a bowl from the kitchen, using a mortar and pestle she'd found—no doubt illegal for Dagric to own—to grind them into a sort of paste.

Dagric's moans turned to mutterings, then gasps as the dusk ivy performed its dark work on his lungs.

Jayce spooned the mixture into Dagric's mouth and waited. It could take several moments for the symptoms to subside, but the longer the time stretched, the more she worried. What if she'd been fooled by the plants again? What if the wrong plant had grown and told her it was the one she sought?

No. She knew this plant. Knew what it looked like, what it felt like, even what it tasted like. Her knowledge, combined with her magic, had accomplished the impossible.

Dagric coughed and sat up. He heaved but nothing came out.

Jayce patted his back to reassure him, but the touch only startled the man, who twisted in his seated position and scooted away from her.

"Who are ya? What are ya doin' in my house?" Dagric asked, eyes wide and terrified.

"Please, calm down. You're still ill from the dusk ivy, and I'll need to give you another dose soon." Jayce held up her hands and softened her voice, trying to appear unthreatening.

"Dusk ivy? I was poisoned." Dagric froze as the revelation dawned on him. He wheezed, then coughed, a hand going to his chest.

"Do you have any pain in your chest?" Jayce asked, concerned for the man's heart. Dusk ivy could sometimes adversely affect the heart, and honey pilewort wouldn't do anything for that.

"I feel a massive weight on me chest. What did you use to cure me? What dosage?"

"Three spoonfuls of honey pilewort in a paste. I would have used carrier oil, but I couldn't find any. So just the leaves and some water," Jayce said.

Dagric grunted but didn't say anything, critical or otherwise. No thanks, just a grunt as he scooted himself toward the wall and leaned against it.

Jayce didn't need his thanks, just confirmation that he was who she thought he was and the remedy for noxbrosia.

"I'm Jayce Keenstone, an apothecary from Lothian," she started, hoping her identity would help put him at ease.

Dagric's eyes opened as slits, eyeing her from the side. He said nothing.

Jayce licked her lips and sat up on her knees. "I came to ask you for a remedy for noxbrosia."

That got his attention. "I don't do plant work anymore. I was banned, don't you know?"

"I saw your alchemy set in the back room, there. I know your garden is burned, but it seems you're still doing something. Besides, you don't need to be working with plants to know them. Someone is poisoning people with the plague using noxbrosia. I know they got it from you." She gave him a stern look, letting him know he couldn't lie to her.

"How d'ya know all that? I never met ya, don't know ya from Damaris herself. For all I know, ya could be workin' with Dray, sent to poison me."

"So, Dray did contact you about the noxbrosia. Did you give it to him?" Jayce asked, straightening.

Dagric moaned. "There I go, blabbing all my secrets. Never was good at keepin' stuff secret. Part of the reason I ended up like this." He wiped a hand down his face, and his shoulders started to shake. First with quiet laughter, and then Jayce realized tears poured down the man's face.

"I-I'm sorry if I made you upset," Jayce said. "It's just really, really important that I get that remedy."

Dagric barked a laugh. "Ironic, that. Fire clove, ruby stem, and golden spore are nearly as illegal as noxbrosia itself. At least, the gathering of them are. And they're damn hard to find. Fortunately for you, I still have some. They didn't take everything from me. Soon as I heard they were comin', I put a few things aside. Fortunate they only burn the garden down twice yearly and not my home."

"Why didn't you move?" Jayce asked.

Dagric raised his eyebrow. "Death sentence if I do. They have to keep an eye on me, see. Can't kill me—they might need me. Like ya do now."

"Who tried to kill you, Dagric?"

"I don't know the bastard that gave me that poison. Ambushed me in my home and forced it down my throat. Goddesses know I deserved it after I sold my soul for an alchemy set and a few packets of seeds."

Dagric fell into a wheezing, coughing fit, and Jayce ran for the kitchen where the rest of the remedy she'd made waited. She brought it back to the hallway and offered Dagric a spoonful. He eyed it warily.

"Didn't ya hear me? I deserve to die. I betrayed the realm, betrayed the people. Innocent people." Dagric's voice trailed off into muttering, and he seemed lost inside himself for a moment.

"It's my duty to do no harm, Dagric. If I let you die, I'll be breaking the first and foremost oath I made when I became an apothecary," Jayce insisted, holding the spoon out again. "Besides, you haven't told me where you keep the remedy yet."

Dagric chuckled. "I can see how ya found me, with grit like that." He gestured toward the bedroom with his chin. "Beneath the bed, there's a cut out bit of floor. Pull it out, and ye'll find my stash. Fire symbol on it, for the cloves. I should have a few bottles. I'd wager a smart woman like yourself can figure out the ratios from that."

"You could come with me, become a hero for the realm again," Jayce said, anxiety twisting her insides. The man talked like he wanted her to leave him here alone to die, and she wasn't sure she could do that.

"How long before someone finds out I had a hand in the noxbrosia getting passed around? I've done a lot of bad things in my life, lass. This lifelong ban from my work is well-deserved, despite what you may think. I'll live, for now, but I'd rather stay here and continue my work as long as I'm able, until they send the soldiers for me and finish it off once and for all."

"I'll tell them you gave me the remedy," Jayce insisted, scooting closer to Dagric. "They'll know you're still good."

"They'll know that I broke the terms of my ban, that I kept my concoctions. Not all of them are innocent, lass. Not all of them are remedies meant to heal. I'm too proud for that. Couldn't let my life's work get destroyed. Had to keep the poisons, too. Mother nature don't discriminate, and I don't either. All plants are fascinating. All plants are wondrous. Even those that kill."

Jayce shuddered. She wasn't sure she could agree with the alchemist, who slumped over on the floor as if exhausted by the brief conversation.

"I'll just... go get that remedy first," Jayce said, implying that she wasn't done trying to convince him to come with her. Not that she had any ideas for getting the weakened alchemist to the capital, even if he wanted to come.

She took the lantern with her to the back room, set it on the floor, and knelt to look under the bed. She could just make out the outline of a roughly cut rectangle in the wood slats.

Using her fingertips, she pried up the wooden piece and slid it to the side, then scooted the lantern closer to get a look inside the hole. Even with the lantern, the hole was filled with shadows.

Hoping there weren't any spiders, Jayce reached her hand inside the floor and grasped the first glass bottle she touched. She held it up in the light. A hand-drawn fire symbol was sketched onto the worn parchment pasted onto the bottle. The fire clove remedy for noxbrosia.

Jayce set it beside her and fished around for another bottle. The next one felt like a different shape and size, and it had several symbols on it that Jayce didn't understand. She put that bottle on the other side of the opening and reached in again. The sound of a gate creaking outside made her pause.

Footsteps on the path outside, running. Jayce grabbed the next bottle she could reach and saw the fire symbol. Two would have to be enough. She grabbed a bottle in each hand and ran back to the hallway, accidentally leaving the lantern in her haste.

She knelt beside her pack, jammed the bottles into a space by her cloak, hoping they wouldn't fall out, and swung it onto her back, then reached for Dagric's arm.

"Someone is coming," she hissed.

"Probably want to see if they finished the job. Leave me," Dagric said, shaking her off his arm.

"I'm not leav—" Jayce's words were cut off by the *bang* of the front door as a man strode in, holding a crossbow.

He raised it and shot before Jayce could even react. The bolt went through Dagric's throat and into the wall behind him.

The man with the crossbow had killed him, and now his sights were set on Jayce.

CHAPTER THIRTY-TWO

With nowhere else to run, Jayce turned and sprinted back to the bedroom behind her. She slammed the door shut. She glanced hurriedly around the room for anything she could use to defend herself, but all she saw was alchemy equipment, papers, and a single chair.

She grabbed the chair, dragged it in front of the door, and propped it against the handle. It would delay the man with the crossbow a few moments, perhaps.

The door handle jiggled, and the man outside thudded into the door, grunting. Jayce backed away, mind reeling.

She had nothing. No weapons or knowledge to use them. She didn't even have any trees to talk to. What did she have?

The man thudded into the door again, bellowing now. Had Dray sent him, or someone else? Jayce truly didn't want to find out. She backed against the bed, then moved around it toward the room's only window. She undid the latch, struggling against the rusted metal, then tried to shove the window up.

It didn't budge. She gasped and pushed again, heaving with all her might, rattling the window panes as she slammed into the wooden frame again.

The door behind her crashed open, and the man with the crossbow stepped into the room. He reloaded and aimed the bolt at her.

Jayce pressed her back flat against the wall under the window, fully aware she had nothing to protect herself with and nowhere to go. She licked her lips, thinking fast. The only thing she had left was her mind. Could she distract or confuse the man?

"Who sent you?" she demanded. Her voice sounded so fierce it was foreign even to her.

The man's lip curled into a sneer. "I suppose telling a dead woman doesn't count for much." He spread his legs and took a solid stance, still holding the crossbow up. "And I like seeing the looks on their faces when they find out who betrayed them. He has your pretty baron, too, though he won't meet the same fate as you. At least, not yet. He's more valuable alive than dead. Unlike you."

Her pretty baron...

Jayce blinked rapidly. Whoever the crossbow man was talking about had to be *Sav*!

"But... why?" she stammered, moving slowly from the window toward the nearest table filled with alchemy equipment. The liquids and gasses were still now, having long cooled.

The crossbow man spat. "You think I know all the plans of those that pay me to do their dirty work? Foolish woman. Dray wouldn't even waste his time to come kill you himself, once he heard you were in the city."

Dray. Sir Dray, the bailiff who had handled her debts, had captured Sav and sent this mercenary to kill Jayce—and finish the job with Dagric. How had Dray gotten to Musport, and when? He must have left the day after he hunted Jayce down at The Silver Gardner, bypassing the monastery and getting a lead on Jayce and Sav. They had followed him to Musport, seeking the very man Dray had intended to kill.

Had succeeded in killing. And he would succeed in killing Jayce, too, if she didn't find a way to escape.

"He hired me to make sure we finished the job with the alchemist, and to find you, if you were foolish enough to be sniffing about," the crossbow man continued with a drawl, like he was bored, but by the gleam in his eyes reflecting the lantern light, Jayce knew he enjoyed every moment. "Dray took Sav back to the capital, where he'll live out a decently long life, so long as he cooperates and gives Dray what he wants."

She reached the desk and her fingers closed around the nearest beaker filled with a slightly yellowish liquid. A quick sniff told her it was sulfurous in nature.

"And what does Dray want?" Jayce asked, stalling for a few more moments.

The crossbow man snorted. "What everyone wants. Money."

Jayce drew her hand back and threw the beaker.

It shattered on the floor between her and the man with the crossbow. A hiss of steam went up as it bubbled on the floor, reacting perhaps with the finish on the wood.

"What did you do?" The crossbow man growled, the tip of his arrow lowering slightly as he examined the floor.

"I wouldn't breathe too deeply, if I were you. That's a noxious gas. It can take a grown man out in moments." Jayce slid her hand along the desk's surface watching the panic form in the man's eyes in the orange lantern light coming from the floor. His pupils dilated and his crossbow trembled in his hands. He seemed to have taken her advice to heart—his chest puffed out with air, his lips shut tight, and his face began to redden.

He still held the crossbow up, adjusting the center of his aim back to Jayce's chest.

Her fingers closed around another, smaller beaker.

"You don't want to die. However much they paid you isn't worth that, not if you wouldn't live to use the money. I have the cure for the gas here. Let me go, and I'll disappear. You'll never see me again." She kept her gaze steady on the man as she walked toward him, holding the smaller beaker, this one with a clear liquid she was almost certain was water, though it swirled with a transparent additive that could have been salt.

The man's face darkened to purple, and he edged farther away from the broken beaker and its contents, eyes almost bugging out of his head.

"I give you the remedy for the gas, you let me leave this house. Do we have a deal?" Jayce asked, handing the beaker out to the man, close enough to the room's doorway she could see Dagric's legs in the hall.

The man with the crossbow nodded frantically, lowering his weapon, and reached out for the beaker.

The moment his fingers wrapped around it, Jayce let go and bolted for the door. Mercenaries were not known for keeping their word, and sure enough, as she jumped over Dagric's body—may he rest with the Three—and sprinted down the darkened hall, she heard him sputter behind her. Then the sputter turned into a roar of rage.

Jayce raced across the porch and leapt down the steps, her feet pounding on the path. She couldn't possibly outrun the man, and at the late hour, no one was around she could seek help from.

Fortunately, the man had ridden a horse. The animal's coat was so dark she almost missed it, but it was tied up on the bent iron gate at the front of Dagric's property. Jayce adjusted the straps of her pack on her shoulders and frantically untied the horse's reins, praying it was a gentle animal.

It bent over her and lipped her hair, standing steady as she climbed up on the short stone wall and swung her leg over the saddle.

The man with the crossbow saw her from the door, took sight, and released a bolt.

Jayce ducked, but she didn't need to, as the bolt went wide. She urged the horse forward with a press of her legs and a click of her tongue like she'd seen Sav do. It leapt into a trot, then a gallop as she squeezed harder.

Another bolt whizzed through the air, close enough to her ear that she felt the wind of it brush by her and saw it clatter into the cobblestones before the horse galloped past it. She let the horse take her through the mostly sleeping city, relief and guilt flooding through her at the same time.

She had escaped, but Sav hadn't. At least not that she knew of. And if the mercenary could be believed, Dray had already left the city with Sav as his prisoner.

Her heart sank further as the horse's hooves carried her through the city square and toward the Oakmist Woods.

The document with the proof of Dray's contact with Dagric had been left on the desk back at Dagric's house. She should have grabbed it when she'd had the chance, but her mind had been too occupied with trying to figure out what had poisoned Dagric. And he had died anyway, with a crossbow bolt through his throat.

She slowed the horse down, not wanting to break its legs on the uneven ground, certain she'd lost the crossbow man at least for now, although she didn't let herself relax. For all she knew, he had another horse at his disposal and would be on her trail within moments, but she needed to walk the horse, calm them both down so she could think of a plan.

All she could think of were Dagric's pained eyes in the moment before he'd died.

She'd seen a lot of death as someone who attended the sick, but she'd never seen someone killed by another person in front of her eyes, not directly. Her heart seemed to shrivel with the pain of the loss of so much wisdom and life. All that was left of Dagric and the legacy of his life's work was now contained in the little black journal in her pack.

She closed her eyes as tree branches crossed over her, and they entered the forest, humming the only song of lamenting she knew.

Legend had it that the goddess Dacia had sung the song for the first time when her two sisters Delain and Damaris had been killed in the battle over the marshes of Thorgor. That song had traveled the realm and shaken even the frigid, rocky shores of Norwast at the height of the realm.

It had reached into the soul of Thengroff the necromancer, and life had taken root there, destroying Thengroff and turning the tide of the battle in the marshes.

That song had become the Dawn Chant and the Evening Song that Queen Lyra sang every morning and every night from the capital. Her voice did not reach so far as the goddess' had, but it reached far enough to make the areas around the capital thrive.

Jayce hummed it now, unable to bring herself to sing in her shaky, warbling voice made worse by grief for a man that she'd barely met.

CHAPTER THIRTY-THREE

By the next afternoon, Jayce knew she wouldn't make it by herself. The road was easy enough to follow with few opportunities to turn off and get lost, but it had taken her three full days of travel to reach Musport with Sav in the first place, not including the time they'd spent at the monastery.

And she didn't have that kind of time. The only reassurance she had was that Dray wouldn't be able to ride straight through without stopping either, and the long ride would give her time to think of a plan.

Because she needed a plan. Without the document proving his association with Dagric and the poison noxbrosia remedy, she couldn't confront Dray directly. Not without trying to bluff her way through blackmailing him to get him to set Sav free, and he would probably just kill her if it came to that.

She would have to get an audience with the queen. And to do that, she would have to leverage her position, a position that five years ago, she had rejected and hadn't spoken of since.

Fear clutched her heart, but her greater fear—of Sav being in danger—drove her forward. She stopped to sleep in brief fits, take care of the horse, drink from the creek, and eat whatever she could forage in the woods: berries that sang and roots that whispered and mushrooms that she could hear the quiet, rumbling voices of, despite their separate classification as fungi. Although she couldn't understand them as clearly as plant voices, and she'd often wondered if they were somehow connected.

She had to eat to live, and without the ability to hunt, plants were her only source of food. But every time she consumed them, the whispers threatened to overwhelm her, and the cold numbed her hands, lips, and even her insides momentarily.

Discomfort rode with her, a silent companion, but she refused to turn from it, refused to be cowed away from her sole purpose—to reach the queen and tell her everything she knew about Dray's involvement with the noxbrosia remedy that would kill innocent people.

She saw no sign of Dray or the crossbow man, and on the morning of the third day, she passed The Silver Gardner and crested the hill that led down into the capital city of Lothian. The white towers of the castle shone in the cold dawn light, and the eerie, ancient melody of the Dawn Chant wove around her, invigorating her soul and making everything seem brighter. Hope flooded into her, and she urged the horse—which she'd decided to call Chaser—down toward the city.

The line to see the queen already stretched down the road some way from the palace steps when Jayce arrived. The sight weighed on her already weary bones, and she nearly gave in to her desperate desire to find food and sleep for half the day. But she couldn't give in, not when Sav needed her.

She dismounted, walking Chaser through the crowd and taking him straight to the guards standing at the bottom of the steps.

The guards eyed her as she approached, and Jayce recognized one of them from when she'd come before she left.

"Back again? You'll have to get in line," the female guard said, gesturing down the snaking line of people, backed up so far now Jayce couldn't see the end.

Jayce straightened her shoulders, drawing in a deep breath to steady her nerves. She could do this. She could do it for Sav. But as she opened her mouth to speak the words, her vision tunneled in on her. She hadn't stepped foot in the palace since the day she'd returned to tell the queen what had happened to her brother when... when...

"End of the line," the other guard said, stepping closer and looming over Jayce threateningly.

Jayce licked her lips, thinking of Sav in an attempt to banish the memories that threatened to overwhelm her.

"I-I am Jayce Keenstone," she announced clearly. "Chosen one of the prophecy, anointed by her majesty as an apothecary of the realm. I seek an audience with Queen Lyra, with critical information regarding a matter of great importance to her and all the residents of the capital."

The guards blinked, stunned by her declaration. Whispers carried down the line, and Jayce tried to close her ears to them as her mind swarmed with panicked thoughts.

"She can come with me," a third guard said from the top of the stairs. He had black hair and a beard, his armor gleaming despite its scuffs. Jayce did not recognize him, and he didn't look at her with familiarity or even a smile.

Her instincts told her to flee. She didn't know what this guard wanted, but she had a feeling it wasn't good.

"Sir Rorick, I—" one of the guards started.

"Her presence is anticipated. I'll take it from here," Sir Rorick said, his dark brown eyes flashing. His entire presence reeked with authority.

"Yes, Captain," the female guard said. She took Jayce by the arm, marched her up the stairs toward Sir Rorick, and passed her off to him.

His hand clamped down on her arm, and he abruptly turned to face the doors without explanation.

"Open," he commanded.

The guards on either side of the doors opened them wide.

Jayce wanted to ask a dozen questions, but she had the good sense to keep her mouth shut. Sir Rorick didn't seem the type to entertain her curiosity, and if he was taking her straight to the queen, she wouldn't question it. She only hoped she wasn't too late, that the noxbrosia remedy hadn't killed too many people, and that she still had a chance to save Sav.

They walked down a long, wide corridor, straight to the throne hall. Guards on either side of the doors confirmed

Sir Rorik's identity, then drew open the heavy, etched metal doors.

Jayce walked down the pristine purple rug, keeping her eyes ahead. The first time she'd been there, she'd gawked at the chandeliers gleaming with crystalline, fractured light, and the long tapestries sewn with the royal crest in silver thread.

This time, she focused on not being cowed by the powerful presence sitting on the throne. Her pale, curling blond hair flowed down her back. An elegant silver and blue gown with enormous sleeves piled in the woman's lap and on the floor at the feet of the throne.

Her face held more lines, but her smile had stayed the same, a kind smile that still somehow didn't reach her eyes.

"Miss Keenstone. I wondered when I would see you again. You've kept to yourself these past years," Queen Lyra said, even her speaking voice containing a musical quality that had a calming affect Jayce could feel even through the tension in the room.

Jayce swallowed, the words she'd prepared on the three-day ride vanishing under the panic filling her mind. She had the mind to curtsey, but Sir Rorick still held her arm, and all she could manage was a quick bob.

"Your majesty, I've preferred the solitude to the memories," she said, her mouth drying up. She kept forcing herself to think of Sav. Not the training she'd had here in the castle, not the journey she'd gone on to the Hobhorn. Not what had happened there.

Sav, only Sav. With his quick, dimpled smile, his curls, his humor, his—

One of the counselors sitting on the dais leaned over and whispered in the queen's ear. She frowned, all cozy familiarity suddenly gone from her smile. She pursed her lips as she sat up.

"I am told that you are responsible for a great trial that has fallen upon our capital. That not only did you cause great ill to fall upon its people, but you also fled to evade capture as well, leaving your debt unpaid. A crime worthy of imprisonment on its own. I find it hard to believe, knowing your work ethic, but time can turn a heart bitter, and I see the potential for motive. Tell me, Jayce Keenstone, did you create a remedy meant to poison plague victims and kill them before they turned moribund?"

Jayce's mouth worked like a fish's, opening and closing without sound.

"N-n-no, your majesty. I left to find a cure. One of my patients died after taking the remedy, and I discovered it was poison and left to—" She stopped, her tongue falling silent as she scanned the hardened faces looking down at her. None of them believed her. None of them would believe her, and she had no evidence to speak of other than her own experience.

"I paid off my debt," she tried again. "I met this baron, Savage Alighieri, and he paid my debt in exchange for..." She trailed off again. In exchange for information about the plague? That would sound suspicious. Like she was trading secrets from her time in the castle for money.

The queen raised her eyebrows. "I'd find your erratic story-telling more amusing if I didn't know for a fact that your debt remains unpaid."

"Then Dray did something with the money. And he's taken Sav—the baron. You have to believe me!"

The queen leaned forward on her throne, clasping her hands together. "You are quickly losing my interest, Miss Keenstone. Do you, or do you not, have evidence for any of the outlandish claims you're making?"

Jayce licked her lips, glancing again at the gathered council, the queen, and their faces hard, as if set in stone. A flash of reflected light caught her eye, and she noticed one of the queen's councilors seemed to be nodding subtly, an older gentleman with a kind face…

She had to try. For Sav's sake, she had to tell the queen what she knew.

"I went to the library at the Draigh monastery to research the plants in the concoction. I knew of noxbrosia because of my…" She licked her lips, maintaining eye contact with the queen. "Because of my ability to hear plants speak. But I didn't know much about it, only that it was an illegal substance to grow or sell. At the monastery, I discovered a book that led me to speak with Dagric Wortcunning, and he gave me—"

"Dagric Wortcunning? You've been consorting with that murderer?" Queen Lyra's eyes flashed with anger, and she raised her right hand, the one containing her seal ring, the hand with which she would gesture to make a decree that would decide Jayce's fate.

"It isn't what you think," Jayce said in a rush. "I was only there to ask about a cure, and to find out if anyone had gotten noxbrosia from him, since it's incredibly rare. And someone did. It wasn't me. It was Sir Dray Wilhelm." The name tumbled from her lips in a rush, like an avalanche she couldn't have stopped if she'd tried, but the moment it fell from her mouth, she wished she could take it back.

Several of the counselors at the top of dais gasped. One leaned over and whispered to the other.

The queen's eyes closed, and a knowing smile spread on her lips, and then those sea-green eyes flashed open again, and her hands gripped the edges of her throne as she leaned forward.

"Intriguing. It's just as he said it would be. Tell me, Miss Keenstone, why Sir Dray would come to me late last night and warn me of your pending arrival, saying he didn't know when you would come, but that if you did, you would spout lies about him committing treason to the realm. That you would insist you were innocent in all doings, when he had evidence that you have been consorting with the criminal alchemist from Musport all this time, creating a toxic remedy for the plague that would cause the capital residents to have false hope, consume the remedy, and die. Despite their deaths, you could claim you had rid the city of moribund, knowing I would offer just about any reward to someone who was able to accomplish such a feat."

"But killing them is wrong. Not everyone turns to moribund. What about those who would recover?" Jayce said desperately. "I never would have created a remedy that killed."

"And yet this letter would say otherwise," the queen said, accepting a folded document from the spectacled counselor on her left. She opened it and cleared her throat. "It details your request to Dagric for some noxbrosia, with a promise to grant him anything he desires in return, including items that he is banned from ever touching again, for good reason. It bears your signature, which matches those we have from your life-debt agreement and invoices from your payments."

Jayce stared at the document, dumbfounded, hardly able to believe she was looking at her own signature.

"The letter has to be forged. I found a similar one at Dagric's house, but with Sir Dray's signature..." Jayce trailed off.

The queen lowered the letter and passed it back to the counselor. "Do you have this letter with you?"

"No, I had to leave it behind. Sir Dray hired a mercenary to kill both me and Dagric. A man with a crossbow—"

The queen laughed. "Sir Dray hired a mercenary? Do you hear yourself? Sir Dray is loyal to the crown, to the realm. He has served me for decades. You may have played a part in attempting to aid the realm once, but you and your brother failed. I'm sure that failure has stuck with you. I've seen how you plunged yourself into debt to buy the materials to seek a cure for the plague. When that failed, you turned to murder. You would do anything to clear the Keenstone name of your ultimate failure to rid us of the Plague King."

Jayce couldn't think of the words to defend herself against such an accusation. Rage and fear combined within her, rendering her mute. She'd said her piece, and they hadn't given it a second thought. Dray had beat her, poisoning their minds against her, going so far as to forge her signature and provide false evidence against her.

Her head dropped to her chest, her breath coming in shallow gasps.

"Jayce Keenstone, I sentence you to a lifetime in the salt mines. You will remain imprisoned until such time the overseer comes to collect prisoners. I only regret that you let so much potential go to waste in your selfish desire to prove yourself."

Sir Rorick's hand tightened on Jayce's arm, and another guard took her pack and then gripped her other arm. They marched her away from the queen and out of the throne hall, into an area of the castle she hadn't been before: the dungeons.

CHAPTER THIRTY-FOUR

Sir Rorick and the other guard unceremoniously escorted Jayce down a winding staircase, through a maze of storage rooms and corridors, until they reached the dungeons, where several guards sat playing cards in front of a large iron-wrought door.

"Jayce Keenstone, by the queen's orders," Sir Rorick intoned.

One of the guards stood, tugging a keyring off his belt and selecting a larger key to unlock the door. It complained loudly as it swung open into a row of relatively neat cells.

Jayce was impressed. She'd always envisioned prisons to be damp, smelly places, filled with vagabonds and murderers.

Each of these cells stood at attention like a soldier awaiting inspection, swept clean with uneven lime-washed walls and flooring, a single mattress with a blanket, and a bucket. Considering criminals were either sent to the salt mines of the Hobhorn or executed in Lothian, perhaps it wasn't difficult to keep them relatively clean.

She likely wouldn't be there more than a few days, herself.

The guard ahead of Sir Rorick opened a cell toward the center of the prison. A shadow moved in a cell at the end, but Jayce didn't get more than a glance before Sir Rorick pushed against her back and sent her stumbling into the cell.

The lock clicked with a finality that made Jayce's heart sink, and she said nothing as the guards walked away.

She paced her cell a few times, noting the mattress was stuffed with straw and the blanket was linen, which whispered to her through a hole in the pinky finger of one glove. When had that gotten there? She hadn't noticed it at Dagric's.

She paced around a final time, then slid against the wall. Cold stone bit into her back. She watched a slanting patch of sunlight move gradually across the floor for a while, too exhausted to move or even think.

And then a cough echoed down the center corridor of the dungeons, and Jayce's curiosity piqued. Who else was down there with her?

She pushed to standing and crossed her cell to grip the bars of the iron-wrought door and peer as far as she could toward the end of the corridor. She couldn't see all the way down, but she did catch sight of a matted head of blond curls four cells down and across the corridor, and her heart leapt into a terrifying gallop.

She licked her lips. "Sav?"

His head turned toward her, and a smile broke out across his face, practically creating its own version of sunlight that lit up the inside of the dungeon and sent a thrill all the way to Jayce's toes.

"Jayce! I shouldn't be excited or relieved to see you in here, but if it means that Dray didn't kill you the way he kept going on about, I'd rather see you here than dead."

"I'm sorry he captured you. That's all my fault. If I'd gone with you instead of needing to find out the truth about the noxbrosia—"

"You would have been captured, too. Dray was there for Dagric, and we had terrible timing. If we'd moved slower on the road or spent more time at Draigh... It's not worth even thinking about, much less assigning blame. He still might have caught us on our way to Musport when he headed back. There's only one main road through the Oakmist, after all."

"You're not hurt?" Jayce asked, adjusting her grip on the bars, trying to look over Sav's entire body.

"Sprained an ankle trying to get away. Tripped over my own donkey, if you'd believe it," Sav said dryly. "Just a limp. I'll be skipping soon enough. How about you?"

"Just scared," Jayce admitted. And it was true. Despite getting chased by a mercenary with a crossbow and galloping the entire way to Lothian, she had little more than sore muscles and a healthy dose of fear for what would come next.

"How did you end up in here? I didn't think Dray got you."

"He didn't, but you beat me here. He told the queen to expect me, that I was behind the noxbrosia remedy, and that I wanted to redeem my family name by destroying the moribund. The queen believed him—he had falsified evidence, and I had nothing."

"Did you talk to Dagric? Did he give you any evidence?" Sav asked, his feet shuffling across the stone.

Jayce closed her eyes, feeling a headache come on. She'd avoided thinking much of Dagric's fate the past couple days, but now that she'd stopped and the adrenaline had worn off, it all came crashing down.

Quietly, her face pressed into the cool cell bars as the crooked box of light moved behind her on the floor, Jayce told Sav about what had happened to the infamous alchemist of Musport.

Sav whistled when she finished. "You're doubly lucky to have escaped death after all that. I can't believe you did it. I mean, I can, because I saw how great you were at surviving in the forest and all that, but I would pay money to see you pitted against a trained mercenary."

"None of it matters," Jayce said, moving away from the bars, rubbing the spot on her forehead that was no doubt red from pressing into the hard metal. "I didn't prove anything. I didn't get any evidence. All I got was a remedy for the noxbrosia, and I can't do anything with it from in here."

"We're going to find a way out of here. Legally or not. We broke into the restricted section of the library and thwarted a warrior monk. I'm sure there's a plant around here somewhere you can summon."

Jayce scuffed her boot on the dusty, but clean, flagstones. None of the ones she kicked were cracked or even loose, the mortar binding them tightly together.

"I don't think anything could grow here if it wanted to. There's not enough light, and it's too well-made," Jayce said, despair squeezing her chest. She swallowed past a tight throat and took several deep breaths, trying not to let panic overwhelm her. She'd come too far to give up now, but she couldn't convince her mind to believe something her eyes disproved with every moment.

"What about outside your window? Grass or a tree, even a rosebush?" Sav asked.

Jayce went to the window and stood on tiptoes, trying to see outside.

The castle was paved all the way around for several stretches, and the gardens stood beyond that. She made out the tops of some rose bushes and an ornate fountain, but her instinct told her they were too far away.

"Sav, I don't think—"

"Have you tried? You know, when I met you, you wore gloves all the time and were terrified of touching plants. I watched you literally eat around them, except for the occasional herb. The last night we spent together, I watched you wake up an entire forest to scare off that herd of moon stags. Don't tell me you don't think you can do it until you've tried."

His words surged inside Jayce, and she felt a renewed energy that reminded her of a plant perking up after it had been watered. She sat down on the flagstone floor and yanked off her gloves, putting them in her lap as she placed her hands palms-down on the ground.

Vines. I need vines, Jayce thought, stretching the limits of her senses, trying to reach any dormant seed, any bit of plant matter that might reside in the soil beneath the floor.

The moments stretched on, and the square of sunlight crawled up the wall of her cell, its color changing from butter yellow to a deep goldenrod.

Jayce slumped over, exhausted, her mind echoing with the emptiness of no response. Not a single plant had heard her, or if they had, they were too dormant to respond.

"It's no use, Sav. There isn't—"

Male voices exchanged, flooding down the prison corridor, and the main prison door followed with a loud creak, slamming shut behind whoever had entered.

Jayce's eyes opened, but she didn't move from her spot on the floor, watching with curiosity that flared to life as fury when the visitor waltzed into view through her barred door.

Dray.

The man chewed a small, pointed stick as he stared at Jayce, arms crossed over his broad chest, a sneer pulling his lips into thin, lopsided lines.

"Bet you wish you'd taken up my offer of marriage now, don't you?"

Jayce moved her hands into her lap, tired of touching the lifeless, dusty floor, and glared at Dray. "Bet you wish you'd killed me when you had the chance. I'm sure I've caused you plenty of trouble with your benefactor. Or is he—perhaps she—your boss? What are they paying you?"

Dray took the stick out of his mouth, the mirth vanishing from his expression. "Careful, missy. It won't take much to convince the queen your sentence ought to be changed to something more deadly. I have a direct line to her ear."

"Does your direct line have the initials L.A., by chance?" Jayce asked, enjoying the look of shock that crossed Dray's face.

"What did that fool alchemist tell you?" he growled.

"Very little, really. But I found your letter to him. It proved everything."

"Too bad you left in such a hurry. My *friend* make leaving stressful for you?"

Jayce just glared, refusing to play into Dray's desire to hear about what he'd cost her.

"What are you going to do with Sav? Send him to the mines?"

"Oh no. You won't be together. He has a purpose he is far better suited to, with that seemingly endless fortune of his and all. Not everyone has enough wealth to throw at paying off the debts of random, otherwise insignificant women, even noblemen. He somehow has the wealth of a king at his disposal, and I intend to find out why, and how I can get my hands on more of it."

Jayce's hands curled into fists.

Down the corridor, Sav chuckled. "I've already told you, Dray. I can't just give you money. It's meant to be used for wise purposes. My schooling, research, my needs."

"I think your family will see preserving your life as a need, in that case," Dray shot back, glancing sideways toward Sav's cell. "If they can approve it to save this wench's life."

"Hey, watch how you speak to her," Sav said, his voice bristling with anger.

"Does the queen know you make it a habit to imprison the innocent?" Jayce demanded, changing the subject before Sav started a fight he couldn't win. Dray had the political and physical advantage here, and he bore a grudge against Sav a league wide already.

Dray turned his attention back toward her. "Oh, your baron isn't innocent. He's an accomplice. Yours, to be precise, and I did a little research into him. Turns out he's using a borrowed name, which has to be a cover up for other nefarious activity. I'm retaining him for questioning while we investigate."

Jayce's mind reeled. A borrowed name? What did Dray mean? But the queen's bailiff continued before she could ask about it, and Sav had fallen completely silent.

"You know what's ironic, Miss Keenstone? You traveled days to obtain evidence that was right under your nose, in this very castle, this entire time. I suggest you get comfortable, enjoy these amenities. The Hobhorn is a much less cozy place, though I suspect you would remember that. Such a shame, really. You would have made a lovely wife."

Dray pushed away from the bars, spitting the little stick out of his mouth into her cell and walking away with a chuckle.

Jayce listened to his bootsteps, following them with her hearing until the main prison door squeaked open and slammed shut and she was certain he'd left.

She stood, crossed to the cell door, and peered out toward Sav, whose arms hung out of his cell as he slumped forward, head pressed against the bars like hers had been before Dray had come to taunt them.

Jayce rapped on the bars of her cell until Sav looked up.

"Start that brilliant mind up again, Baron Alighieri. We're going to come up with a plan to get out of here."

CHAPTER THIRTY-FIVE

Jayce woke up to a clanging sound, her face pressed against the hard stone floor. She sat upright, yawning. She'd fallen asleep trying to summon plants from outside the prison, and exhaustion had gotten the better of her.

The clanging, it turned out, was a man in a dirty apron and hairy arms, brandishing a cart filled with bowls. He waited for the guard to unlock Jayce's door, then dropped one of the bowls with a grunt and hurried to finish his rounds.

Jayce scooted forward, stomach grumbling, and grabbed the bowl. Some of it had sloshed onto the floor—a sort of cracked corn gruel with chunks of gristly meat that she had to suck clean and spit out unless she wanted to break her teeth. She considered the cracked corn, wondering, for a moment, if she could make it sprout even after it had been cooked, but a brief bout of fruitless concentration convinced her to eat it instead.

Numb with the cold of eating plants, and her mind swirling with their words, Jayce crawled to the mattress and tried to find a spot that didn't have straw poking through so she could try to get warm. She lay there shivering for a time, watching the square of golden sunlight pinken and vanish, having dropped too close to the horizon to reach her tiny window anymore.

The queen would sing the Evening Song, soon. How many more of those would Jayce hear before she was carted off to the salt mines?

She closed her eyes for a moment, breathing in the smell of stone and straw and unwashed human. Beneath her, the stones began to vibrate slightly, and she frowned, reaching her hand over the side of the mattress and pressing it against the flagstone floor.

Sure enough, the stones seemed to hum under her hand.

"Jayce?" a familiar voice called from above. No, outside, through the window of her cell.

Jayce sat upright and moved to stand below her window, looking up into the concerned face of her friend, Nels Martin.

Nels' face relaxed, spreading with a wide, relieved grin. He crouched down, reaching for the bars and pulling himself closer. "Jayce! I found you. I tried to get in for a proper visit, but they wouldn't allow it. I've been asking the stones where they were keeping you and calling your name like an idiot."

"Asking the stones?" Jayce wished she were tall enough to reach the bars and touch her friend.

Nels rubbed his chin on his shoulder. "It's part of my ability. What, you think I visit the Hobhorn and mine stones and gems like any other rockhound? They sing to me. And when they sing about you, it's the most beautiful—"

"Nels," Jayce said with exasperation.

"It's true," he said simply, unashamed. Then his expression went grim. "We've got to get you out of there."

"You'd be breaking the law," Jayce warned. "The queen put me in here. She thinks I created the poisonous remedy, and that I defaulted on my debt by leaving the city without permission. I think Dray siphoned the funds, and I know he had a part in creating the remedy. I just have to get out of here and prove it."

She considered Nels for a moment. "Can you talk to the stones? Make them move?"

Nels shook his head, brown hair flopping in front of his face. "No, it's more of a sensing thing. I hear... tones from the rocks and minerals underground. Those tones sometimes tell me things, but I can't make them move."

Jayce rubbed the bald spot on her eyebrow and turned from the window to pace. Her foot stopped short of landing as her eyes spotted something she hadn't expected to see, even with all her efforts in summoning it.

A green sprout with curling tendrils waved at her from between two flagstones, the finest, hairline crack broken through the mortar.

Jayce grinned, crouching to admire the tiny green thing, a sense of pride washing through her. She had done that, through impossible odds.

She straightened, glancing at Nels again. "I need you to get Dray out of the castle. Distract him any way you know how; make something up. Do it after the Evening Song, when the sky darkens, then meet me inside. You can get in through the south servants' entrance."

"I don't know where that is," Nels said.

"It's on the south side of the castle," Jayce replied. "A plain brown door in a recessed stone doorway. You can't miss it, really. They're not hidden."

Nels leaned away from the barred window, glancing left and right nervously before bringing his worried eyes back to her. "How are you going to get out?"

Jayce looked at the little sprout, her heart near beating out of her chest. "Don't worry, I've got that covered."

After Nels left, Jayce got to work, concentrating on the sprout, stroking it with her fingers, thanking it for growing. The candlestick vine had reached a foot high, and the bottom stem had gone from pale green and flexible to woody and stiff. Candlestick vine earned its name from the way it grew up straight, then branched out along any vertical surface, looking like numerous candles in a candelabra. It was often pruned in fancy, ornamental ways.

Jayce guided a single strand of the vine to grow along the floor, urging it toward Sav's cell, where she sent it through the bars and searched until the vine found his warm, sleeping body and jabbed him awake.

Sav sputtered, his mattress rustling frantically, and then he exclaimed.

Jayce watched him arrive at the door of his cell. He looked out at her with a stunned expression on his face.

"Did you... *make* that?" he asked.

"I asked it to grow, yes," Jayce said, laughing at his stunned expression. "Its bark is wooden. I think I can ask it to grow small branches you could use to pick the locks on your cell, if you can describe what you need."

Sav grinned and examined the lock for a moment, then gave her a description of what shape he needed grown out of the wood.

Jayce sat on the floor, feeling the need to ground herself so she could concentrate on what to tell the plant. As she closed her eyes and rested her bare fingers on the bark of the candlestick vine, Queen Lyra's voice wound its way through the air and into her cell.

The Evening Song. She would have to work fast. She sent her thoughts through her hand into the vine, asking it to grow the uniquely shaped part from its wood.

"It's working!" Sav whispered loudly.

Sweat dripped down Jayce's face from the effort of maintaining her connection with the vine, and the tendrils inside her cell kept growing as well, almost as if they fed off her, growing far faster than would ever be possible in nature. She pushed at it, hot and somehow still freezing through her entire body, until Sav exclaimed that the pieces were ready.

Jayce took her hand away and rubbed at her fingers and arms to bring life back into them. Across the corridor, two quiet snaps told her Sav had harvested his lock picks.

"I don't know if they'll be strong enough," he admitted.

Jayce scooted toward the cell door, sitting cross-legged on the floor and watching him work on the lock.

It took longer than she expected, and tension rose inside of her. What if it didn't work? What if the candlestick vine wood wasn't strong enough and it broke?

She was about to tell Sav to give up when he let out a quiet whoop and the lock sprung. He eased his cell door open as quietly as he could manage to avoid alerting the guards beyond the main door, then made his way across the corridor to Jayce.

"What's our plan for getting past those guys?" Sav asked, gesturing with his chin toward the guards as he angled the wooden picks into Jayce's lock.

"Knock them out with something?" Jayce asked with a shrug.

Sav gave her a concerned look. "Four grown men with combat training?"

"Tie them up with my vines?" Jayce replied, only half-serious. She felt exhausted, as if she'd been running for days. All she wanted to do was eat and take a nap, not summon more vines to immobilize the guards. "Besides, I think there are only two now. The others left after they finished their card game."

"Two guards is still more than we can handle. We need a distraction."

"We'll think of something," Jayce said, forcing herself to stand. "For now, concentrate on—"

Footsteps echoed down the stairs to the prison. Voices carried down the corridor as the guards addressed whoever had arrived. Had Dray come back to gloat some more?

"Sav!" Jayce hissed warningly. She glanced in alarm at the plant growing out of the stone behind her. Its trunk was rather thick now, almost too wide for her hand to fit around, and it had several branches trailing on the ground, searching for a wall to grip onto. Whoever came down would see that for certain. Could she hide it?

Sav slipped away from her door, creeping down the corridor closer to the main door, then slipped into one of the other empty cells. He pressed himself against the wall on the same side as the main door, so whoever entered would pass him and hopefully not see him.

Jayce dragged the scratchy brown blanket from her mattress and tossed it over the plant, then stood in the doorway, wishing she were taller and wider to better hide the view of the plant that definitely shouldn't have grown in the middle of her cell.

Long, dark blue and silver robes swished over matching slippered feet. Jayce dragged her gaze up the entire length of the fancy robes, and her eyes landed on a wide-eyed, bespectacled face that she hadn't seen before that morning.

One of Queen Lyra's counselors.

He stopped in front of Jayce's cell, looking her up and down, then peering curiously behind her. He removed one hand from inside his voluminous sleeves, pointing. "You didn't think you could hide that, did you?"

Jayce licked her lips and readjusted her grip on the bars on the door. "I thought the cell looked drab. A bit of green freshened it right up."

The counselor looked over his glasses at her. "You're that woman who can hear plants."

Jayce nodded.

"You probably don't remember me. I first met you five years ago. You came to the castle with your brother."

Jayce froze, hardly daring to look the man in the eyes. If he knew about Javin, he knew about the failures of her past. Had he come to rub it in? To blame her for the continuation of the plague? Or did he want something from her?

"Who are you?" she asked, hoping he wouldn't choose to talk about her past, and also hoping she could distract him so Sav could get out.

She glanced towards where she'd last seen him and caught a glimpse of the back of his green vest as it vanished towards the stairs. He'd gotten out. But what about the guards? What about her, still stuck in her cell? Those questions would have to wait.

The counselor bowed slightly. "Counselor Leopold Castellan. You may call me Leopold." He readjusted his stance, straightening, but even so his eyes were even with hers, their heights roughly the same. Then he leaned in conspiratorially. "I have come to give you aid."

"What?" Jayce asked in shock. The last thing she had expected was aid from one of the queen's own counselors.

"I believe you have been falsely accused. I've long suspected Sir Dray of nefarious acts. He must be working with someone, but I've never been able to prove it. If you could get some evidence to present the queen and her council, I'd like to help you."

Was this a trick? How could anything get worse from this? She was already accused, already headed for the mines unless she got exactly what Leopold wanted her to get—proof that Dray, or whoever he worked for, was behind the noxbrosia remedy, not her.

"What do you have to offer?" Jayce asked, rather than tell him outright they planned to escape. He had probably guessed as much already, but she wasn't about to hand him the information if he might still use it against her.

"I couldn't get my hands on a set of prison keys to free you, but if you could get out of there, I have a master key that can open most other rooms in the palace. One of the perks of being the Key Keeper." Leopold shrugged as if it were no big deal to be entrusted with something so powerful.

"You have a master key?" Jayce gripped the bars tighter, pulling herself close enough her nose nearly touched the metal. "I need to get into Dray's private quarters."

Leopold nodded. "I assumed as much. All I ask in return is that you help me uncover who is working with him. It is someone from within the castle, possibly one of my fellow counselors. If there is evidence in Dray's rooms, I want it."

Jayce hardly needed to consider. She wanted Dray caught, and whoever he worked with. "Deal," she said, reaching her hand through the bars.

Leopold grasped it, his thin fingers stronger than they looked. He smiled at her with satisfaction. "You are quite the amenable and intelligent young lady, as I knew you would be. Now, how will you escape?"

Jayce turned and glanced around her cell, focusing on the candlestick vine at the center. Could she make it grow fast enough to break through the stone wall? Maybe break the bars? She didn't have Sav's skill to pick locks, so going that route would be a waste of time. If only he hadn't left! She had to trust that he had seen an opportunity to avoid the guards, somehow.

"I have an idea. You shouldn't stay here. Can you meet me at the servants' entrance outside?" Jayce asked.

"There are three. Would you like the east, south, or west?" Leopold asked matter-of-factly.

"South. I have a friend waiting there, Nels Martin. Tell him you've spoken to me. Tell him the password is amethyst, so he'll trust you." It was the stone Nels had given her to pass messages, and she hoped he would get the reference.

She shook out her hands, nerves and anticipation making them tremble.

Leopold bowed. "I will meet you there."

"Leopold," Jayce said as the man turned away.

He glanced back at her.

"Thank you for coming here. For taking such a risk."

"It is you who are taking the bigger risk. I should be thanking you." Leopold's robes swished as he walked down the corridor toward the main door to the prison.

Jayce rolled up her blouse sleeves and shoved her gloves into the pocket of the breeches she wore. It was time to see exactly what her magic could do.

CHAPTER THIRTY-SIX

The cell had nearly darkened by the time Jayce convinced the candlestick vines to climb the wall and grip the iron window bars. She stood with her hands on the plant's smooth bark, gritting her teeth against the whispers and the numbing cold.

"Come on," she pleaded out loud, her mind exhausted from chanting instruction to the vines. There had to be an easier way, but if there was one, she didn't know it. She wanted to wrap her hands around the vines and rip them from the walls in frustration, but it wouldn't solve anything.

Besides, every time she got frustrated, the vines shrank back a bit as if affected by her emotions.

If that was the case, maybe she needed a different emotion.

Jayce thought about everything that she'd been through to get to this point. She thought about the queen sentencing her, she thought about Dray and everything he'd gotten away with. She pushed past the lines drawn in her mind and thought about the moribund, the plague, and the source of it all—the Plague King and how she had failed to save her brother when he'd gone to destroy that being of darkness and malaise.

Anger coursed through her, hot and devastating. She hadn't let herself feel angry about Javin. She'd shoved it all down. But now it had a clear path to rage through her heart, into her hands, and into the plant. With her rage, she called upon the vines to pull. To use the destructive force of hundreds of years of erosion compounded into a few brief moments to pull on the bars.

The wall exploded.

Jayce gasped and crouched, covering her face as rock and rubble rained down on her. Then the dust cleared, and she stood, gaping at the wide hole where the window had once been.

"Good plant," she said, sprinting past the vine and using the branches that had grown along the wall to pull herself up out of the cell and onto the grass.

She rolled across it, laughing at the whispers of the tiny leaf blades, at the cold that had once bothered her so much it had made her ill.

Even with this grand use of her powers, the cold hardly bothered her. Perhaps it was the heat of her anger, still coursing through her veins and mind, or maybe she had somehow grown acclimated. She would have to conduct more controlled experiments to know for certain, but for now she had to meet with Leopold before someone noticed the massive hole in her cell and that she was missing from it.

Jayce sat up, brushing the grass off, not bothering to don her gloves. She didn't need them at the moment. She walked swiftly toward the southern servants' entrance. She'd chosen it because it was closest to the prisons.

Shadows grew long and chilly as the last sliver of sunlight vanished from the sky, and Jayce used those shadows to her advantage, creeping along the stone wall of the castle. With her dust-covered clothes and mussed-up hair, she might pass for a servant coming inside from working in the gardens. At that thought, she straightened and tried to look more weary as she made her way to the nondescript wooden door under the arched stone doorframe built into the castle.

The latch opened readily under her hand, and the door creaked open. Two figures moved in the corridor just beyond, covered in shadows.

"Nels?" Jayce whispered.

"Present. Plus, this old guy you told to meet me here?"

Jayce aimed her elbow at the thinner shadow and made a satisfying connection with his side. "Be nice! Leopold has the key," she said.

"Indeed," Leopold replied.

"Why aren't there any lights down here?" Jayce asked.

"We put them out to avoid being identified in case anyone other than you used the entrance," Nels said.

"He'd already done it when I arrived," Leopold said, his shadow moving. Jayce lost sight of him against the dark stone.

Nels fumbled for her hand and eventually grasped it. "It's a straight hall. I'll lead you if you want."

"Hurry. Sav is somewhere in the castle. He got out before Leopold and I spoke."

"Sav?" Leopold asked.

"I haven't met him either," Nels said. "Is he handsome, Jayce?"

She was tempted to elbow him again but resisted since she needed to focus on not tripping in the dark.

Eventually, the corridor turned into a staircase, and they went up. At the top, a lit torch flickered, and they all paused before the door.

"I'll take a peek," Nels offered, cracking the door. He waved his hand. "Coast is clear."

Leopold pushed in front of Nels and turned to face them, adjusting his robes. "There's no need to sneak around like criminals. Straighten up, walk behind me with purpose, look no one in the eye. If we're stopped, I will say you are assisting me with some work, and we will pray to the Three that we don't run into the queen or Dray himself."

Leopold's plan made Jayce's heart rate double, but she followed his instructions. To her relief, they only passed a handful of servants as they ascended to the second floor of the castle and passed through a maze of corridors until they reached one at the far back.

"Sir Dray will tell anyone who so much as looks at him that he simply prefers privacy, but I played a part in getting him these rooms so far removed from everything else. Forgotten in a corner," Leopold said proudly, gesturing to a door at the end of the last hall they passed through.

"Forgotten and allowed to scheme without being suspected," Jayce said, crossing her arms over her chest.

A look of realization passed over Leopold's face. "Ah, yes. It would have that effect as well, I suppose." His voice dropped to a mutter as he searched his pockets and finally produced a ring of keys with only three keys on it. He selected one and used it to unlock the door.

"My part here has finished. May the Three be with you. And remember, any evidence you discover about who Dray is working with comes to me."

Jayce nodded and slipped into the room, Nels behind her. They closed the door, pausing to listen. The room they'd entered stood silent and empty, a sitting room with lanterns lit on the walls. Jayce passed through, knowing with a glance that Dray wouldn't keep private information on public display where he entertained guests.

There were two other doors leading off the main chamber. One led to Dray's bedroom, a sparsely furnished and well-kept room, no doubt cleaned regularly by the castle maids.

"You look through here. I'll check the other room," Jayce told Nels, ducking out of the room.

She glanced at the first door they'd come through, anxiously watching for both Dray and Sav. Had Sav been caught? Or delayed somewhere?

She had to hope he would be all right. She had to focus on finding the information that would incriminate Dray, that way even if Sav did get caught, she would have the evidence to free him.

Jayce turned to the third door and moved to push it open. The door stuck fast. She wiggled the latch, pulling harder, but it remained stuck.

"It's locked!" she hissed toward the room Nels was in.

Nels poked his head out. "Have you checked for a key? Under the rug, in that table over there?"

Jayce rolled back the piece of carpet she stood on. Nothing. She rummaged through the single drawer in the tiny table next to an armchair nearest the last door. She even checked for a false back and a false bottom, running her fingers along the drawer seems and knocking.

Nothing.

Panic filled her. What would they do? No doubt everything they needed was behind this door.

"Need some help?"

The male voice made Jayce jump and whirl around. She came face to face with Sav.

He gave her a wicked grin, seemingly pleased he'd startled her.

Jayce put a hand over her heart. "Don't do that!" she hissed, managing to keep her voice down. "Yes, I need your help. Did you keep the lockpicks I made you?"

Sav held up the two twisted sticks. "I'm not sure how many uses they have left, but I'll give it a go."

He passed by her, his arm brushing hers, and she shivered in a good way, then stepped back from the door so he'd have enough room to work.

Nels came out of the bedroom a moment later and glanced from her to Sav. "Is this him, then?" Nels asked.

"Yes. Be nice," Jayce said, tapping her foot, impatience getting to her. "How exactly did you get Dray out of the castle?"

Nels kept staring at Sav a moment, then leaned over close to Jayce. "Does his front end look as nice as his back end?"

"Nels!" Jayce exclaimed quietly, shoving his shoulder.

Nels laughed behind his hand, then collected himself. "I told Dray that Mistress Millie was doing free drinks down at her tavern. I've seen him there a lot, all the way in Midtown."

"Good. A few drinks, at least."

"That was just after the Evening Song. Unless he gets utterly sodden tonight, he'll be back soon," Nels said. "I don't want to rush your friend, but he needs to hurry."

Sav straightened, somewhat red-faced, and brushed several curled strands out of his eyes. He held out a hand toward Nels. "Baron Savage Alighieri. I don't believe I have made your acquaintance, Mister—?"

"Nels. Nels Martin," Nels said, taking Sav's hand.

Was it just Jayce, or did their grip seem unnecessarily hard and their stare unnecessarily long?

She cleared her throat. "Sav? The door?"

Sav broke eye contact with Nels and put his hands on his hips. "Ah, yes. Well, it'll be just a moment, if your friend can keep his pants on."

Nels put up his hands and gestured. "Don't mind me. I'm just here for moral support." He winked at Jayce, and she rolled her eyes, then glanced at the door again, unable to keep from worrying.

There was no telling what Dray would do if he found the three of them invading his private space.

"Ah ha!" Sav said, loud enough to make Jayce wince. He moved the latch effortlessly, and the door swung open without a sound.

"Sav, you're a genius," Jayce said, planting a quick kiss on his cheek as she passed him.

"What do I have to do to get one of those?" Nels asked, following her into the room, which appeared to be Dray's office.

Jayce ignored his teasing, heading immediately for the desk. "He told us himself that everything we need to convict him is right here under our noses. Check everything, don't worry about making a mess. If we find it, we'll be pardoned. If we don't..."

"We're doomed," Sav finished for her, going to a row of shelves behind the desk, which filled half the wall, each square cubby stuffed with papers.

"What are we looking for, exactly?" Nels asked, moving toward a wardrobe-like cupboard off to the side of the room.

"Letters, especially with Dagric's name on them, or the initials L.A.. Inventory sheets, falsified documents, receipts for purchases for potion ingredients. Anything that looks suspicious for a bailiff to have on hand," Jayce said, pulling the desk drawer and dumping it on top. The papers were all personal letters, apparently from women. She leafed through them, growing more disgusted by the moment that Dray had ever proposed to her.

"What about this?" Nels said, dragging something off the top of the wardrobe. He removed the cloth drape and revealed an alchemy set, glistening with copper pipes and flexible tubing.

"Yes! Exactly. But we'll need more to convict him. It's not a crime to own an alchemy set, just odd for a man who mainly handles debts to the realm. Sav, have you found anything?"

"Not yet," Sav called back. "This man really needs a secretary. His desk is a mess, and it looks like he's kept every paper he's ever gotten."

"Keep looking. Put anything that looks relevant on the center table. I want to take him for all he's worth," Jayce said, shoving the letters back in the drawer.

"Too bad you won't get the chance," a deep voice said from the doorway.

Jayce gripped the side of the shelf, knees suddenly weak with terror.

Sir Dray had returned to his quarters.

CHAPTER THIRTY-SEVEN

A long dagger gleamed wickedly in one of Dray's hands. He lunged at Nels, who was closest to the door by the wardrobe-like cupboard.

Nels ducked and leapt for Dray's legs, but Dray stumbled back.

Jayce glanced around frantically for anything she could use to throw at Dray, and her eyes landed on the bronze paperweight on the desk. She grabbed it, heaving, and it went wide, forcing Nels to duck again as he tried to stand. He shot a wide-eyed look her way as Dray swiped at him again with the dagger.

"Keep looking! I'll distract him!" Nels said, catching Dray's arm and forcing him back, showing surprising strength for as thin as he was. But Dray trumped him in both size and training, and Jayce knew Nels was in serious trouble, no matter how confident he sounded.

She started flinging papers out of their shelves, letting them fall to the floor in a snow-like flurry.

Most were debt invoices, like she'd once received, and most of them looked legitimate. She wanted to scream in frustration.

A loud crash pulled her eyes from the papers to the two fighting men. Nels had crashed into the wardrobe's open door and sat dazed inside, a waistcoat covering his face.

"Nels, look out!" Jayce shouted as Dray raised the knife again.

"Jayce, over here!" Sav said excitedly. "I think I found something."

A sickening *thud* and a loud groan from Nels made Jayce's heart clench, but she ran for Sav and the document he held in his hand. She wouldn't make the same mistake she'd made before and miss her chance to get evidence against Dray into her grasp.

Dray's arm grabbed around her middle, yanking her back against him. She thrashed, trying to get him to loosen his grip, but he held tighter, making her stomach and ribs ache.

The cool metal of his blade found her neck, and Jayce went limp. Dray adjusted his grip, getting a stronger hold on her midsection, and he walked backward toward the door.

"The papers. You can either hand them to me or put them in the fire yourself," Dray said, gesturing with his head.

Sav stared at Jayce as if frozen, his face a mask of terror.

"Move!" Dray snarled, pressing the knife harder against Jayce's throat.

She made a choking, protesting sound, and Sav's gaze grew desperate.

"Don't—" she started.

"You be quiet," Dray said into her ear, his breath hot and damp on her cheek. "Unless you want to be left to bleed out on my floor."

Sav breathed in, then seemed to make some kind of decision. He stepped forward, holding the papers toward Dray.

Dray glanced from the papers to his hold on Jayce, realizing he would have to let her go in order to free one hand to hold the evidence.

He kept the knife at her throat and released her midsection.

"No funny business, now," he said to no one in particular, snatching the papers from Sav. He glanced over them and started laughing. "This is nothing. You thought you could convict me with this? You, Baron, third row down, second shelf from the right. That stack. Grab the whole thing."

Dray cackled with undisguised glee as Sav obeyed, crouching down on the floor to retrieve the requested stack of papers. He glanced at it, licking his lips, then looked at Jayce.

"This is it. This is what we would have needed."

"And now you can watch it burn. Give it here," Dray said, gesturing wildly with his free hand.

Jayce tried to signal with her eyes that Sav shouldn't listen, that he should take the papers and run to Leopold, or the queen, whoever he could convince to listen.

"Why are you doing this, Sir Dray?" Jayce cried, trying to distract him so Sav could get away.

Sav didn't move, staring at the papers in his hand.

Dray's hand tightened around Jayce. "Because I'm being paid more djewls than you could even dream of, and ridding the capital of those moribund once and for all. As soon as we can increase production and send it out to the rest of the city, the moribund will be eradicated and we can come forward to the queen with proof our remedy works to end that terror."

"It isn't a remedy at all," Jayce spat. "It's poison. You're killing people who might survive the plague!"

"And saving those who would get killed by those who change into the undead and prey on their families," Dray snarled.

Jayce closed her eyes. She could see his reasoning. Had been through it herself. But as someone who had sworn to do no harm, she couldn't condone killing innocent people, especially when they didn't understand what the so-called remedy they were taking would do to them.

"Enough talking," Dray snarled, adjusting his grip on the blade at Jayce's throat. "Bring me the papers."

Sav ignored Jayce's pleading gaze and approached anyway, regret in his eyes.

Jayce felt Dray's hand holding the knife fall away and move toward Sav, too late to stop what was about to happen.

Dray snatched the papers from Sav's hand and plunged his dagger into him with the other.

Sav grunted, hands going to the dagger in his side, and fell to his knees.

All the air rushed out of Jayce. She moved forward to attend him, to stop the bleeding, but Dray stopped her.

"He's a dead man. Come with me. There's something I want you to see." He grabbed her arm, his knife stuck inside Sav, and pulled her from the room.

Her last glimpse of the room was of Sav, blood blossoming through his shirt and his shocked, pain-filled expression. On the other side, Nels lay prostrate on the floor.

"Let me go!" Jayce screamed, tugging on her arm.

Dray reeled her in, trapping her with his arm around her midsection, her face so close to his she could smell the silvertop ale on his breath.

"I said, you're coming with me," he breathed, his voice laced with threats.

Jayce went with him, eyeing the documents clutched in his other hand, which he held opposite her, his arm outstretched in the air. She could wrench out from under his hold, knock him over, maybe make him drop the papers?

They passed the half-circle of armchairs and the loveseat at the center of the room, and a familiar, cold whisper rushed through Jayce as a leaf brushed her arm.

Dusk ivy. I still the breath and stop the heart—

Confidence surged through her. She'd summoned the protection of a forest, used vines to break out of prison.

She stepped down hard on the inner side of Dray's foot, forcing him to loosen his grip enough that she spun out of his hold and reached back toward the potted plant on the mosaic table behind her.

Her hand plunged into the pot, grabbing leaves and dirt in a frantic fistful.

Grow! Jayce urged, and her body trembled as cold surged through her.

The plant responded, its leafy tendrils dipping over the table edge and onto the floor.

Dray saw the plant move of its own accord, and his eyes widened with fear. He stumbled toward the fireplace, documents in hand, reaching for the hungry flames.

The dusk ivy wrapped around his wrist, then shot out to grab his waist, dragging him away from the fire.

Jayce gripped the plant's pot in her arms, her hand gripping the plant's roots to keep them from pulling straight out of the pot. If it were in the ground, she wouldn't have to brace it, but with Dray's struggling, the plant had nothing to brace itself against, except Jayce. She felt its scratchy roots wrap around her hand and between her fingers.

"Stop struggling, Dray," Jayce said, as Dray's second arm was wrapped up and pulled into his side. The documents fluttered to the floor, unharmed.

Jayce stepped up beside him, careful not to get close enough for him to lunge at her, and scooped up the documents. The evidence she had promised to deliver to Leopold, the queen's counselor.

Dray increased his agitated movements as if trying to break free. The dusk ivy responded by reeling him in tighter, wrapping him up like a caterpillar in a cocoon.

"If you don't stop struggling, I'll force feed you one of these leaves. You should know what it feels like to die of suffocation after your lungs collapse. After all, it's the fate you left to Dagric Wortcunning when you ordered him poisoned."

"I made no such order," Dray said. "I was following orders."

"Given by whom?" Jayce demanded. She well and truly could not feel her fingers now, either from the cold of touching the dusk ivy or its roots cutting off her circulation, she couldn't quite tell. She just had to hold Dray long enough to get help.

Dray pressed his lips together in response.

"Never mind. You can tell the queen. Or maybe we'll find the identity of L.A. in these papers," Jayce said, waving the documents.

Dray said something muffled as the dusk ivy curled around his jaw, covering his mouth, and he clammed up to avoid getting any of the leaves in his mouth.

Don't kill him, Jayce told the plant, noticing its tendrils trying to pry Sav's jaw open.

We just make him sleep, the dusk ivy insisted.

I need him alive, Jayce said firmly.

To her relief, the plant relented, its tendrils stopping their attempts to part his lips.

She couldn't set the pot down without giving Dray the chance to escape, but it was a large, ceramic pot that weighed on her arm, and it was growing tired. She lifted the dusk ivy root ball out of the pot, spilling dirt across the rug and causing Dray to make muffled sounds of protest.

"A clean rug is the least of your worries, Sir Dray," she muttered, eyeing the roots that had entwined her hand so much, they were practically a glove.

You're going to need to let me go, she told the plant.

If we let you go, we let the man go, the dusk ivy responded.

It made sense to Jayce—without direct contact with her magic, the dusk ivy would go inanimate once more, and Dray would shake off the vines like he would any plant. She was stuck with a plant-glove for the time being.

She shrugged and walked toward the room, Dray hobbling along behind her, half-dragged by the rope-like vines tightened around him like a vice.

In the back room, Nels was on all fours, shaking his head side to side.

"You all right, Nels?" Jayce asked from the doorway, her eyes going to Sav, who lay slumped over on his side, unmoving.

"Dizzy. Should I be seeing dark spots?" he asked.

"They should go away shortly," Jayce said absently as she knelt next to Sav and nudged his shoulder.

"Sav?" she called, shaking him a second time.

He moaned and rolled over, his hand over a growing, damp patch of blood soaking through his white shirt.

"You're not supposed to take the knife out," Jayce chided, moving his hand and examining the wound. "Nels, can you help me over here?"

Sav's eyes blinked open, looking at her upside-down. "You have a plant for a hand," he said, words slurring.

"It's temporary," she assured him. "Unlike organ damage. What hurts?"

Sav licked his lips. "My stomach." He lifted his hand again to show her.

Jayce sighed, and Nels scooted up beside her, squinting slightly.

"What do you need me to do?"

"Take off his shirt and use it to staunch the bleeding. I'll hold it there while you get help. I'm just a little tied up at the moment."

Nels' gaze traveled from her hand to where Dray stood, vine-bound, behind her.

"Goddesses above, Jayce. What did you do?"

Jayce hardly spared Dray a glance, keeping her eyes instead on Sav's face, trying to gauge how much blood he'd lost based on his pallor and the steady thump of his heartbeat beneath her fingertips on his neck.

"His blood pressure is good, but I don't like how much blood he's losing. Nels, his shirt."

"My fingers work," Sav complained.

"Lay there and shut up," Jayce snapped, fatigue, pain, and worry making her anger rise.

"You're bossy when you're fixing people," Sav grumbled, shifting slightly as Nels undid the buttons on his shirt and tugged it over each arm.

Nels balled up the material and pressed it against the wound. Jayce laid her hand across it.

"I'll go find Leopold," Nels said, standing up and swaying slightly.

"Are you certain you feel well enough?" Jayce asked, not taking her eyes off Sav, suddenly worried she had asked too much of her friend.

"I'll be back," Nels said in response, glancing between the two of them before slipping out of the room.

Jayce worried about him, but pushed that concern to the back of her mind to better focus on Sav's wounds.

Sav's gaze locked into Jayce's. "Am I going to live?"

Jayce's breath left her in a rush. "Yes, you're going to live. I swear, you are the most dramatic patient I've ever had."

Sav watched her with a gaze that made Jayce feel as if he'd stripped her bare.

"You saved my life, Jayce. Again."

"Just repaying my debt," Jayce said, smiling. She realized she'd let the pressure off his wound and checked beneath the bundle of cloth before reapplying it and pressing down again. Still bleeding, but it had slowed.

For once, Sav didn't object to her mention of a debt between them.

Jayce found herself nodding off as adrenaline left her body, and almost slept, but the need to keep Sav's bleeding down kept her awake.

"Are you hurt?" Sav said after some time.

"No. But my hand is numb." She held up her root-bound hand.

"Is that... is it going to cause a problem?"

Jayce sent a nudge to the dusk ivy to loosen its grip on her hand so the blood would flow properly.

"I don't know. I've never held a plant this long before," she said, suppressing a yawn. It was getting late, and she barely had enough energy to remain upright, much less theorize about whether her magic would cause permanent damage to her hand.

"I'm sorry for what I said to you before Musport. I should have said this sooner, but I chickened out." Sav took a deep breath, gazing at her still slightly upside-down from his position on the floor. "You're not a burden. You're worth every investment I've made, and I would do it all again just for the chance to meet you."

"I know," Jayce said. She bit her lip, breathing in slowly to gather courage for the next part she had to say. "I'm coming with you, Sav. To the Ivory Guilds."

Sav shifted beneath her. "You are?" he said, tone surprised. "You don't have to. I know what I'm researching makes you uncomfortable."

"If anything, you've taught me that a little discomfort"—she held up her root-bound hand—"won't kill me. Even if it feels like it might."

"That's going in my book," he said at last.

Jayce's breath caught. "Your book?"

"The one I'm writing. You were already going to be in it, but this whole adventure is too good to leave out. Someone should know what we've been through."

Jayce couldn't have agreed more.

CHAPTER THIRTY-EIGHT

In the days that had followed her encounter with Dray, Jayce Sav, and Nels had been called to give testimony before the queen. Fortunately, with the evidence presented by Counselor Leopold, both Jayce and Sav had been pardoned of any crime, including their intrusion of the restricted section at the monastery.

Dray, on the other hand, had been stripped of his title and sent to the salt mines, a fate that Jayce didn't envy one bit.

Sav, once he'd been deemed healed enough to move about, had been in and out of the apothecary, sending letters and making arrangements for their journey across the sea to Enterea. And then he had left Lothian, going ahead of Jayce to finalize the details of their journey. An unavoidable inconvenience, he had said, before kissing her hand and driving off to the port at Crotos.

It was almost worse than when he'd left her at Musport before, except this time she had the reassurance that she would see him again.

Jayce kept busy making more of the cure Dagric had given her to counter the noxbrosia, sharing what she discovered with the castle apothecaries and instructing them to give it to anyone who was in possession of the noxbrosia poison.

Once that was done, she did not return to her rounds, instead spending time cleaning and preparing her apothecary to be vacant once more, this time for far longer.

Now, afternoon sun streamed through the windows of the apothecary in peaceful, swirling beams of light, and Jayce could rest easy knowing that the noxbrosia concoction had been banned, and a statement made about the danger of taking it. The mysterious L.A. that had corresponded with Dray, however, had not been identified.

Jayce tried not to think about that as she rubbed a soft cloth across the copper of a funnel to her alchemistry set before she pressed it into the designated spot in the leather carrying case the set had come in.

With a sigh, she closed the case, twisted the latches so they held tight, then added the suitcase to the growing pile near her front door.

She flexed her left hand, which still held strange marks like twisted, purple scars from where the dusk ivy had gripped her. She couldn't feel half of it, most of the numbness in her fingers, but fortunately it didn't seem muscular, just nerve-based. She could use her hand, she just couldn't feel it properly, and that sometimes meant she dropped things or ran into them more than she had before.

A small price to pay to escape Dray.

It already seemed like a lifetime ago that she had taken on the powerful bailiff, and together with Nels and Sav, had gotten him put where he belonged—prison.

He would have many ages there, and then many more working to pay off his own, newly accrued life-debt to the capital to replace the debt payment he'd stolen from Jayce instead of turning it in to the realm.

She would never have to face him again, and that made her smile through the strange numbness in her fingers.

A rapid knock came at her door, and Jayce almost fell over the pile of luggage in her haste to answer. It opened before she got to it, a familiar, grinning face poking into the apothecary entrance.

"Oh good, you haven't left yet. Any chance I could convince you to stay in Lothian? Set up a stall next to mine in the Midtown market now that you're free of other obligations?"

Jayce laughed. "As incredible as that sounds, no, you won't convince me to stay. I'm already packed." She swept a hand over the bags and bundles on the ground. All the herbs and equipment, clothing, and belongings she'd need to spend a significant amount of time in the realm of Enterea across the sea.

"I can see that," Nels said, the mirth vanishing from his face.

The corners of his mouth turned down, and Jayce's heart sank. She reached for his hands, taking them in hers.

"Don't. Please. Can you be happy for me?"

Nels snorted. "What kind of friend would I be if I didn't cry when my friend left me to go on another insane adventure, and right after the most recent adventure tried to do her in?" He tugged her in for a hug, wrapping his lanky arms around her.

Jayce sank into her friend's embrace, burying her face so the tears fell silently into his shirt. They stood like that for a good long while, until Jayce finally pulled away, sniffing.

"Going to miss my carriage," she said, rubbing away the wetness on her face.

"Ah, darn, you found out my plan," Nels said. "You know, marrying me is still on the table."

Jayce gave him a disparaging look, and his expression softened.

"I know you don't want to marry me," he said.

"That's not—" Jayce started.

Nels held up a hand, stopping her. "You don't have to explain. My proposal was meant as an out for you to take in the face of Dray's threats, but it seems you've gone and dealt with that on your own." He breathed out through his nose, a nearly silent sound of amusement. "I should have known a woman like you would be able to fight her own tyrants."

"Someday, someone is going to come along who deserves you, Nels," Jayce said, blinking away tears that surprised her with their force. She didn't want to think about leaving him behind, because every time she did, she was reduced to a sappy mess.

"Now that's all settled, we can go back to being friends, yeah?" He grinned and Jayce nodded, relieved that the awkwardness between them might be able to fade now.

"In that case, who is this chap you've brought home, Jayce? Are you sure there's nothing, you know, romantic going on?"

Jayce laughed and shoved Nels, making him step back away from her, laughing.

"Lay off him, okay? He's had a rough few cycles."

"Totally. I know what it's like being around you. Honestly, I don't envy the man."

Nels cackled with glee, and Jayce took off after him, trying to knock his hat off his head. He held her off with his long arms.

Jayce stopped trying to reach Nels' hat, a futile effort anyway, and caught her breath.

He approached her, arms up in surrender. "All right, all right. I'll be good. All I'm good for now is a bag boy anyway."

Jayce did so with gusto, piling her belongings high in his arms and grabbing the last few things to take out herself. She paused at the door, glancing one last time around the apothecary. Saying goodbye felt like deception—the last time she'd left thinking she wouldn't be back, she'd returned after all. But this time...

Jayce shook her head. No final goodbyes.

Nels chatted with the carriage driver, a well-dressed man with a jolly demeanor. Jayce glanced in the back of the carriage, noticing a small pile of luggage already there. She glanced at Nels.

"Those aren't my bags," she said.

"No, they're mine," Nels said, hands casually in his pockets, bouncing on his heels as a grin formed on his face. He couldn't keep a straight face if he tried.

"You're not... you're coming?" Jayce asked, her voice becoming high-pitched with excitement.

Nels nodded, and she ran and embraced him again, laughing.

"Why? How?" she asked. Then she punched him. "You let me think you weren't!"

"I wanted it to be a surprise!" Nels said, smirking.

Jayce laughed, wiping moisture from her eyes and trying to calm her pounding heart.

Nels continued, handing one of her bags to the carriage driver. "Sav invited me, if you'll believe it. He said there's a Master at the Ivory Guilds I should talk to, one that has spent their life researching rocks across the realms. They have magic like mine, and they can show me all the great places to find rocks in Enterea. Can you imagine what business will be like when I bring stones and gems back from across the sea?" He rubbed his hands together.

Jayce laughed again. "You could open up a real shop next to mine."

Nels raised his eyebrows. "Or maybe I'll become a famous traveling merchant."

"I'm glad you're coming," Jayce said at last.

"Sure I'm not going to spoil things between you and that fancy baron of yours?" Nels asked.

Jayce elbowed him. "There's nothing going on between us." Despite her words, her heart beat faster at the thought of Sav. It had been seven days since she'd cleared him to travel ahead to Crotos so he could charter a ship that would take them to Enterea.

"Yet," Nels teased. "And now I'll be there to witness all of it. And beat him up if he breaks your heart."

Jayce's retort was stopped by the next thought that crossed her mind. *What about the apothecary*?

She grabbed the key from her pocket and held it up. "Nels, you were going to watch my apothecary. Who's going to look after it while we're gone?"

"Don't worry, I made some arrangements. The baker's wife is going to keep the key safe and the garden tended in exchange for using anything she would like to use in her breads and an age's worth of free remedies when you return. Put it in your garden box out front, she'll be by to collect it after the midday rush."

The driver tugged a time-keeper from his pocket and tapped it, eyeing Jayce with an expression that she could easily read.

Jayce hid the key in the petunias growing in the garden box beneath the window and bid a silent farewell to the place she'd called home for most of her life, then turned back to the carriage.

Nels helped her into the seat next to the driver, then climbed in himself.

It was a long ride to the sea—four cycles of travel by carriage, listening to Nels prattle on about rocks while the road jostled them on hard seats. They camped at night at Jayce's request. Despite the queen having pardoned her and Sav with the Draigh monastery, Jayce wasn't ready to look Elder Vambi in the eyes again after leaving the way they had.

Jayce passed the days and nights restlessly, both too excited and too terrified to enjoy it, but she never looked back on the road that had passed under the wide, wooden wheels of the wagon that bore her and her possessions toward the sea.

On the morning of the fifth cycle, she took a deep breath of salt-scented air as the wagon rolled into Crotos.

The city was filled with bustling people from all sorts of places, some coming, some going. The wagon halted at the check-in station just before the docks, and Jayce clambered down, eager to get through the line and find the boat she was going to travel on, the *Dover*.

The official checking her looked down his pointed nose at her paperwork. A letter of recommendation to study in the Ivory Guilds, signed by Baron Savage Alighieri, and paperwork indicating she had been born in Lothian. He sniffed, then stamped them both.

"Step over to the side, miss," he said, gesturing toward a little wooden booth opposite his.

Everyone had to be given approval from a certified border physician before being allowed to sail.

Jayce passed the health check with an official seal of approval on her paperwork and met back up with Nels, who had undergone his own check and waited for her, surrounded by all their bags.

"The driver left," he said by way of explanation. "You pass?"

"Never healthier," Jayce said, tucking away her papers.

She picked up several pieces of her luggage, and together they made their way down the docks.

They passed three sterns, two belonging to boats that had just docked and were unloading, and the third just pushing off amid shouts of the sailors. A merchant ship, by the look of it. In his letter, Sav had said theirs was much bigger...

Jayce halted, almost running into a woman with a feather hat several feet tall. The woman straightened her handsome waistcoat and huffed away as Jayce gaped at the amazing vessel before her.

The *Dover*'s prow dwarfed nearly every other in the bay, and standing atop it was a man with curling, wind-tossed blond hair blown in his face. He glanced her way and did a double take, and Jayce laughed, jumping up and down and waving.

Sav waved back, then cupped his hands over his mouth. "Ready for another adventure?"

"Yes!" Jayce yelled back, grabbing her skirts and running for the plank, trusting that her luggage would soon follow.

She walked swiftly up the gangplank, dodging men and women with bulging muscles as they brought supplies aboard. Nels came behind.

She met Sav at the prow and glanced around breathlessly. It was quite possibly the most incredible sight she'd ever seen, aside from the peaks of the Hobhorn, but those had instilled feelings of trepidation and even terror inside her. The ocean was something else entirely—the promise of new opportunities and fresh starts.

"It's incredible. You know, I've never seen the ocean," she said, looking out across the ship toward the endless teal water that met the blue horizon in a barely visible line.

"You're going to love it," Sav said, resting his arm on the side of the ship behind her. "Did you have to bring him?"

He nodded toward Nels, who had set the luggage down on the deck to get a breather.

"You invited me, if you'll recall," Nels said, hands on his narrow hips.

Sav slapped him on the shoulder. "I owe you my life. It's the least I can do. Forgive me a few friendly jibes."

A stiff sea breeze swept across Jayce's skin, and every part of her it brushed chilled the way it did when she touched a plant. Indiscernible whispers tickled her mind, as if the flora on the other side of the sea knew she was coming and wanted her to know that they awaited her.

She shivered, rubbing her hands over her exposed arms.

Sav, ever the gentleman, noticed she was chilled and swept off his handsome coat. He draped it over her shoulders. "It's a good thing I packed plenty of hot chocolate," he said, grinning at her.

Jayce grinned back. "A good thing indeed."

Keep reading to see pages from Jayce's apothecary journal and follow me to hear about the release of *Plague King Chronicles Book Two: The Arrow and the Ivy*

the apothecary
KEENSTONE

Nightlock

I came across a rather sinister discovery today in the western woodlands. A small bush bearing opaque white berries was found growing along the riverbank. At first glance it seemed harmless enough, but upon further inspection I found it to be Baccae mortiferae, commonly known as nightlock.

Nightlock berries are deceptively sweet, but contain deadly poisons. Ingestion of even a few berries results in violent purging, cramping, sweating and restricted blood flow, eventually leading to death if left untreated. The telltale sign of nightlock poisoning is a bluish-purple discoloration of the extremities due to lack of circulation.

Thankfully, Sunpetal provides the antidote for nightlock if administered quickly enough. Sunpetal leaves must be brewed into a tonic and given immediately to any poisoning victims to neutralize the toxins. I have harvested a supply of Sunpetal leaves to have on hand should there be any cases of accidental nightlock ingestion.

"Chill the blood. Empty the stomach. Cure indigestion. Stop the senses."

Sunpetal

While surveying the riverbank for any further signs of Nightlock, I came upon a low-growing plant with broad, rounded leaves and vibrant yellow veins. Upon closer inspection I found it to be Solispetalum curatum, commonly known as Sunpetal.

Sunpetal is a beneficial plant with medicinal properties. When the leaves are brewed into a tea, tincture or tonic, it acts as an antidote for Nightlock poisoning and can save lives if administered in time. It also works as a remedy for melancholy when taken as a tea. The leaves are edible and can be a nutritious addition to salads or cooked dishes.

One must be careful not to mistake Sunpetal for the similar-looking Eveseed, which has rounded single-lobed leaves but lacks the distinctive thick yellow veins. Eveseed is harmless but will not counteract the deadly nightlock toxins.

I have harvested a large supply of Sunpetal leaves which I will dry, prepare and store for use as an antidote and remedy. Sunpetal's medicinal properties and edible leaves will serve the village well. There may be darkness in the forest, but also light which gives me hope. With the aid of Sunpetal, nightlock's threat may be conquered.

"I wander the forest in search of sunlight to imbue its light into my veins. I flush the bloodstream and ease cramping. I can sense your distress. Let me ease your mind..."

Honey Pilewort

Today while walking through the Oakmist I came upon a creeping vine with small pale leaves and a sweet scent that I remembered from my childhood. Upon tasting one of the leaves, I found its flavor to be sickly sweet, like honey. After further study, I identified it as Mellis dulcis vitis, commonly known as Honey Pilewort.

Honey Pilewort has useful medicinal properties. When brewed into a tea, its sweet flavor makes it appealing to children and masks the need for extra honey or sugar. A paste of the plant can remedy the deadly symptoms caused by Dusk Ivy, and can cure mild melancholia or stomach upset. The scent itself seems to have mood-boosting qualities.

Due to its common nature and the enjoyment children find in its flavor, Honey Pilewort may prove useful as a treatment for the young ones. Its remedies are simple, natural and pleasant-tasting. I shall harvest leaves to be dried for teas and tonics, especially with the threat of Dusk Ivy nearby.

Even in darkness, sweetness and light can be found if one knows where to look. Honey Pilewort may be a small comfort, but comfort nonetheless.

"I grow where I want and flourish in the sun. I am the sweetest of plants."

Noxbrosia

While studying texts at the Draigh Monastery, I discovered a rare plant worth further research.

Scientific name: Noxbrosia Vespera Florum, commonly known as Duskshade or Nightbloom
Location: Frigid mountain regions, particularly the Norwas region in Neldor.

Leaf and flower shape: Long dark green stems with alternating long, thin leaves. Flowers are an iridescent indigo color and bloom only at night.

Properties: The compounds within the noxbrosia plant contain a poison so deadly, it was made illegal to cultivate or obtain in any manner by His Highness King Alaric Donovanu.

Cure by Dagric Wortcunning, adapted and improved by Jayce Keenstone: A tincture of fire clove, goldenspore, and ruby stem in a suspension of alcohol. Give three dropperfuls daily for five days after exposure, then reduce to one for another week.

Sources: Alchemist's Encylopedia, Botanist's Compendium, The Alchemist's Encyclopedia, The studies, formulas, and musings of D. Wortcunning.

"I cling to the mind and muddle the senses. I disturb the nerves and lock the bones. I clear the skin and drain the blood."

ACKNOWLEDGEMENTS

This book was the product of so many wonderful people supporting me and cheering me on! Firstly, I'd like to thank you, dear reader, for joining me on Jayce's journey. I hope you loved reading it as much as I loved writing it! Please consider leaving a review on your favorite book platform so others will give it a chance. I'd also love to hear from you! You can email me any comments you have at authorbreemoore@gmail.com

Thank you to those who read *The Quill and the Vial* when it was first published on Kindle Vella as *The Plague King Chronicles*. Your comments and reactions were so motivating! And thank you to Teshelle Combs and Jamie Dalton, fellow authors who answered all of my Vella questions!

Shoutout to my Kickstarter Backers! You are incredible! Thank you for joining me on this awesome publishing adventure, I hope the book and your special goodies are everything you hoped they'd be and more. I'm looking forward to many more Kickstarter projects, especially for book two in this series.

An ultra-special thanks to my beta readers: Rachel W., Amy W., Beth K., and Heather Q. You saw the gem that needed polishing and shaping and gave me the perfect advice to make this book everything it could be!

Shoutout to my local library and coffee shops – Swede & Co. and The Lost Canvas. Thanks for your strawberry boba lemonade, delightful herbal teas, and tasty treats that kept me going while writing and revising my book.

The ultimate thank you goes to my husband, Tyler, for spending hours after work, on weekends and during the summer with our six kids, giving me time to write and edit and make my dreams come true. You might not read my books, but I know you're my number one fan.

ALSO BY BREE MOORE

Bree Moore lives in Iowa with her husband, six children, and two cats. When she's not busy homeschooling or folding laundry, she sneaks off to write more fantasy.

Bree writes urban and epic fantasy to explore different worlds with amazing creatures and magic systems. She enjoys giving her readers a story that is both entertaining and emotional, with a healthy dose of romance. When she's not writing, Bree can be found foraging for edible plants, watching fantasy shows and movies, or hanging out with her husband and kids.

Previously published works include: *The Shadowed Minds* series, the *Lost Souls* series, and *Shadows of Camelot* series. She's currently working on *The Plague King Chronicles.*

Visit www.authorbreemoore.com for a FREE fantasy book!

tiktok.com/@breenovels

instagram.com/breenovels

Printed in the USA
CPSIA information can be obtained
at www.ICGtesting.com
LVHW050925101223
766126LV00038B/679/J

9 781956 668261